WHY YOU WERE TAKEN

JT LAWRENCE

FIRE FINCH
www.firefinchpress.com

Why You Were Taken is a work of fiction.

Names, characters, places and incidents are the product of the author's imagination or are used fictitiously. Any resemblance to actual persons, living or dead, events, or locales is entirely coincidental.

2017 Paperback edition

ISBN-13: 978-0-620-74654-0

2nd Edition

Copyright © 2017 JT LAWRENCE

JT Lawrence has asserted her right to be identified as the author of this work. No part of this book may be reproduced or transmitted in any form or by any means, mechanical or electronic without written permission from the author.

All rights reserved.

Published in South Africa by Fire Finch Press, an imprint of Pulp Books.

www.jt-lawrence.com

Cover design by Stuart Bache of Books Covered

Set in Bell MT

DEDICATION

Every word of this novel is dedicated to my
late writing mentor & very dear friend, Laurence Cramer,
who taught me to never walk slowly.

Mister L, you packed more sap and spirit
into your short time on earth than most people do in a lifetime.
I'll never forget feeling my baby boy kicking inside me
at your funeral; asserting the cycle of life. Easing my devastation.
How I ached to see your sons struck fatherless.
How it burned to see how much you were loved by so many.

A lifetime lesson in your passing, too:
'Grab Life by the Balls,' I can hear you say,
late at night when the darkness pulls at my sleeves.
I see your light, Mister L.
Thank you for the writing. To me, you'll live forever.

WHY YOU WERE TAKEN

BRIDE IN
THE BATH

1

Johannesburg, 2021

A well-built man in grimy blue overalls waits outside the front door of a Mr Edward Blanco, number 28, Rosebank Heights. He's on a short stepladder, and is pretending to fix the corridor ceiling light, the bulb of which he unscrewed the day before, causing the old lady at the end of the passage to call general maintenance, the number which he has temporarily diverted to himself.

He would smirk, but he takes himself too seriously. People in his occupation are often thought of having little brain-to-brawn ratio, but in his case it isn't true. You have to be clever to survive in this game, to stay out of the Crim

Colonies.

Clever, and vigilant, he thinks, as he hears someone climbing the stairs behind him and holds an impotent screwdriver up to an already tightened screw. The unseen person doesn't stop at his landing but keeps ascending.

The man in overalls lowers his screwdriver and listens. He's waiting for Mr Blanco to run his evening bath. If he doesn't start it during the next few minutes he'll have to leave and find another reason to visit the building; he has already been here for twenty minutes, and even the pocket granny would know that you don't need more than half an hour to fix a broken light.

At five minutes left, he checks the lightbulb again and fastens the fitting around it, dusts it with an exhalation, folds up his ladder. As he closes his dinged metal toolbox, he hears the movement of water flowing through the pipes in the ceiling. He uses a wireless device in his pocket to momentarily scramble the access card entrance mechanism on the door. It's as simple as the red light changing to green, a muted click, and he silently opens the door at 28, enters, and closes it behind him. In the entrance hall of Blanco's flat he eases off his workman boots, strips off his overalls to reveal his sleeker outfit of a tight black shirt and belted black pants.

The burn scar on his right arm is now visible. The skin is mottled, shiny. He no longer notices it; it's as much part of him as his eyes, or his nose. Perhaps subconsciously it is his constant reminder as to why his does what he does. Perhaps not.

He stands in his black stockinged feet, biding his time until he hears the taps being turned off. Mr Blanco is half whistling, half humming. A small man; effeminate.

What is that song? So familiar. Something from the 1990s? No, a bit later than that. Melancholy. A perfect choice, really, for how his evening will turn out.

He hears the not-quite-splashing of the man lowering himself into the bath. Tentative. Is the water too hot or too cold? Or perhaps it's the colour of the water putting him off. Recycled water has a murkiness to it, a suspiciousness. Who knows where that water has been, what it has seen? The public service announcements, now planted everywhere, urge you to shower instead of bath, to save water. It does seem like the cleaner option. If you do insist on bathing, they preach, you don't need more than five fingers. And then, only every second day. His nose wrinkles slightly at that. He takes his cleanliness very seriously.

Mr Blanco settles in and starts humming again. The man with the burnt arm glides over the parquet flooring and enters the bathroom. Even though his eyes are shut, the man in the bath senses his presence and starts, his face stamped with confusion. The scarred man sweeps Blanco up by his ankles in a graceful one-armed movement, causing water to rush up his nose and into his mouth. As he chokes and writhes upside-down, the man gently holds his head under the water with his free hand.

It's a technique he learnt from watching a rerun on the crime channel. In the early 1900s a grey-eyed George Joseph Smith, dressed in colourful bow ties and hands flashing with gold rings, married and killed at least three women for their life insurance. He would prowl promenades in the evenings looking for lonely spinsters and pounce at any sign of vulnerability. His charisma, likened to a magnetic field, ensured the women would do as he told them, one of his wives even buying the bath in which she was to be murdered. His technique in killing them was cold-blooded, clean: he'd grip their ankles to pull their bodies under—submerge them so swiftly that they would lose consciousness immediately—and they would never show a bruise. But where such care had been taken in the actual murders, Smith was careless with originality, and was caught and hanged before he could kill another bride in the bath.

A moment is all it takes, and soon Mr Blanco is reclining in the bath again, slack-jawed, and just a little paler than before. The man in black turns on the taps and fills the tub. Turns out five fingers is enough in which to drown, but it would be better if it looks like an accident, or suicide.

Mr Blanco's face is a porcelain mask, an ivory island in the milky grey water. Perhaps the person who finds him will think he fell asleep in the bath. Which he has, in a way. He washes his hands in the basin, wipes down the room. He throws on the white-collared shirt he brought with him and within five minutes he is out of the building and walking to the bus station, dumping the dummy toolbox and overalls on the way. He manages to hop on a bus just as it's pulling out onto the road. He's in a good mood, but he doesn't show it. This was one of his easier jobs. He wonders if the other six names on the list will be as effortless.

He slides his hand into his pocket and pulls out the curiosity he lifted from Blanco's mantelpiece: a worn piece of ivory—a finger-polished piano key. Engraved on the underside: 'Love you always, my Plinky Plonky.' It's smooth in his palm and retains the warmth of his skin. A melody enters his head. Coldplay: that's what Blanco was humming. The man finds this very satisfying.

RAINBOW VOM

2

Johannesburg, September 2021

Kirsten, late for the appointment she's been dreading for weeks, taps her sneakers on the scuffed concrete of the communal taxi stop on Oxford Road. The taxis are supposed to collect passengers every fifteen minutes but the drivers don't pay much attention to the official timetable. Most of them are passive aggressive which, Kirsten thinks, is better than just plain aggressive, which they were in the old days. Taxi bosses, South Africa's own mafia, used to gun down their rivals—blood in the streets—as if our history doesn't have enough of that already.

They stay with her, the pictures. She doesn't know if it's part of her synaesthesia or if she just has a more visual memory than most. It comes in handy with her job as a photographer.

The exception, of course, is her early childhood, of which she can remember very little. It was before you could download and back up your memories. Her parents used to tell her what she was like when she was a child, describe her first word, her first steps, the outings they had been on, but Kirsten's early memory remains an odourless, flavourless blank.

One year, for their anniversary, Marmalade James gave her the first book she had ever read cover to cover. A hardbound, beautifully illustrated, vintage edition of a Grimms' fairy tale: 'Hansel and Gretel'. The pages are foxed, the cover bumped. When she holds it she can feel that the book contains more than one story. She was so touched by the gesture: as if he's trying to give her a small part of those early years back. She treasures the book. Reads it carefully, is appalled by it, falls in love with it, can't bear to read it again. Still dreams of toaster waffle tiles.

Kirsten's watch beeps with a reminder just as a minibus rolls up. She's supposed to be at the clinic already. She double-clicks the message and it dials through to the reception machine, letting them know she's running late. People are more flexible now that personal cars are practically extinct and almost everyone relies on public transport. At least that's what Kirsten hopes, seeing as she's terminally late. The irony of her period being precisely on time every month is never lost on her.

She lets a few passengers push in front of her in the queue so that she's last to board and gets a seat in the front row. She hates sitting at the back. All the smells: the perfume and aftershave and shampoo and worn pleather shoes and smudge and *atchar* and chewing gum. All the sounds: the tinny *kwaito*, jazz and retro-*marabi* on the radio; the different languages and dialects; the shades of skin; the mad hooting.

The close fabric of different textures and colours makes her giddy, sometimes ill. Overwhelming: like having to see, smell, touch and taste all the colours of the rainbow, in 3D, at the same time. At its worst, it mixes together to become a thick, soupy, smelly, bubbling, multi-coloured mess.

Normally she closes her eyes, pictures herself in a clean white room, and tries to cut herself off from her senses, but fellow passengers never like that. They either take offence or move a little away from her, afraid, perhaps rightly so, that she will hurl on them. Rainbow Vom, she thinks, and smiles, although the idea doesn't make the trip any easier.

With her LocketCam she takes a quick snap of the miniature disco-ball hanging off the taxi's rear-view mirror, which swings as they stop to pick up passengers. The driver makes a dangerous stop at a dogleg to offer a woman a ride. Probably because she's pretty, Kirsten thinks, till the door opens and she sees the woman's bulging stomach.

Christ. As if this morning isn't difficult enough.

The other passengers all snap to and make the appropriate noises. Not gasps, not quite, but something similar. They shift up in their seats, making space for her, dusting invisible crumbs off the cheap cracked upholstery seat.

The pregnant woman smiles shyly, thanks them in vernacular. The people on either side of her beam as she sits, and steal shy glances at her bump. The woman smiles, puts her hand on her belly. A special kind of smug, the way only pregnant women can be. Kirsten stares out of the hair oil smeared window.

The Infertility Crisis has hit the lower socio-economic groups the hardest, with nine out of ten couples battling to conceive. As the salaries climb, though, the infertility—bizarrely—decreases, with top earners having the reversed fortune.

Declining fertility rates are a problem the world over but nowhere is it as dire as in South Africa. No one knows the definitive reasons behind the crisis. Billions have been spent testing the various hypotheses: cell tower radiation, Tile and/or Patch use, hormones used in farming and agriculture, high stress levels, bad diets, GMO, people waiting too long to start their families. While there is some correlation, they still can't figure out why South Africa is so badly affected compared to other countries. The population is declining rapidly, and those fortunate few who do manage to conceive are treated like queens.

When they draw near to where she's going, Kirsten lets the driver know by shoving a hundred rand at him. They're supposed to use government tokens to pay for community taxis but drivers always appreciate cash. Old school style. She doesn't do this for the sake of the driver, but more as a small act of rebellion against the incumbent ruling party, the New ANC—known, regrettably, as the Nancies—because the idea of a nanny state makes the hair on the back of her neck stand up.

She jumps off onto the pavement, glad to put distance between herself and the bun in the oven. Digital street posters call her name and tell her to wait, they have a message for her.

'Kirsten,' a recorded voice says in an American accent, 'have you done something for yourself today?'

Bilchen knows her favourite ice cream flavour—rose petal—and showers her with 4D rose petals and a blast of cool air. A travel agency tells her that it's been 206 days since her last holiday—doesn't she need another one? Bolivia? Mozambique? The Cape Republic? The soundtrack is vaguely island style and she can smell rum and coconut. Has she considered a travelbattical? Workcation?

Tuk-tuks zoom past her, hooting as they go. The sky darkens. Kirsten shields her eyes and looks up to see a drone-swarm fly overhead. She doesn't like them, doesn't like the shadow they cast. Hates that they have cameras, as if she's living in someone else's bleak futuristic imaginings. Already she feels as if she's being watched, always has. She shakes her brain, tries to focus on the task ahead. The time has come.

Carpe diem, and all of that.

For as long as she can remember, she's always hated doctors. And hospitals, but doesn't everyone? She abhors it when someone says they hate hospitals. That's like saying you hate stepping in dog shit, or wetting your pants in public. Obvious. Or in local slang, *obvi-ass:* the stating of which usually just shows how little you know.

Yuck, I'm just grouchy. Nervous.

Her underarms are damp so she slows her pace, and thinks about the ice cream, the Piña Colada.

Besides, how can she say she hates doctors when she's practically married to one? Just one example of how conflicted (read: crap) her personality is. Anyway, Marmalade is different. He's a paediatric cardiologist and goes around fixing kids' hearts, like some kind of golden-haired scalpel-bearing angel. And it's not like he has ever been *her* doctor. Never going to happen (No, not even then).

inVitro looms before her. It's bigger than she expected. The pictures on the website made it look less intimidating. The architecture is beautiful, inspired by Petri: the disc-shaped building is built out of attenuated glass (Crystal Whisper), strangely transparent and reflective at the same time: as if the architect meant for it to look invisible.

Kirsten wipes her clammy hands on her jeans, wonders if she really wants to go ahead with this. All the electronic poster-projectors near her apartment have been advertising this place; it seems to be the best of the hundreds of fertility clinics around. The spambots hack your online social status, and as soon as they see you are in a relationship they bombard you with wedding messages. As if anyone gets married anymore. After a while they give up on you getting married and start with the fertility and baby *spiel*. A bit like parents.

Or—Kirsten sniffs—how parents used to be. Her pain is still jagged.

Two heavily armed guards stand at the entrance. They look more like American militants than security: top-of-the-range automatic rifles, Kevlarskin, tortoise-shell-shaped helmets that make them sweat. They don't take their eyes off the pedestrians walking past. Seeing-eye cameras swivel in Kirsten's direction and blink at her. A bit further in, a lesser-armed female guard scans Kirsten for anything suspicious, then points where to go.

The reception area of inVitro is plush but anaemic: decorated in the kind of soulless way a five-star hotel is. The walls are covered in vanilla wallpaper that feels flat, dry, and tastes sweet, like a wafer. Kirsten hears the whisper of air sanitiser as she approaches the empty smiles at the desk.

The waiting room is packed; this place must be printing money. A woman, camouflaged in beige, hands her a stylus and a glass tablet with a form to fill out. She looks for an empty seat in the crowded room. Mainly couples: some scrubbed-looking and hopeful, some carrying the stale air of defeat, a few pinkly embarrassed, although Kirsten sees no reason to be. As difficult as it is, it's generally accepted that everyone in South Africa is IUPO nowadays: Infertile Until Proven Otherwise. At least Kirsten, and the other people in the room, have the money for treatment—most aren't that lucky, hence the huge skew in the latest population stats.

Some of the patients are wearing SuperBug masks. Kirsten supposes she should be wearing hers too but reckons she has to draw a line somewhere. If she has to choose between wearing a mask over her face every day for the rest of her life or getting sick she'd rather take her chances with The Bug. Besides, the government-issue masks are revolting to look at. Perhaps if she can get hold of one of the designer masks… she's about to sit next to a resigned-looking pair when her name is called.

The gold nameplate on the half-ajar door is blank. The nurse knocks and they enter. *Now or never.* Kirsten takes a deep breath.

The doctor takes the electronic clipboard, dismisses the nurse, and looks with interest at Kirsten over the top of his black-rimmed glasses.

'Miss Lovell?'

His eyes are the palest blue (Quinine) (Arctic Icecaps). They drill through her, make her feel intensely uncomfortable.

'I'm Doctor Van der Heever.'

Kirsten's nerves stretch her smile wide. She feels like running. He motions for her to take a seat and ignores her for the next two minutes while he scans her form, pinching and paging. She focuses on her breathing and casts her eyes around: one side of the office is floor-to-ceiling glass, with an uninspiring view of ChinaCity/Sandton. Glinting certificates take up most of the opposite wall. What kind of specialist feels the need to wallpaper half of his office with certificates? What's he trying to make up for?

'So… you've been trying for around three years?'

Kirsten jumps to attention. 'Three years. Yes.'

He grunts acknowledgement, keeps paging.

'You have children?' she blurts, without really meaning to. She thinks he'll say no, that he's married to his job. There are no framed prints of family on his desk.

He looks up at her, stares. Moistens his lips. 'I do. A boy. Well, he used to be a boy. A grown man, now. A doctor.'

Yuck. 'You must be proud.'

He blinks at her; his eyes magnified by his glasses. 'Your family's medical history –'

'It's patchy. I'm working on getting more information. I'm actually –'

'No matter,' he says, 'we'll do the standard primary diagnostic tests on you and your partner.'

The mention of tests sock Kirsten in the stomach. It's true she doesn't have many memories of her early childhood, but what she does remember is having endless examinations, specialist after specialist, x-rays, MRIs, CAT scans, blood tests. Breathing in gas to trace the blood flow to her brain, a hot flush of an iodine IV to examine her renal system.

It had made her hate her condition. Only once she'd been free of the weekly appointments did she finally start to accept the way she is: regard it as a gift instead of a disability. Now it seems as if it's starting all over again and she is heavy with foreboding.

'What kind of tests?' Kirsten tries to keep her voice even.

'Nothing too invasive, for now. Bloods, HSG, PCT. Then maybe a laparoscopy, hysteroscopy, depending on what we find.'

Using a stylus, he writes something on the glass, then clicks a button to bump the prescription to her watch. Her wrist buzzes as it comes through. A spray of tiny blue polka dots.

'It's a prenatal supplement. Folic acid, DHEA, Pycnogenol, royal jelly, omegas.'

Dr Van der Heever stands up, as if to see her out.

Is that it? Nine thousand rand sure doesn't buy you much specialist.

'Don't look so worried,' he says with a sidelong glance, one Kirsten can't help but to find menacing. 'We'll take good care of you.'

THEY MUST BE PLAYING WITH THE WEATHER AGAIN

3

Johannesburg, September 2021

Everyone holds their breath. The pale, painted puppet-like bodies keep still while the light flashes bright white.

'And it's a wrap,' Kirsten announces, lowering her camera and looking around at her team. The models, tired of holding their stomachs in and being pestered by the make-up artist, pout and blink at her gratefully. She rides her swivel chair to the 24" screen to file her shots.

She's happy with the day's grind. There is a luxury that comes with advertising shoots, compared to the journalistic and proactive stuff she usually does. It makes for an easy day, and she feels good because she knows she's got some excellent cinegraphs. Highly stylised, super slick, this job is definitely going into her portfolio. She feels hopped up, Mint Green.

'Stunning,' her assistant hisses over her shoulder, making her start. She closes the file. 'Seriously, that's some bang tidy work.'

'I'm off,' says Kirsten. 'Will you give the models some of this food?'

Shoots for brands like this are always over-catered. She slips a packet of Blacksalt crisps and a CaraCrunch chocolate bar into her pocket, grabs a bottle of water.

'Tell them to eat something. Models love being told to eat something.'

The sun is sinking behind the jagged downtown skyline when Kirsten walks towards the Gautrain station, and a warm drop of rain on her cheek makes her look up at the sky. She always expects the rain to be perfumed by the data in The Cloud. She imagines all the pictures there, all the poetry and music. Surely the rain should taste of something? Mummatus clouds are gathering in the east. They must be playing with the weather again. It feels wrong to her that the government is allowed to. The country needs rain desperately but influencing the weather just seems wrong. Unnatural.

In her experience, forcing an outcome rarely works. It's one of the reasons she has waited so long to visit a fertility clinic. Surely if it's meant to happen, it would just happen? But it hasn't. So now she guesses she is in the same boat as the weather manipulators.

It's not the first time she's drawn a parallel between the drought and the fertility crisis. Human bodies, after all, are 87% water. Without water there can be no life. Perhaps this is the next step in human evolution—Learnings from Lemmings—our natural resources are coming to an end but instead of diving off cliffs and walking into the sea to control our population, we just became infertile. A neater solution. Civilised.

Although lemming-inspired people still exist on the fringe of society: the suicide stats are soaring. They call it the Suicide Contagion, as if it's infectious. As if you're coasting along nicely, happy with your little patch of life, until the guy in the cubicle next to you decides to take a bottle of TranX to bed with him and the next thing you're contemplating doing it too. Like it never crossed your mind that you could end your life until you hear that someone else has done it. So on your way home from work you buy a bottle of TranX and a box of toaster waffles. You eat the waffles.

Kirsten gets on the train and sits as far away from everyone else as she can so that she can furtively eat her pocket-softened chocolate. The doors slide closed and they start to move. The sugar paints her mouth bright yellow (Cadmium Candy).

The projection looming above her interrupts the 7 o'clock news with snaps of contrived family moments: a father playing soccer with his IVF triplet sons, a mother gardening with her mixed-race daughter, a double amputee with bionic legs graduating from university. Then a slogan in bold typography appears over the picture: "A Future For All!"

It's the global slogan for 2021, but what does it even mean? Kirsten finds it especially ironic given the fertility crisis. She would laugh if it was funny. Ever since The Net shrunk the planet and the rich countries 'adopted' the poor countries, the UN is going around thinking that the Earth is some crazy-quilt version of Shangri-La.

In the mean time South Africa has serious problems; the news broadcast returns to show her cases in point: crippling rolling blackouts for those still stuck on the Eishkom grid; people dying of dehydration, cholera, and the SuperBug; strike after strike in the labour force retarding the already dismal service delivery; townships being razed to the ground to make space for factories and soulless, culture-barren RDP grids; a violent spike in hijackings; and prisoners dying in the Crim Colonies.

The global news: more ocean innocents disappearing on a regular basis, most likely nabbed by Somali pirates. More casualties at Hoover Dam as China continues its invasion of the US in search of water supplies.

Ha-ha, future for all. Kirsten looks down at the wrapper in her hand and realises her chocolate is missing. She checks her lap, her bag, the floor. Surely she hasn't eaten the whole thing?

Now the news shows some square-jawed businessman cutting a shiny blue ribbon, and people flashing their teeth and applauding. His name comes up: Christopher Walden, CEO of Fontus. Airbrushed pictures of Fontus trucks offloading crates of bottled water to impoverished-looking schools and remote villages. Cuts to Walden handing a bottle of Hydra to a lollipop child and showing the cameraman a thumbs-up.

It's good PR, but they don't really need to advertise. Apart from being the largest soda- and water-bottler in the country, Fontus has had the sole government contract to supply subsidised bottled water nationwide since it became unsafe to drink tap water. They practically own the country.

There are portable water purification systems available, towers and billboards and bottles and straws where nanoparticles in the filter remove heavy metals and biohazards, but they are slow and the water still tastes grey. Most homes have them but it's just easier to buy bottled when the world is spinning so fast no one feels they have the time to wait for something as basic and essential as water.

Kirsten and James have recently begun to make a point of drinking Hydra and not the more expensive brands, Tethys, or the luxurious 27-flavoured 'champagne of waters' Anahita, despite their friends' teasing for being 'neo-pinko socialists.' More than the price tag, they reject the notion that water is becoming a status symbol. She would drink tap water if she could, if it was safe. People still do of course, dirt-poor people, and those who shirk the warnings on homescreen and radio, people who believe it is all just a money-making racket, or worse, an post-Illuminati conspiracy. People who consider bottled water as the new Kool-Aid, wear Talking Tees that shout 'Don't Drink the Water!' that make you jump as you walk past.

The thought makes Kirsten feel navy (Blackbeard Blue); she can't wait to get home. She hasn't realised how tired she is, after the demanding shoot and this morning's anxious appointment. She pulls the plaster off the crook of her arm, revealing a light bruise and a blood freckle where the nurse took a sample at inVitro. The train slows to a stop. She surreptitiously drops the plaster and the CaraCrunch wrapper into a litterbin on her way out.

Kirsten loves the flat she shares with James in Illovo. It's an old building with high, ornate pressed ceilings, parquet floors, and decorated in her shabby chic bohemian style, accentuated with knickknacks from their travelling and orphaned props from previous shoots.

It's an old block, aged but sturdy. It has soul, she tells Marmalade, not like those new edge-of-cutting-edge buildings going up in town with their moving walls and pollution-sucking paint. Superglass everywhere so that you are constantly walking into walls. Hundreds of pivoting cameras to catch you walking into said walls. Not a comfortable chair in sight. Fake pebble fireplaces. Not like theirs, which they light with actual matches and feed with solid hunks of wood, and watch the florescent flames slowly work away at the grain.

God knows she likes this brick-and-mortar building, she

thinks, punching the worn-out elevator button for the third time, *but this lift could really do with a(nother) service.*

Eventually it cranks into life, something whirrs and settles with a dull thud from above, and it begins its unhurried descent. *Good thing I'm not in a hurry.* The numbers-caught-in-amber buttons light up painfully slowly: 4.

There is another noise, closer, a shuffling behind her and Kirsten whirls around, expecting to see someone, but the lobby is empty. 3.

The overhead lights flicker, and she thinks: just perfect. She is in just the mood to walk up three flights of stairs in the dark. 2.

The lights seem to stabilise, and then they go out. The elevator stops mid-groan. She hopes no one is stuck inside. The auto-generator will kick in any minute but the person trapped might not know it.

She flicks her watch's torch function on and begins climbing the stairs. It's hardly a searchlight, but it will do. She wishes James was home but he touched down in Zimbabwe a few hours ago, to work at the new surgery they've set up there. He has always spent a lot of his time grinding out of the country, but lately it seems he is never home.

They often discuss emigrating: James will be cooking some wholesome dinner while she reads the Echo.news tickertape out to him, and on bad-news days, which seemed more frequent lately, they invariably end up wondering to each other how much worse South Africa can get before they seriously consider moving to a safer place. Sometimes, sitting in the dark of loadshedding, talking by candlelight, eating olive sourdough and cheese, they say all they want is a more efficient place, a country that doesn't seem as inherently broken. And while James is always ready to leave, eager to leave, Kirsten can't bring herself to, as if bound by some stubborn magnetic force.

Kirsten is slightly out of breath when she reaches the third floor (Wheatgrass Shooter). When they first moved in she would say she lived on the green floor, or tell visitors to press the green button in the elevator, and they would think she was crackers. Of course there is no green button, and there is nothing green about the floor on which she lives. Marmalade understands her colours though: If he asks her how many slices of toast she'd like and she answers 'red' he knows that means two. Or yellow: one. Isn't it obvious? No, he says, I'm just used to your type of crazy.

She walks down the dim corridor and fumbles at the door, dropping her access card. Swearing purple (Aubergine Aura), she bends down to pick it up and a dark figure steps towards her.

JOURNAL ENTRY 7

20 February 1987

Westville

In the news: *South Africa is reeling in the wake of a grenade attack that killed a number of SADF personnel at Tladi Secondary School. A second Unabomber bomb explodes at a Salt Lake City computer store, injuring the owner.*

What I'm listening to: *Slippery When Wet - Bon Jovi!*

What I'm reading: *'Echoes in the Darkness' — non-fiction about the murder of a teacher and the disappearance of her two children. Heartbreaking.*

What I'm watching: *The Bedroom Window. Bow-chicka-wow-wow!*

Can you believe the news? Seems there are bombs going off everywhere.

Today was the worst and most shocking day of my life.

After fainting yesterday in the photocopy room at work, I went to the doctor down the road, at the corner clinic. All the girls here go to him, although I don't know why! He is downright creepy! I won't be going back there again. Told him about the nausea, dizziness etc. Can't keep any food down. Thought I had a tummy bug. Felt like he could see my secret through my skin. He asked me if I was sexually active as he looked at my naked ring finger. SRP. Self-Righteous Prick. And hypocrite. Everyone knows he's been having it off with Susan Beyers since her diagnosis. He's way too young to be such a SRP. Maybe even too young to be a doctor?! He can eat my shorts. Argh, I hate them. Doctors, I mean. They give me the creeps!

So yes, I know you've guessed already. I had too, although I was in serious denial. The nurse phones me today (at work!) and tells me the test was POSITIVE. Not positive, as in, Good News, but positive as in PREGNANT.

I AM PREGNANT (!!!)

I was (am) completely shocked. I'm practically a virgin! Plus P and I have always been so careful. I'm on the pill AND we use condoms. Well, we use condoms most of the time. There was that time at the beach after the concert when we didn't have one. And that once in my Citi Golf when I had that vicious bruise on my left knee from the hand brake and had to wear stockings to work in the middle of summer. Oh, God. Oh God.

A miracle/tragedy. A tragic miracle. Shoot, was all I could say into the phone. Shoot. Shoot. I wanted to say a lot worse!

They wanted me to go in immediately to get prenatal care:

vitamins I think. She said something about ultrasounds and folic acid. Acid is right. My life is over! I said I wasn't going back to that clinic and then she tried to refer me to an obstetrician but I just, like, put down the phone. There is NO WAY I can have this baby. P will think I'm trying to trap him. Get him to leave his wife.

P aside, what on earth am I going to do with a baby?!! I'm 24, still kind of new in town, and trying to make a good impression at work and in the neighbourhood. This was supposed to be my new beginning, my Big Break. How am I going to explain being single and knocked up?!

And, more importantly, what about taking care of the little anklebiter? Screaming sprog and dirty nappies? No way, I'm supposed to be a career girl! It's the 80s for God's sake! I left home so that I could make a life for myself, not tie myself down. Not be a gin-swilling housewife. I've dreamt for years of perms and power-suits and matching pumps, and having my own computer. And a telephone that I can dial with the back of my pencil so that I don't ruin my new manicure. Why am I so damned fertile?! It's a curse!

I don't know what to do. Very stressed and there's no one I can tell. Except Becky back home but then she'll think she was right: that the Big City would change me. Oh my God, can you imagine what she'd think of me now? I could never tell her! The girls around the office are great but I'm not close enough to anyone yet. Besides, they all obviously know P and it would be too dangerous. This will make me sound like a hypocrite but I really don't want to hurt P's wife. That would be terrible. I'm a terrible person. This is probably a punishment. As they say, Karma's a bitch.

Also, my family would be totally horrified. I can just imagine the look on Dad's face. He lives in this whacky reality where the 60s didn't happen and we're all still pre-sexual-revolution conservatives. I guess I was, too, until six months ago.

F*CK! He'll disown me in an instant. And Mom. I'll be an orphan.

F*CK F*CK F*CK!!

It feels like the world is tumbling down around me.

I feel like jumping off a bridge! I may as well! Then at least I could rest. My mind could rest. Who would miss me, anyway?

I feel so sick. Anxiety, guilt, morning sickness: all turning my stomach into a washing machine. I can't eat. I can't sleep. I don't know what to do.

I think I'm going to throw up again.

God help me. I don't deserve it, but please help me anyway!

A BIG RED BLOOM OVER HIS HEART

4

Johannesburg, 2021

Kirsten gasps, clutches her chest.

'Jesus Christ!'

'I've been called worse,' says the dark figure. The overhead lights flicker back on.

'The fuck are you doing here?'

'*Hai wena*. Is that the way you would greet the son of God Almighty?'

'As far as I know, the son of God doesn't skulk in dark corridors with inflatable motorbike helmets.'

'And how would you know, being the infidel that you are?' asks Kekeletso, arms akimbo. 'And, bless you, *sista*, still such a filthy mouth.'

She holds up a black bag. 'Is it okay if I shoot up in your place?'

Kirsten leans forward and hugs her, smells nutmeg in her cornrows, and warm leather. She loves the way Keke dresses. She seems to pull off a look that is sexy, hardcore, and feminine, all at the same time. Kirsten always feels like a tomboy in her company, in her uniform of tee, denim and kicks. She swipes her card and opens the door.

While Keke is dosing herself with insulin in the lounge, Kirsten opens the door of her antique aqua Smeg and roots around for a couple of craft beers. The idea of needles makes her *gril*, so she's never been able to watch Keke do it. Just hearing the beeping of Keke's SugarApp on her phone makes her shudder. There is the zip of the black bag (Squid Sable), which means she's finished, and when Keke comes through to the kitchen her nano-ink tattoo is already fading. The white ink is sensitive to blood sugar: when Keke's level is normal the tattoo is a faded grey; antique-looking. When she needs a shot it turns white, and the dramatic contrast with her dark skin is quite unsettling.

Kirsten twists off a cap with a hiss and hands the bottle to

Keke, who looks like she needs to say something.

'So,' says Kirsten, 'never known you to be lost for words.'

Keke says, 'I think you're going to need something stronger.'

She opens her black leather jacket and slides out a folder, laying it on the kitchen table. Kirsten puts her hand on it. It's warm. Keke moves it away from her.

'Drinks first.'

'At least you've got your priorities straight.' Kirsten forces a smile. The folder burns a slow hole in the kitchen table. Finally, she thinks: finally some explanation, some kind of way forward. She grabs a bottle of Japanese whiskey by its neck, and hooks two crystal tumblers with her fingers. With her free hand she gets some transparent silicone ice cubes from the freezer.

'Do you ever miss real ice?' she asks, 'I mean old-fashioned ice, made out of frozen, you know, water?' She sits down, across from Keke, across from the folder.

'Nope,' says Keke. 'That's like saying you miss coal-powered electricity. Or cables. Or teleconferencing. Or hashtags. Or church. Or Pro-Lifers.'

'Or condoms. Or tanning,' adds Kirsten.

'I wouldn't know,' says Keke.

'I hope you're referring to tanning.'

Keke laughs.

Kirsten says, 'You know what I don't miss? Handshakes. I always hated shaking people's hands. I found it bizarre even before the Bug, before people stopped doing it. It's too... intimate... to do with a stranger. Which is when you usually had to do it. I'm no germophobe, but...'

'I know! You're taught as a kid to catch your sneeze with your hand—'

'—and cover your mouth when you cough—'

'And then the next moment you're shaking everyone in the room's hands.'

They both pull faces at each other.

'Some people still do it, you know.'

'Ja, well, bad habits die hard.'

They drink.

'So,' she says, 'how're you doing?'

It makes Kirsten squirm to talk about herself when she isn't in a good place, when her Black Hole is gaping, trying to swallow her. Who wants to hear about her hollowness? Who wants to be bored with her First World Problems when they have enough of their own? When someone asks her how she is when she feels like this she is always tempted to yell 'Fine!' and change the subject as quickly as possible. But Keke knows her better than that.

The Black Hole is Kirsten's name for the empty space she has always felt deep within herself. She has never known a time without it, only that it shrinks and expands depending on what was happens in her life. When she fell for Marmalade James, for example, it was pocket-sized: a small blushing apricot. When it sunk in that her parents were dead: a brittle plastic vacuum cleaner, emphasis on the vacuum. Not being able to get pregnant is the size of a tightly formed fist, which free-floats around inside her body but is mostly lodged between her ribcage and her heart. Sometimes the hole grows or narrows inexplicably, and makes her wonder if there is another version of her walking around, falling in and out of love and otherwise experiencing the rollercoaster of (a parallel) life. She has always had The Black Hole, it is part of who she is, and it hurts her insides just thinking that she will most likely carry it to her grave.

Keke, sensing her discomfort, says, 'Your plants are doing well.'

'Yes.' Kirsten looks around as if she has forgotten they are there. 'They're happy.'

'Happy may be an understatement. Your flat is a veritable jungle.'

Kirsten laughs. 'It's not.'

'It is! There's a lot of fucking oxygen in here. Do you even remember what colour the walls are?'

'Don't be ridiculous.'

'If I ever run out of news stories I'm going to come back here and do an ultra-reality segment on you. The crazy plant lady. Living in a Jozi Jungle. Madame Green Fingers.'

'Ha,' says Kirsten.

Keke puts on her important-news-headline voice: 'Most lonely women get cats, but Kirsten Lovell is a fan of... flora.'

'Ha. Ha.'

'Most hoarders are content with keeping mountains of old take-away containers, but this woman can't get enough of The Green Stuff.'

'That makes me sound like a blunt-vaper.'

'Her neighbours called the authorities when the vines began creeping through the walls and into their kitchens... it was clear: time for an intervention.'

'Okay, hilarious. You can stop now.'

'Really? I was having fun.'

'I could tell.'

'It started off innocently, you know. A fern here, an orchid there.'

'Ah, yes, those orchids. Gateway plants.'

They smile at each other. Kirsten is surprised at how grateful she is for the company.

'Earl Grey.'

'Er, what?'

'The colour of the walls,' says Kirsten. 'Earl Grey. The colour you get in your head when you taste bergamot.'

'You'd better not say that on camera. They'll cart you off to somewhere you can't hurt yourself.'

'Hm. That doesn't sound too bad.'

Keke leans forward again. Business time. 'So. Is there any news from your side about the... burglary—from the cops? Any leads?'

Kirsten shakes her head. *'Niks nie.'*

God, she hates talking about it, thinking about it. Pictures, unbidden, flash in on her mind. The broken glass and splinters on the floor, the up-ended furniture. Pillows ripped apart. The hungry-looking safe wrenched open and plundered.

The blood was the worst. There wasn't a lot of it—in a kind of detached way she had noticed how little actual blood was spilt—but the vividness of the colour (Fresh Crimson), like leaked oil paint, it was as if it had come alive and advanced on her, misting her vision and strangling her: and that unforgettable assailing metallic smell. An avalanche of a thousand copper spheres.

'Nothing? Not one lead?' presses Keke.

'If they have one, they're not sharing it. All I know is what they said upfront, that it looks like it was a house robbery gone wrong. Looks like it was two guys who broke in. Something about bullet trajectories and blood spatter.'

Keke frowns at her. She knows it must sound bizarre to hear someone talk so technically about the murder of her own parents. But Keke knows that Kirsten doesn't cry. She describes Kirsten as 'immune to face-melting'.

'There will definitely be some kind of... forensic evidence. Crime scenes of botched burglaries are usually teeming with the stuff.'

The bodies had looked like jointed paper dolls, the vintage ones you dress with paper clothes, 2D. Her father's body drawn as if he were a runner in a comic book. A big red bloom over his heart. Her mother, unusually pious, hands secured in prayer position with a bracelet of black cable-tie (Salted Liquorice). A small hole in her forehead. Both lying on their sides, their waxen faces resting on the dull, dirty carpet.

There is a cool palm on Kirsten's arm and she flinches, looks up and blinks past the pictures in her head.

'Are you okay? I'm sure you're still very shaken up, it hasn't even been—'

'I'm fine. I'll be fine.'

'You shouldn't be alone. Where's Marmalade?'

'It's been long enough.'

'Long enough? It hasn't even a month, Kitty Cat. The last time I saw you was at the funeral, for God's sake.'

They sit in silence. The funeral: twin coffins and the cloying scent of lilies. Pollen stains on white tablecloths. Clammy hugs.

'Zim,' says Kirsten. 'James is in Zimbabwe, at that new clinic.'

'Then who is all this healthy food for?' She motions at the toppling fruit bowl, the mountain of bright green apples, and vegetable stand.

For thirteen years James has tried to stud Kirsten's junk food diet with healthy alternatives. If she is going to eat that CaraCrunch, then she should have a low-fruc Minneola too. *Slap* chips? The mitigating snack is a handful of edamame. He tempts her with fresh chilli gazpachos, honeyed veg-juices spiked with galangal, wild salmon salami. He eats as if he can reverse the diseases he sees in the world.

'He always stocks up the house before he goes, hoping I'll run out of junk and resort to eating some kind of plant matter. He says we should buy shares in Bilchen and then at least we'll have money for the double bypass surgery I'll need one day.'

Bilchen is the Swiss-owned megacorp that produces the majority of processed food in the world: cheap, tasty, and full of unpronounceable ingredients. In addition to their plants in China and Indonesia they own hundreds of factories in SA, producing mountains of consumables, from food to hygiene products to pet snacks.

When James sees her eating something like her staple Tato-Mato crispheres he says to her: 'You know that there is no *actual* food in there, right?' and she laughs her fake laugh to annoy him, licks her fingers, and points at the pictures on the foil packet. 'Tato-Mato, Doctor Killjoy. It's made out of potatoes and tomatoes. *A vegetable and a fruit.* You heard it here first,' and he shakes his head as if Kirsten is beyond help.

Bilchen is perennially in the news for one scandal or another. Anti-freeze contamination in their iguana food, horse-DNA in their schmeat rolls, sweat-shopping kids in Sri Lanka, big bad GMO. They own so many brands they can just kill whichever has caused the controversy and re-label their product, market it as 'new' to hook the early adopters, and deep-discount it to the couponers. The leftovers feed the freegans. *Et Voila*, a new brand is born. P-banners and virtual stickers plead with you to 'vote with your feet' and 'consume consciously': 'Boycott Bilchen' is the new 'Save the Rhino.'

Keke sighs theatrically. 'How lucky does a girl get?'

'Ja, yum, look at all those... shiny green apples.'

'No, I meant Marmalade. Kind, generous, god-like in appearance, saves little children, *and* does the grocery shopping!'

'Well, he gets cars loaned to him all the time, for his job, so it's easier for him.'

'Pssh. There is a Man-Lotto and you won. *uLula.*'

'He also has his faults, you know.'

'Ha! Not likely.'

Kirsten hides her smile.

'Seriously though,' says Keke, 'his parental units did an amazing job.'

'They didn't, actually,' says Kirsten.

'*Hai, stoppit.*'

'I'm not kidding. His mother was never around and his father is a real nutcase. Horrible guy.'

'I can't imagine that.'

'He left home at fifteen. He just couldn't live with his dad any more. He won't even talk about him. Cut all ties.'

'An evil father… so is that why he keeps trying to save the world?'

'Probably. Good premise for a superhero story, anyway,' says Kirsten.

'It's been done before.'

'What hasn't?'

'Funny you should say that,' says Keke.

'Huh?'

'I have a… story for you.'

'You found something? About my parents?' Kirsten turns the ring on her finger.

'I tried to get something out of the cops, anything, but they completely closed ranks. Even my contact there, in profiling, said only certain creeps are allowed access to the case. Who's that inspector?'

'The thug? Mouton. Marius Mouton.'

'Yes, Mouton is handling the thing, doesn't want too

many other creeps involved. Can't have any leaks jeopardising the investigation. Apparently this happens sometimes on high-profile cases, according to my guy, but it's not like your parents were, like, diplomats or anything? But then he said it could be that the criminal is high profile, you know, like a serial killer, or in this case, maybe a terror gang. So maybe they're close to getting someone, and they want the case to be really tight.'

'Ack. We'll never get anything out of Mouton.'

'Ja, we'd have better luck asking a gorilla.'

'The gorilla would have more manners.'

'A better vocabulary.'

'Better teeth. And smell better. A gorilla would smell better.'

'More sex appeal?'

'Okay, I think you just crossed a line there,' laughs Kirsten, 'as in, a legal one.'

'It wouldn't be the first time. Anyway, I don't see us getting much out of them, so I asked my FWB, Hackerboy Genius, to see what he could find, under the radar.'

'Remind me?'

'Friend With Benefits. Marko. The hacktivist.'

Keke is the only person Kirsten knows who's gone bi-curious speed-dating to gather work contacts. The fact that they come in useful for her journalistic grind doesn't mean there is no sex on the table. From Keke's cryptic hints Kirsten gathers there is, indeed, a great deal—and variety—of sex on the table. As well as being 'a raging bisexual,' ('Isn't everyone bi these days?') she is what she likes to call 'ambisextrous'.

'Marko is a very—talented—individual,' she sparkles, sitting up a little straighter.

Uh-huh, Kirsten thinks. 'Speed dating?'

'Yawn! Speed dating is so last season, old lady. How ancient are you? Now it's DNA dating. Very New York.'

Kirsten is glad she doesn't have to date anymore. The dating pool in Joburg makes her think of a tank of Piranhas; Keke loves it.

'Chemically compatible couples, what's not to love? And boy, are we... compatible. You'd never believe it if you met him. Anyway, so he's actually the one who found this for me.' She puts her hand on the folder.

'It's big. Really big. Cosmic. You ready for a mind-fuck?'

Kirsten's fingers tingle. Keke slides it over to her, and she opens it.

JOURNAL ENTRY

3 March 1987

Westville

In the news: *a guerrilla is shot dead by Gugulethu police after firing at them with an AK47.*

What I'm listening to: *The new Compact Disc (CD) of 'A Hard Day's Night' by the Beatles*

What I'm reading: *'Watchers' by Dean R Koontz. It's about two creatures that emerge from a secret government laboratory, one to spread love, the other doom.*

What I'm watching: *Nightmare on Elm Street 3. Totally gnarly. Usually I enjoy scary movies but I had to walk out of the cinema. Life is grisly enough.*

I went in for my abortion (hate that word!) today. I felt so trapped and alone but it seemed like the only solution. I got up really early, I had to be at the 'family planning clinic' at 7 and after waiting for a while in a grubby room with two other girls with shame-flamed cheeks they gave me a depressing pink gown to change into. Had to take off all make-up and jewellery, even my new nail polish. There was a mirror in the fluorescent room and I just looked at my face and I was so pale and looked so terrible. I kept thinking 'what have I become? What have I become?'

I am NOT the kind of person who sleeps with married men, and definitely not the kind of person who has an abortion! And once these things are done they can never be undone. I will be forever bruised. My soul will be dented. I was looking into that mirror thinking that I didn't even recognise myself, and I just started crying. Weeping, really. That hyperventilating ugly-cry.

Shame, the nurse was so kind to me, she could see that I was really shaken up. She held my hand. Told me if I didn't want the baby then I was doing the right thing. That the world doesn't need another unwanted child. It would be best for everyone, if I was sure that I didn't want it. It's not that I don't 'want it' I wanted to say to her. It's that I can't have it. Look at me, I may be 24 but I'm just a child myself.

So I was on the operating table after taking the pre-med and feeling totally woozy and my legs were in stirrups when something just happened, like a bolt of lightning. All of a sudden the abstract idea of pregnancy became a real idea of a little baby (a little baby!) instead of an 'it,' and the thought was there as clear as day that there was no way I could go through with the termination. Mine and P's baby!! A little pink gurgly precious baby! The anxiety fell away (I blame the drugs) and revealed my true wish, even if it was clouded by conflicted emotions.

I felt so embarrassed telling the doctor but he didn't mind. Usually I absolutely hate doctors but he was really nice: said it was better to be sure, and that I still had another 3 weeks to change my mind if I wanted to, said he'd take care of me. But I won't. Something happened to me on that table and it totally wasn't what I planned.

The nurse squeezed my arm and gave me her number in case I wanted to talk. I started crying again – something about the unexpected kindness of strangers in hard times. Also, the meds! I am going to have to tell P about the baby. I'm sure he will be angry and end things. I will probably have to find a new job, a new town. My parents will, like, never speak to me again! No duh. My life as I know it is over. Never felt so lonely before!

All that said I can't help feeling a tiny jab of excitement (stress?) when I think of the baby. Eeeek! An actual baby. What was I thinking? I'm totally terrified.

Bon Jovi's song is constantly playing on every radio and in my head. I'm living on a prayer!!

TOMMYKNOCKERS

5

Johannesburg, 2021

Seth sits in the lab. It's late, but he feels as if he's on the point of a breakthrough in the project he's grinding. It's his second-last day at the smart drugs company and he wants to leave with a bang. It will be good for his—already enhanced—ego. He adds another molecule to the compound he's configuring on the screen of his Tile, subtracts one then adds another. It's almost ready.

Seth is the best chemgineer at Pharmax and he knows it. No one can map out new pharmaceuticals like he can. To add to his professional allure——and to his considerable salary—he is known to be mercurial. No one company can pin him down for more than a year, despite offers of fast-tracking and bonuses. Some colleagues blame his exceptional intelligence, saying he bores easily, others, his drug problem. While both hold some truth, there's a much more pressing reason Seth moves around as often as he does, which he keeps well hidden.

During the short ten months he'd been at the pharmaceutical company he had already composed two first-class psychoactive drugs, and is now on the brink of a third. His biggest hit to date has been named TranX by the resident marketing team. It's a tranquiliser, but modelled in such a way that while it relieves anxiety, it doesn't make you feel detached or drowsy. After the tranquiliser hits your bloodstream, making you feel warm and mellow, it's followed by a sweet and clean kick.

It's all in the delivery system, he told his beady-eyed supervisor and the nodding interns as he showed them the plan. All about levels, layers, the way they interact with each other and the chemicals in the brain. The molecular expression is beautiful, they all agreed.

The drug before that was a painkiller. It doesn't just take away your physiological pain, it takes away *all* your pain: abusive childhood, bad marriage, low self-esteem, you name it. It is one of his favourites, but then he has a soft spot for analgesics. With the drug based on the ever-delicious tramadol, Seth had used the evergreen African pincushion tree for its naturally occurring tramadol-like chemspider, allowing for a rounder, softer, full-body relief, without the miosis or cotton mouth.

Genius, if he doesn't say so himself. The formula isn't perfect though: too much of it is taxing on the liver. And he isn't sure what the long-term effects on the brain might be, but that is for the Food & Safety kids to figure out.

Seth moves to an appliance on the counter, clicks 'print,' and after a rattling he takes out a tray of pills. Shakes them down a plastic funnel and into an empty bottle, catching the last one before it disappears and popping it into his mouth. The bottle makes its way into his inside pocket after he scribbles on it with a pen. These particular pills are green; they look innocuous enough, like chlorophyll supplements, or spirulina. His latest project involves experimenting with salvia, or diviner's sage, as the hippies used to call it. Mexican mint.

On his way out, his tickertape blinks with a news update. A minister has been fired for having a secret swimming pool. The NANC is contrite and apologetic; they don't know how this could have happened. They have hard lines for mouths and use words like 'shocking,' 'unacceptable,' 'unconscionable,' and say they will certainly press charges. The journalist reporting the story looks familiar: a young, uncommonly attractive woman in cornrows and a tank top, leather bottoms. Biker? A white lace tattoo covers her shoulder; she has kohl eyes and an attitude. Just his type.

He thinks of the swimming pool and remembers a sunblock-slathered childhood of running in the sprinklers, drinking from the hose, water fights with pistols and super-soakers. Having long showers and deep bubble baths. Flushing the toilet with drinking water. Chlorine-scented nostalgia: kidney-shaped pools, dive-bombing, playing Marco Polo. The feeling of lying on the hot brick paving to warm up goose-pimpled skin. Then one day they weren't allowed to water the garden, then domestic pools were banned, then all pools were illegal, then, then, then. It had been so long, he'd do anything for a swim. For a tumble-turn in drinking water. How decadent that all seems to him now. The next news story is about a famous pianist found drowned in his bath. Seth switches it off.

He shrugs off his lab-coat, replaces his eyebrow ring and snaps on a silver-spiked leather wrist cuff. He puts on his black hoodie, applies some Smudge to his eyes, ruffles his hair into bed-head, and checks his appearance in the glass door on the way out. His mood starts climbing; he can feel the beginning of the slow-release high.

Thunder in winter, he thinks as he walks outside: they must be playing with the weather again. His superblack jacket renders him almost invisible, and his compact silver-tipped umbrella shields his face from the unseasonal shower. The city street is dark and slick, highlighted only occasionally by pops of lightning and the reflection of neon shop signs on the tar's uneven surface. Algaetrees, green streetlights, flicker on and off as he moves beneath them. There's jubilant shouting in the distance; a wave of music; a car backfires. A building's clockologram blinks an error message.

Jutting edges of the pavement interrupt the man's usually elegant stride: missing bricks, gaping manholes, roots of trees smashing their way through crumbling concrete. Undulating and decorated by shimmering litter, the walkway seems to take on a life of its own.

A group of people is up ahead, walking in his direction. Coal-skinned men dressed in oiled leathers and animal skins. Sandals and scarred faces. He sees their determined foreheads in blasts of light as they pass under the streetlights. *Gadawan Kura.* Ivory bracelets click as they walk.

When they get closer, Seth lifts his chin at the leader. He doesn't step aside, as most people would. Instead he brushes an arm and keeps moving. Once they're clear, one of the men starts shrieking, imitating the hyenas they are known for keeping, and the rest of the men cackle. Seth adjusts his hood and walks on.

A stranger in rags jumps out of a side alley and into his path. A hobo? Impossible. There were no more homeless creeps in the city: they had all been 'enrolled' in the Penal Labour Colonies. The faint whiff of matches and booze. Seth's hand tightens around the gun in his pocket, snicks off the safety. Water droplets glisten on the ragman's dark skin and hair; he pats himself down with twirling hands and a gap-toothed smile to show his tattered pockets are empty. He smells like the street.

'Jog on,' says Seth. 'Scram.'

'Jus' asking for a smoke, *bra.*' One of his eyes is black, bottomless. The other is overcast.

A cigarette? You've got to be kidding. It's 2021 – nobody smokes anymore.

He closes his umbrella.

'Get out of my way.'

A spark of defiance as the obstacle opens his mouth to speak. There's a glint of a blade. Instinctively Seth knees the stranger in the crotch, and when he's off-balance, raps him sideways on the jaw with the handle of the umbrella. The ragman falls backwards onto the shining road, knocked out cold, his trench knife clattering on the pavement beside him.

Seth keeps moving, and the Algaetrees flicker. He turns into a back street scented by tar and trash. A rat scurries out in front of him, but he doesn't flinch, which he takes as a good sign. He expects the drug to peak in two hours, maybe three. Optimism in a bottle. With one click of his earbutton his life has a soundtrack, and he's ready for a bright night.

Once he reaches his block the microchip in his ID card automatically opens the main access gate. A new biomorphic building, cool with smoked emerald glass and metal; glittering charcoal porcelain tiles. Smog-eating exterior paint and a solar Cool Roof with water catchment tanks. It's the ultimate lock-up-and-go: wholesale security, self-regulating, pet-free. He ignores the open mouth of the elevator and runs up the stairs, punches in his code—52Hz—and has his retina scanned to open his front door. The entry panel blinks and the door unlocks. A woman's voice purrs from the speaker above the door in a neutral accent: 'Welcome home, Seth.'

The main lights glow; the temperature is set to 24 degrees. He pops a pill, locks away his gun and checks his Tile for messages. Just as he hoped, the green rabbit blinks on his screen. He has a new job to do. A thrill tugs at his guts. It's his most important post yet. Dangerous. He can't wait to get started.

*

The TommyKnockers club is underground. You have to know a person who knows a person to get in. There isn't any secret code word to gain access; the club is so difficult to find, you either know where it is or you don't. That, and a giant Yoruba bouncer called Rolo, ensure that only the right kind of people get in. As Seth approaches the nondescript front door, Rolo steps into the grey frame and tips his invisible hat to him. Diamond fingers catch the light.

'Mister Denicker,' he says in a voice as deep as a platinum mineshaft.

'Rolo.' Seth nods back. He glances behind him before entering. Despite leaving the ragman in the gutter, he has the distinct feeling that someone is following him.

On the other side of the door is another world. You step from the bleak and broken inner city street into a gaudy 1940s Parisian-style steampunk bordello, replete with scarlet velvet bolted in gold, chain tassels, and oiled men and women wearing very little in the way of clothes and too much eye make-up. The twist comes later: as you move from room to room, and deeper underground, the imagery becomes more exaggerated, bizarre, sinister, as if someone has decided to cross a brothel with a spooky amusement ride. As if TommyKnockers is the representation of someone's erotic dream turning into a nightmare.

The deeper you go, the less mainstream the dancers

become, catering to more exotic tastes: a voluptuous woman with three breasts, a freakishly well-endowed man, a heavily inked hermaphrodite with a clock etched into her back. The art on the walls changes from *chat noir* and *Marmorhaus* prints to surreal landscapes, obscured faces, bizarre vintage pornography, disturbing portraits hung at strange angles. Luminous sex toys alongside hallucinogenic shooters at the spinning bars, lit by deranged copper pipe chandeliers. Sex shows featuring Dali-esque hardcore fuckbots.

Seth doesn't usually go further than the first few rooms. He is no prude, enjoys a bit of kink, but his insomnia doesn't need encouragement. He has enough to keep him up at night.

This evening, as soon as he crosses the threshold, he heads directly to an attractive blonde standing against a wall. It's an old tactic, one that frequently pays off. None of that seedy languishing at the bar, surveying all the available meat on offer and later trying to hook up. This technique is cleaner. It shows you are a man who knows what he wants. The woman, caught off guard, invariably accepts the offer of a drink, and from then on it's usually green lights all the way to the bedroom. Or club restroom. Or taxi. Or White Lobster den. Or wherever else they happen to find themselves.

This particular blonde is wearing a belt for a skirt and black boots with heels so high he wonders how she manages to stay vertical. Masses of teased hair, powdered with fine glitter.

'Hello there,' says Seth. Not too friendly, not too distant.

'Er,' she says. Where has he come from?

He looks at the glass in her metallic-taloned hand: 'Campari?'

The rose-coloured sequins above her eyes blink in the uneven light. He has a coldness in his eyes. A hardness. She tries to size him up. A drug dealer? A psychopath? A rufer? Does she, after her countless drinks, even care? She looks him up and down, nods. He leads her to the bar and orders her a double, vodka for himself, and two ShadowShots, which are not, strictly speaking, legal.

The Campari comes on the rocks—it's one of the few clubs that still offer actual ice in drinks—despite the cost, instead of frozen silicone shapes. He grinds a block between his molars; he likes real ice. She purses her lips at the shooters, as if to say he's naughty. He presses one into her hand; they touch glasses and down the drinks. Both feel the rush of the warm spirit as it washes through them.

A man arrives at the bar and pretends to not watch them.

The woman blinks at Seth; sighs as her pupils dilate. With a cool and gentle hand he propels her by her lower back to a more private area, with brocade curtains and oversized couches. An oil painting of a man with a patchwork blazer and rivets for eyes gazes over them.

'Let's get you out of those dreadful shoes.'

*

Kirsten opens the folder while Kekeletso watches her. Inside: her parents' autopsy reports. Keke has removed the photos taken by the forensic team *in situ*. It is enough that Kirsten found them dead, without having to see their death-grimaces again. Not that it makes much difference to Kirsten: a picture on glossy paper won't be much more vivid than the images in her head.

The reports aren't long. Kirsten skims a few pages describing what she already knows: bullet in brain, bullet in heart. .22 calibre Remingtons: one to stop thinking, one to stop feeling. Fired at arm's length distance for her mom, half a room for her dad. Her mother was most likely kneeling there when the killer squeezed a round into her head. Execution style, but face-to-face. The police say it is a botched burglary, but this creep isn't a stranger to murder.

Kirsten scans the medical jargon: entry wound of the mid-forehead; collapsed calvarium with multiple fractures; exit wound of occipital region. Official cause of death: Massive craniocerebral trauma due to gunshot wound.

There are diagrams on one of the final pages, similar to what you might find in a biology textbook: line drawings of people dissected lengthways so that you can see their bones and organs. Kirsten is always better with pictures. She strokes the diagrams with her finger, following the coroner's notes and asides. When she finishes with her father's she starts on her mother's. Immediately something looks wrong.

'Do you see it?' asks Kekeletso. Kirsten has been so absorbed she has almost forgotten Keke is there. She looks up, her finger glued to the illustration of her mother's abdomen. The ceiling rains cerise spirals down on them.

'She had a… hysterectomy?'

'Yes.'

'How come I didn't know that? Did she do it when I was too young to remember?' This is entirely possible given her sketchy childhood memories.

'Turn to the last page. I found it in her private medical file.'

Kirsten locates the last page in the folder and holds it up, pushing the others away. It is a record of an elective surgical procedure undergone by her mother in 1982. A full hysterectomy, five years before Kirsten's birth.

JOURNAL ENTRY

12 March 1987

Westville

In the news: *Sweden announces a total boycott on trading with South Africa. Les Miserables opens at Broadway.*

What I'm listening to: *The Joshua Tree by U2. Radical.*

What I'm reading: *The scariest book known to man: IT by Stephen King.*

What I'm watching: *Lethal Weapon*

I am, like, the happiest person in the world right now. When I told P about the baby I thought the worst, but I am right to love him because he is the nicest, sweetest, strongest man ever. Okay he was totally shocked but after a few minutes he hugged me so tightly and said that he would take care of the baby and me. I thought that he meant having us holed up somewhere as a secret lover and lovechild (which would have been totally fine by me!) but he is a better man than that. Said he wants to be a good father and you can't do that not living in the same house. He asked me to MARRY HIM!!!

It wasn't, like, the romantic picture I had in my head, the proposal. I guess I thought that when the day arrived it would be all champagne and roses and candlelight. Maybe on a tropical beach somewhere (Mauritius?), or a fancy restaurant. And the man would be taller and have more hair and he'd be rich (and not married!) and I... well, I wouldn't be knocked up. It was more of a discussion than a proposal, and then he, like, blurted it out. Not as a question, but as what we should do, and I agreed.

My mind is swirling right now. I mean I feel bad that he is going to leave his wife, that's so gnarly, but it has been over for a long time and I know that he will take care of her. Still, I feel sick about it. I hope she never finds out the truth. But I'm going to have his child and that is the most important thing right now. I hope that she will forgive him/us one day, and that I will be able to forgive myself. I am going to be a better person. I am going to stop being selfish and be the best wife and mother that I can be. I'm going to make P so happy.

MAD FURNITURE WHISPERER

6

Johannesburg, 2021

Seeing as James is away in Zimbabwe and Kirsten has no grind planned for the day, she decides it is time to do something she has been putting off for too long. She catches a *boerepunk*-blasting taxi to the south of Johannesburg and takes a long, brooding walk from the bus stop to the storage garages in Ormonde.

As she walks she snaps pictures with her locket. She used to have a superphone with a built-in camera, had a collection of lenses for it, but lugging a phone around when you could snap a Snakewatch on your arm just seems archaic. Now smartwatches are being replaced with Tiles and Tiles are being replaced with Patches. It seemed impossible to keep up.

The LocketCam is tiny, smaller than a matchbox, and is really only a lens and a shutter release. She'll get the pictures later from her SkyBox. It is great for scenes like this: an old bus depot painted white by the ratty pigeons that have adopted it as their home; a mechanic's cheerful advertising mural painted on a brick wall; a poster for a Nigerian doctor with an unpronounceable name who can enlarge your penis, get your ex-lover back, make your breasts grow, make you 'like what you see in the mirror,' vaccinate you against The Bug, and make you rich. *If he had that power, I'm sure he wouldn't be messing around with other men's junk. Or, on second thoughts, maybe he* wanted *to mess around with other men's junk, and that's why he became a junk doctor.*

When she reaches the storage building it looks all closed up. Not very promising. Then she sees their billboard, and the logo: a smiling rhino. Ironic, and sad. Like a dodo giving a thumbs-up, or a winking coelacanth. Who would choose an extinct animal as their mascot?

Once the cops gave her the go-ahead to put her parents' house on the market she paid a company to move all their possessions here. There is no way she could have faced doing it herself. This is the first place she found online, and she doesn't remember the rhino. Now she wonders if her parents' things really are here or if they were on the first truck out to some dodgy location: Alex, Lonehill, Potchefstroom.

There is no bell to ring or reception to visit. When she calls the number on the faded hoarding, a telebot tells her it is no longer valid. She walks around the building and finds a back entrance, a simple fenced gate closed with a heavy padlock. She has been given two keys she at first thought were identical, but she tries one now and the padlock springs open. She steps inside and locks the gate behind her.

The number on the cheap keyring is pink/purple-blue: 64 (Chewed Cherry Gum; Frozen Blueberry). She walks past a xylophone of colours before she finds her lot. The garage door is rusted and needs some persuading to roll up. It screams all the way and the red chevrons the noise causes in her vision momentarily blinds Kirsten. Then, silence: dust glitters in the sunlight.

She stands still, breathing, blinking, trying to cope with the onslaught of smells, colours, feelings, memories whirling around her. The lounge suite is closest to her, and she focuses on that. She lifts the protective sheeting and glimpses the arm, a familiar tattoo of faded chintz. Pictures in her head: her lying on the couch, eating milky cereal while watching TV, one throw-cushion behind her back, another under her knees. The base ragged where their decrepit cat, Mingi, used to sharpen his claws. She lifts a seat cushion and looks at its stained underside where her mother once spilled tomato soup, never to be forgiven by the stubborn fabric.

The coffee table with a small crack in the glass top that had been there for as long as she could remember. The server; the kitchen table; the counter swivel chairs. The buzz in her head dies down. She can do this. Slowly, methodically, she re-acquaints herself with each object. She lays her hand on them as she goes, acknowledging each piece, like some kind of mad furniture-whisperer.

The huge steel angle poise lamp, the bedside tables, the antique oak bookshelf. Box upon box of books and files and folders. Her parental units were academics and personally responsible, she was sure, for razing at least twenty rugby-field-size portions of rainforests each in the amount of paper they used over their lifetimes.

Despite being part of the original e-reader generation, they preferred their reading style old school, and pen and paper to glass or projections. 'It just feels more *real*,' her mother used to say when Kirsten sighed at her for writing down her shopping lists on the back of old receipts. 'Smartphones exist for a reason,' Kirsten would show her over and over how she could have a virtual shopping list, how she could send it to the store and have her groceries picked and delivered for her. Her mother would give her a tight smile, and she would know that she would never win this particular battle. When Cellpurses and then smart watches came on to the market it was just too much for them. They used to wield those old smartphone bricks as if they were something to be proud of, like the burning bras of the 1960s. An image of a particularly ugly bra in flames comes to Kirsten's mind; she doesn't know where it comes from. One of her university courses? An ancient Fair Lady? Picstream? Webpedia? Flittr? Sometimes she feels as though her brain is a giant, multi-dimensional reflector, filled with the world's random pictures. Where have they come from? A parallel life? A previous life? Someone else's life?

The only exception to her parents' fear of progressive technology was when she had given them a Holograph: a 3D-photo projector loaded with her Somali Pirates pictures. This is before the collection had won any awards. They were so proud of her, kept the projector running on loop, despite its rather macabre content: they had pirates in their lounge for months. The Holograph never moved from the mantelpiece, even when it stopped working.

There, there's a good memory to hold on to, until she remembers that the Holograph was stolen in the burglary, which makes her see the crimson comets again.

She battles to tear open the buff boxtape, cursing herself for not thinking of bringing a pair of scissors, when she finds in the third carton a neat little pocket-knife (Royal Sky). It is, fittingly, a sharp taste, a stab of bitter on her tongue, a hint of cyanide, like chewing an apple seed. She remembers this taste exactly, and gets a poke of nostalgia. Her father would keep this knife in his pocket and bring it out on special occasions: when a bottle of wine needed decorking at a neighbourhood braai, or a loose thread threatened to unravel a dress. There would always be a calm measured-ness on these occasions. A slow inspection of the problem, a thoughtful diagnosis, and the retrieval of the magical object from the deep recesses of his trousers. A slow opening of the blade, a glint of light when it was revealed, and then at last, the careful incising where it was needed. Never forgetting the cleaning of the tool afterwards, a sleeve-shining of its insignia, and its eventual evaporation. Considered, calculating, careful.

She remembers specifically an occasion when she was battling to free a new baby doll from its suffocating plastic shell. The way he had achingly-slowly dismantled the packaging and kneeled to hand the toy to her. The way he had looked at her, almost with sadness, as if he had some kind of prescience that she wouldn't be able to bear children of her own. The memory, before fond and with pretty edges, now stings her with its poignancy. She swallows the hard stone in her throat.

Kirsten was never allowed to touch the knife, it was forbidden. She flicks it open and starts ripping into the boxes.

*

Seth knows before he opens his eyes that he's late for his grind. He groans and stretches for the Anahita water bottle he keeps next to his swingbed. Switches off his dreamrecorder. A few gulps later he turns on his Sunrise. Throughout the apartment all the curtains open, allowing the morning light to bleach the inside of the rooms, and what feels like the inside of his head. The apartment voice, which he has nicknamed 'Sandy,' wishes him a good morning and proceeds to play his Saturday playlist.

It's his last day at Pharmax so it shouldn't be too much of a problem if he's a few hours late. It takes him a while to remember why his head feels like it had been left on a township soccer field: Salvia pills, cocaine drops, ShadowShots, a beautiful girl with sequins for eyes. Having sex with the shining girl behind one of the curtains in the club, but bringing a different girl home. Rolo calling them a private cab. Long chestnut- and blonde-striped hair, palest skin, beautiful tits, cosmic blowjob. He yawns and rearranges himself, has another sip of water.

Shit, I didn't even check her ID for her Hi-Vax status.

That is dumb, but lately he's done worse. He is either getting less paranoid or more self-destructive. Maybe it's the salvia. Stretching his arms above his head, he makes a verbal note for his Pharmax report. Seth reaches over for his jacket, lying on the floor, and checks the inner pocket. He shakes the white bottle: almost half of the pills gone. He'll need to top up today before he says his goodbyes.

The stripey-haired hook-up wasn't happy when he asked her to leave at around 3AM but that was pretty much the standard reaction. He made the night more than worth her while, so he told her to suck it up as he pushed taxi tokens into her hand and closed the door behind her, opening it again just to turf out a lone red boot that smelled of Givenchy and old carpets.

As always, he is surprised by the hurt expression. *Honestly, how could she expect him to get a decent night's sleep with a total stranger in his bed? Some creeps were Fucked Up.*

He gets up and wraps his raw silk dressing gown around himself. He doesn't like walking around the place naked, even though he lives on his own. He finds people doing mundane things in the nude—like eating breakfast—distasteful. Naked is for showering and sex, for God's sake, not for frying eggs and pressing wapple juice. He switches on the kettle, pours Ethiopian javaberry grounds into his antique espresso maker, and puts it on the gas stove to percolate. While he's waiting he supercharges his Tile, steams some double-cream milk. Makes seedtoast with almond butter and wolfs it down. Makes some more, and takes it to his tablet along with his mug of fragrant coffee.

Just as he had hoped, a small green rabbit blinks on his screen. Someone from Alba is online and bumps him. He types in his password to gain access to the thread.

FlowerGrrl> Hey SD. You ready?

He takes a sip of his coffee, dusts crumbs off his fingertips, and types a reply:

SD>> Hello my favourite cyberstalker. Yebo. Starting/F on Monday.

FlowerGrrl> U happy/brief?

SD>> Always.

FlowerGrrl> U did a good job/Pharmax.

SD>> There was nothing 2 do.

Out of nowhere, his left thumb starts tingling. He examines it, rubs it on the top of his thigh, and carries on typing.

SD>> They had nothing for us.

FlowerGrrl> Clean corporate? Thought those went/way/rhinos.

SD>> Me 2. But they R squeaky. Apart/drugging up country & making lds $$ off vuln & desperate.

FlowerGrrl>Hey, we all need 2 earn/living.

SD>> Sure. Any news re anything else? Heard about/stupid politician/pool?

FlowerGrrl> Criminal.

SD>> :)

FlowerGrrl> Sure there are lots of those at F.

SD>> Criminals or pools?

FlowerGrrl> Both. If u find 1 have/swim for me. Haven't swum since/kid.

SD>> Me neither. Probably have heated springs & shit in there. I'll do/fucking backstroke 4 U. YOLO!

FlowerGrrl> LOLZ! LFD. YOLO FOMO FML.

SD>> Congrats on Tabula Rasa bust. Excellent work. Mind-5.

FlowerGrrl> Going 2 break story next week.

SD>> They'll make good miners/farmers/etc at the PLC.

FlowerGrrl> Ha! Can U imagine? 1 day a botox billionaire, the next you're lubing up a cow.

SD>> Karma's a bitch.

FlowerGrrl> U said it, baby.

SD>> Nice/catch up.

FlowerGrrl> Ja, B careful now.

SD>> Always.

FlowerGrrl> Seriously. Watch yourself.

SD>> I am being serious. I'm paranoid, always careful.

FlowerGrrl> LOL! Funny cos iz true. X

The green rabbit disappears.

*

Kirsten's left thumb is bleeding. She hadn't realised you could get a (double) paper cut from double-walled cardboard. After swearing a great deal in every colour she can think of, she kicks the box that had inflicted the damage. She wants it to go flying, but it's heavy and all she manages to do is nudge it off the pile. It lands with a thud of disappointment on the concrete floor.

The corner of a white card sticks out from underneath the box. She pries it loose. Smaller than the palm of her hand, tacky double-sided tape on the back: it's the kind of card that gets sent with flower deliveries. The illustration is of a lily, printed in sparkling pink ink (Strawberry Spangle), which she bleeds on.

Inside, in a script she doesn't recognise, it says 'CL, yours forever, X, EM.'

Her watch beeps. It's a bump from Keke, wanting to meet up for drinks next week. Says she has something to celebrate. Somewhere dark and clubby, she says.

'Affirmative,' Kirsten replies, 'Congratulations in advance for whatever we're celebrating. Let's bask in our mutual claustrophilia.'

Bumps, or chatmail messages, are getting so short nowadays they can be impossible to textlate. Sometimes Kirsten uses the longest word she can think of, just to rebel against the often ridiculously abbreviated chat language.

She realises that this probably makes her old, and wonders if it is the equivalent of wielding a brick for a cellphone. Even her Snakewatch is now old technology. She doesn't have the energy to upgrade devices every season. Maybe she is more like her mother than she has ever realised.

She flicks the card back into the box and sucks the side of her thumb, where the skin is dual-sliced, and waits for the red to stop. She feels hung over, even though she didn't drink *that* much the night before. Another sign of aging? She sometimes feels like she's ninety. And not today's '90 is the new 40!' but real, steel, brittle ninety. Grey-hair, purple-rinse, hip-replacement ninety.

So far she had flipped through what felt like hundreds of files and documents, most written in jargon that she doesn't understand. She had to page through a library of notes before she found her birth certificate. Onionskin paper, slightly wrinkled, low-resolution print, ugly typography, but there her name was in black and white: Kirsten Lovell; daughter of Sebastian and Carol Lovell. Born on the 6th of December 1988 at the Trinity Clinic in Sandton, Johannesburg.

So she does exist, she thinks, *even though it should seem clear. Cogito ergo fucking sum.*

Perhaps the autopsy report was wrong? They could have mixed up her mother's body with someone else's, easy enough to do when so many people are dying of the Bug. Or the discharge note from the hospital could have been wrong; they got the date of her hysterectomy wrong. A sleep-deprived nurse on her midnight shift could easily have written down the wrong year. Perhaps absent-mindedly thinking of her own surgery, or the birth of one of her own kids.

Getting tired of hunting through the boxes now, she finally finds the one she had come all this way for. It's a bit squashed on the edges, and grubby with handprints. Sealed with three different kinds of tape, it has clearly been opened and closed a number of times over the years. 'PHOTO ALBUMS' is scribbled on the side in her mother's terrible handwriting. When Kirsten catches sight of the scrawl she feels a twinge of tenderness and has to sit down for a breath.

She opens the box with a little more care than she had the others. Twelve hardcover photo albums take up the top half of the box, and the bottom is lined with DVDs. They only started taking digital photos when she was in high school, so it was safe to say what she was looking for would be in one of the paper albums.

There is a specific picture of herself as a baby that she wants to find. She guesses the photo was taken when she was around six months old, somewhere outside in the sun with a tree, or trees, in the background. A silly, fabric-flowered headband decorates her hairless moon of a head. Her back is slightly arched and an arm is outstretched to someone off-camera, a pale pink starfish for a hand.

Slowly she pages through each album, trying to not get caught in the webs of emotion they contain: rhubarb crumble, ash grey, peppermint (the colour, not the taste), coconut sunscreen, soggy egg sandwiches (Sulphurous Sponge), some kind of flat sucker with a milky taste – butterscotch? Butterscotch with beach-sand. Marshmallow mice – available only at a game-hall tuckshop at a family holiday resort in the Drakensberg. Ammonia, baby oil, cherry cigars. Silk carnations, flaking slasto, ants that taste like pepper. She snaps shut the last album and looks for another box of photos.

This can't be all there is. We're missing three years. The first three years.

Kirsten, now driven by a fierce energy, attacks what is left of the boxes. Her mind races with possible explanations. Maybe they didn't own a camera. Maybe they believed it was bad luck to photograph a baby. Maybe the photos were lost, stolen, burnt in a fire. There are no baby clothes either. No baby toys, but she's sure they must have been given away—there were hundreds of orphans in those days—abandoned babies: unheard of today. Wet patches bloom under her arms as she scrabbles through the contents. Her hair begins to bother her and she ties it up roughly into an untidy bun. As the boxes start to run out, her anxiety builds. She finds no more albums, but in the second-last box she opens she discovers some framed photographs. *Of course! It was framed! That's why it's not in an album.* A calming finger on her heart.

And there it is, almost exactly how she remembers it. She clutches it, searching it for detail. The heat of her hands mists the silver frame: heavy, decorative, tasteful, the picture not exactly in focus, but close enough. A blue cotton dress (Robin Egg) puckered by the tanned arm holding her up. She has no aunts, no grandmothers; that must be her mom's arm, although she doesn't recognise it.

She expects the photo to make her feel some kind of relief, but it has the opposite effect. Some small idea is tapping at her, whirring in her brain. Something feels off the mark. She scans the picture again.

What is it? The texture. The texture of the paper is wrong. It isn't printed on glossy or matt photo paper, the way it would have been in 1987. It's grainy, pulpy. Kirsten turns the frame over in her hands and pries loose the back. A quarter of a glamorous cigarette print ad stares back at her, its bright blue slashing her vision.

Kirsten turns it over and over again, battling to understand, not wanting to understand. It's not a photo of her. It's not a photo at all, but a cutting from a magazine. The autopsy diagram flits into her mind with its careless cross over her mother's lower abdomen.

She glances over at the cheap-looking birth certificate then down to the piece of paper she holds. Perhaps her photo was published in the magazine for some reason? Living & Loving, the cutting says, 'New Winter Beauties,' July 1991. She was three years old when this issue was printed.

ORGANIC ARSE CARROTS

7

Johannesburg, 2021

'Oh,' his new manager says, greeting Seth with an awkward smile, 'I thought you would be wearing a suit.'

At the behemoth reception of Fontus, the walls are covered in digital 4D wallpaper of waterfalls, streams and lakes. White noise gushes through the sound system: water splashing and birds chirping. Seth doesn't shake his proffered hand.

'I don't wear suits.'

Heavy security guards the front door, which is at odds

with the holograms of rising mist and darting digital hummingbirds. Men with concealed guns and pepper-spray look serenely on as employees and visitors enter through the metal detectors.

As they make their way through the building, the moving images change according to which section they are in: the waters Anahita, Tethys, Hydra, followed by the carbonated soft drinks. Anahita is platinum and crystal, blond hair, and pale, skeletal models. Diamond drops and sleek splashes of mercury. Tethys is dew on grass, rainforests, intelligent-looking people wearing spectacles, good dentures, hands on chins. Cool, humidified air streams past them as they walk.

Wesley doesn't back down. 'It's company policy.'

Hydra is smiling black children, barefoot, dusty. A gospel choir. Fever trees. Optimistic amateur vegetable gardens. Dry red earth. Seth gets thirsty just looking at them.

'No, it's not,' says Seth. 'I would never have signed the contract.'

There is an awkward silence until they reach the section where he will be grinding: Carbonates. As expected, there are bubbles frothing and fizzing all around them. Wesley slows to a stop in the red area: CinnaCola. The décor is like a large tin of red paint has exploded.

'It may not be in the *actual* contract…'

'Well, then, there's no problem. Is this my office?' Seth strides in and slips behind the desk, surveying his stationery. Shrugs off his black hoodie and slings it over his chair. He's never had a proper desk job before; he's used to being in a lab of sorts. He uncaps a brand new permanent marker and sniffs it. Wesley looks at Seth swivelling in his chair and purses his lips. Strokes his soul patch with two fingers.

'We have an 8AM meeting every Monday morning to set up our week's goals,' he says.

Y*eah, I won't be making those*, Seth resists saying.

'A goal not written down is just a dream. What is measured is managed. CinnaCola assembles in the Red Room.'

Seth inspects the contents of his desk drawers. Wesley tries to get his attention.

'But it's not all work-work-work here! On the last Friday of the month, we do a teambuilding activity, where we compete against the other FCs.' Wesley fingers the red lanyard around his neck. 'FC. That's Flavour-Colours,' he says. 'It's teambuilding and fun and all that but it's also a serious competition. It's important that we win. What are you good at? You know, apart from maths? Paintball? Boules? Triathlons? Firewalking? Extreme Frisbee?'

The distaste must have shown on Seth's face because Wesley stops talking and looks uncomfortable. He puffs out his chest and says 'It's compulsory.'

Is it also compulsory to walk around with a carrot shoved up your arse? Do they hand out complimentary organic arse carrots here?

Wesley's cheeks colour, and for a second Seth thinks he

said it out loud, but then realises it's because Wesley has caught sight of his sneakers. They're limited edition, by a local graffiti artist, and have the word *Punani* emblazoned on the sides. He guesses they're worth more than Wesley makes in a month. Seth is tempted to put them up on the desk, but then thinks better of it. Best not to push him too far, too soon. Managers are assholes at the best of times and he can't have anyone deliberately obstructing him. As a peace-making concession he takes out his eyebrow-ring and puts it in his pocket. Rubs off some of the Smudge on his eyes. He sees Wesley soften. It works every time.

'Okay, then,' says Seth, pointing at his giant flatscreen Glass, 'I'd better get started.'

Wesley attempts a smile, and looks immediately like a rodent: his nose crinkles up and his lips reveal his large front teeth. Perfect, Wesley the Weasel. At least now he won't forget his name. A welcome pack on his desk contains his access/ID card, to be clipped onto his very own red lanyard, a CinnaCola shirt in his size, complete with animated fizzing logo, and a blue book of Fontus rules of conduct. The Fontus logo is, unimaginatively, a stylised illustration of a fountain, and the word 'Fontus' is set in a handsome font, uppercase. He turfs the lanyard into his drawer and slides the card into his pocket.

'You have to wear it,' says The Weasel. 'The lanyard, and card. It's for ID as much as it's for access.' He points to the camera in the corner of the room. 'Security, you know.'

Seth retrieves the red lanyard and clips his card onto it. Reluctantly puts it around his neck. The Weasel chortles.

'Besides, we can't have those Greens sneaking around the red section, stealing our brand strategies!'

Posters on the walls feature pictures of the Fourteen Wonders of the world on dark blue backgrounds with slogans like: 'It's Not a Problem, it's a Challenge' and 'Opportunities are Everywhere'.

He waits for The Weasel to go before he dumps the rest of the welcome pack into the bin. The shirt continues to fizz. He swivels his ergochair around, stares out of the window. Someone laughs in the corridor. The grounds are immaculate: the lawn grass smooth and green; perfectly tended bright annuals burst with complimentary colours under canopies of handsome indigenous trees. Cheerful employees pass each other with a smile or a wave. The campus is like a hotbed of high spirits, cleanliness, and efficiency, a bright island in the dark fuss that is the rest of the country. Seth pops a pill. Yes, he thinks, there is definitely something very odd going on around here.

JOURNAL ENTRY 7

28 September 1987

Westville

In the news: *Two bombs explode at the Standard Bank Arena in Johannesburg. John McEnroe is fined for his antics at the US Open. Star Trek: The Next Generation debuts on (American!) TV.*

What I'm listening to: *Michael Jackson's Bad album. Superbad!*

What I'm reading: *Misery by Stephen King: injured and drugged, an author is held captive by a psychotic fan. So-o-o creepy. Make P get up to switch the lights off!*

What I'm watching: *Fatal Attraction. Not the best movie to watch in the week before your wedding! Totally scary, I loved it.*

We got married today at a tiny ceremony at Westville Magistrate's Court. P's best man (Whitey) was there, and both of our parents. I totally thought my folks would boycott the wedding but they were troopers. Dad put on a brave face and Mom took turns crying and fussing with my dress in front, as if a piece of fabric could cover my huge pregnant belly. I mean it's totally gigantic! I never thought it was possible to get this big! The ONLY thing that fits me apart from this big meringue of a wedding dress is my old 'Sex Pistols' T-shirt. I practically live in it!

When I wrote to Dad about it (the pregnancy) he was very cross and I didn't hear from him for ages. Mom phoned me and told me to be patient, and that he would come around. If not before the wedding then definitely once the baby was born, she said. His first grandchild! She was right. When I saw him he hugged me (carefully avoiding the bump), and said: "There's nothing to do but to make the best of a bad situation." I wanted to say to him: a lovely baby is not a 'bad situation', but I was so totally grateful to be forgiven and to feel loved that I just kept quiet and kissed him.

The 'wedding photos' are going to be so funny. We got a certificate right away saying that we are husband and wife. Me, a wife?! Ha! I'm so sure! Our wedding song was our favourite song by Bryan Adams: 'Hearts on Fire'. I got quite emotional, think it's the raging hormones. But when I looked at P I could tell that he had a lump in his throat too.

We went to a seafood restaurant afterwards and my dad ordered lots of platters and sparkling wine. I couldn't, like, have seafood or wine in my state but I didn't feel like eating anyway. I toasted our marriage with Grapetizer in a champagne glass. Totally the Best Grapetizer I have ever tasted.

Afterwards, in bed, exhausted but happy, P lay with his hand on my stomach and we could feel the baby moving.

Happiest day of my life, and I can't wait to meet my baby.

MARY CONTRARY

8

Johannesburg, 2021

Kirsten catches the waiter's attention and motions for another round. She is sitting on her own in Molly Q's, a retro-restaurant, the only one in Johannesburg that still serves molecular cuisine.

It's her best, and James had booked a table for them for his first night back home. Kirsten's favourite gastroventure, she loves the purity of the flavours here; the shapes she sees and feels are so vivid and in focus.

She is drinking their signature cocktail, an unBloody Mary-Contrary. The purest vodka swirled with clear tomato water and essence of pepper. They serve it with a long, slender frozen piece of celery-green glass. Kirsten takes a sip and feels the crystalline shapes appear before her. Not as strong as the first drink, but quite clear nevertheless.

Damn the law of diminishing returns.

They'll get stronger, more palpable, later in the evening; alcohol always makes her synaesthesia more pronounced. Suddenly she feels lips on her forehead, a warm hand on her back, and she blinks past the crystals to see James.

'Kitty! I missed you.'

She springs up to hug him, inhales the tang of his neck. He smells like Zimbabwe: hand sanitiser and aeroplane cabin. Also: miswak chewing gum that has long lost its flavour. They hold onto each other for a while.

'I missed you too.'

Kissing James is always orange: different shades of orange depending on the mood of the kiss. Breakfast kisses are usually a fresh Buttercup Yellow, sex kisses are Burnt-Sky, with a spectrum in between of, among others, loving, friendly, angry, guilty (Pollen, Polished Pine, Rubber Duck, Turmeric). His energy is warm yellow-orange-ruby, sweet, with a sharp echo. Marmalade James.

They sit down, and Kirsten orders a craft beer for him, a hoppy ale; he doesn't drink cocktails. He always laughs out loud when they watch old movies and James Bond drinks a martini.

'How's the clinic?'

He has a slight tan, despite his usually fanatical compulsion to apply SPF100, and crumpled cotton sleeves. He looks tired, but well.

'Understaffed, underfunded, and bursting with sick people: sick children, sick babies. It was difficult to leave.'

Something small in Kirsten splinters. He grabs her hand.

'Of course, I'd rather be with you than anywhere, but there are just so many—'

'I understand,' she says, looking away. It's easier to be with people you can help.

'So many of the babies there are hungry and neglected. Not like here,' he says.

'Not like here,' she agrees. How can you neglect a baby? How come those creeps are fertile, she thinks, when I'm not?

'I mean I can see how the border-baby trade is thriving. When you see kids like that you get the feeling that their parents would gladly part with them for a couple of hundred thousand rand.'

'Awful,' says Kirsten, pulling a face. 'They should write it into law that you need to qualify for a parenting license before you're allowed to procreate.'

'You don't mean that,' James says, but she kind of does.

They order the set menu, and an *amuse bouche* of wooded chardonnay gelée with pink balsamic caviar arrives, then Asian crudo with a brush of avocado silk, and wasabi sorbet.

They keep quiet for the first few bites, allowing Kirsten to appreciate all the shapes, colours and textures of the flavours. The wasabi sorbet in particular sends cool ninja stars into her brain. It feels good.

'How are you?' James asks, 'how have you been holding up?'

'I had a very interesting weekend,' she says, spooning the last of the wasabi into her mouth and feeling the jagged edges of the stars fade away. 'I discovered the reason I'm so, well, fucked up.'

James takes a long, slow sip of his beer. They had been through this so many times before.

One of the problems with long-term mono-relationships, is that listening to the same old issues gets eyeball-bleedingly boring. At least now she has a new angle.

He looks at her, measuring her mood, puts down his glass. She senses him sighing on the inside.

'Kitty, you're not fucked up.'

'I am, a little.'

'Okay, you are, a little, but so is everyone else. You're just more aware of your fucked-up-ness than the average creep, because you're...'

'Special?'

'Not what I was going to say, but let's go with that.'

They smile at each other, and it reminds her of when they

started dating in varsity. When things were still shiny.

'Do you mean your synaesthesia?'

'No, the synaesthesia is my light side. I'm talking about my dark side.'

'The Black Hole,' he says. God, how he hates The Black Hole.

As a child she had tried to explain it to her parents, thinking that they had it too, that is was a necessary human condition, but they would get frustrated and lose their patience, just as James does now. Perhaps The Black Hole on its own would have been fine, but with her synaesthesia it seemed too much for them to handle. It caused a rift: a cool, empty space between them that could easily be ignored; not often navigated.

Once, when she was still in primary school, she tried to explain the emptiness to her mother, who became furious and stormed out, leaving her at home alone. When the minutes streamed into hours and the sun started sinking she went to the neighbour's house: a young couple who, nonplussed, plopped her in front of the television. They fed her milky rooibos and stale Marie biscuits while they whispered into the phone. Afterwards, they sat in the living room with her, making awkward conversation, until the glare of her mother's headlights lit up their sitting room, announcing, with bright hostility, her return. It wasn't the first or the last time her mother had left her on her own.

Eventually, a little desperately, her father had produced Mingi: a meowing yin-yang ball of fluff, hoping the kitten would stitch up The Black Hole, but it didn't. She kept quiet about it after that, not wanting to cause them any more worry. Now they were gone and now James was the worrier.

'And?' he prompts, 'what's the reason?'

She smooths out the polka-dotted tablecloth then says the words out loud: slowly, clearly, listening to her own voice. 'I think I was adopted.'

James frowns at her. 'What?'

'Keke visited while you were away. She found out some… well, to cut a long story short, my mother had a hysterectomy before I was born.'

She lets it sink in. James just looks at her.

'And,' she says, taking the birth certificate and magazine clipping out of her bag, 'look at these. Look at this cheap-ass certificate, probably created in CorelDRAW. Do you know that there is not one photo of me as a baby? Not one.'

She flips the imposter-baby picture over to reveal the magazine name and date on the other side. James looks stunned. She doesn't blame him. She doesn't quite believe it yet, either. He grabs the photo from her hand and studies it.

'I know!' she says, 'isn't it crazy? I'm adopted!' The woman at the next table looks over in interest. Kirsten lowers her voice. 'So there is a reason I never felt properly connected to them. Why I always felt like an outsider.'

'Everyone feels like an outsider. It's inherent, the feeling we don't belong. Ironically, the one thing we all have in common.'

'Yes, okay, but... it's crackers, right? Do you realise what this means? I could have a family out there!'

James is quiet, looks worried.

'Well?' she urges him, as if he has some kind of answer for her.

'I'm sorry, I don't know what to say. I mean, it's pretty shocking. If it's true.'

'I need to find them.'

'What do you mean?'

'What the hell do you think I mean? I'm going to find out who my real parents are. And meet them. Have them over for some fucking cake.'

'I don't think it's a good idea.'

'I knew you'd say that.'

'That's unfair.'

'That night... that night they were killed,' says Kirsten.

James puts his hand over hers.

'My mother called me. She said she had to tell me something. That it couldn't wait.'

'Why didn't you... tell me?'

'She was upset, stumbling over her words. Not making sense. I thought she was... having one of her episodes.'

Carol had been showing signs of early-onset Alzheimer's. She hadn't been diagnosed, but the symptoms of dementia had begun presenting themselves the year before, and were increasing in frequency. Kirsten pictured the disease as a whey-coloured cotton wool cloud over her mother's head (Cirrus Nest). As with most issues, her parents hadn't liked to talk about it. James looks into her ever-changing eyes, the sound of the sea.

'Surely you must get it? This is my chance to find my missing part. Besides, it's not just for me; it's for us. To know my biological mother's medical history… it might help us figure out our… fertility issues.'

'I wish that I was enough for you,' he whispers, turmeric in the air. Kisten gives him a segment of a smile. They both know it will never be true.

He takes a gulp of his beer. 'We don't have fertility issues.'

'Are you being serious? We've been trying for years.'

'That's normal, nowadays.'

A frozen veil descends between them.

'I feel the hope too,' says James. 'And the disappointment. I want a baby as much as you do.'

'Bullshit,' she says, although she knows it hurts him.

'Look, the less you worry about it—'

Kirsten curls her hands into fists. 'Less worry is not an option currently on the table. Please choose another fucking option.'

The chicken truffle with cocoa-chilli reduction and green peppercorn brittle arrives. It is beautifully presented but Kirsten is raging inside and can't imagine she can swallow any of it.

'Look,' she says, pushing her chair back. 'I'm meeting Kex for drinks tonight. I'm going to go.'

'Kitty, please don't be like this.'

She stands up. 'I'll see you later.'

*

Seth leaves the Fontus building at 20:30. He is enjoying the actual work of the new job, the flavour-mapping and production process modelling; it's like grinding at Disney World after the serious chemical engineering he did at Pharmax. Plus they have everything you could possibly want on the campus: a gym, a spa, a drycleaner, a download-den, communal bikes, restaurants, a (mostly empty) childcare centre, a virtual bowling alley, a Lixair chamber, SleepPods, all complimentary for staff. They even have wine tasting and book club evenings. Golf days, gaming nights. Infertility support groups. Overnight accommodation. The huge property is not dissimilar to a full-board holiday resort. It's as if they don't want their employees to leave the premises. Seth is surprised they don't run a matchmaking service to keep all the creeps in the family. Or a brothel.

The employees themselves seem to be extremely clean-cut: professionally dressed, well groomed, clear skinned. Not a lot of individual style—no Smudge or ink in sight. Certainly no recreational drugs as far as he can tell.

The Weasel is turning out to be even more of a pesticle than expected, literally leaning over his shoulder as he works. He finds it difficult to be constructive when he's being watched, especially by a bag of dicks. He needs to experiment and play around, and this includes swapping and swerving in between a host of different programs and apps, and you can't do that when you have those watery eyes glued to your screen.

Worse still, it makes it almost impossible to do his real job—his Alba job—the reason he is here is in the first place. Seth feels a hot rush of irritation, almost anger; he needs to blow off some steam. He has a cocaine drop, his third for the day, and decides to head to the SkyBar.

*

Kirsten catches a tuk-tuk for the short ride into the inner city. She has the feeling someone is watching her, and keeps looking over her shoulder for James, that he must have followed her out of Molly Q's, but each time she thinks she hears something, or sees movement out of the corner of her eye, there is no one there. Despite the reassuring company of her fellow passengers, she starts to feel quite spooked.

Kekeletso is already at the bar when Kirsten gets there, and is getting some girl's number. Once she has it, they smile at each other, and the woman kisses Keke's cheek, strokes her arm. Keke is wearing a lacy tank top that shows off her nano-ink tattoo beautifully. It's an antique grey colour now, so Keke must have shot up quite recently.

The SkyBar is on top of the tallest skyscraper in South Africa. It's five hundred floors, and has a glass elevator on either side. They used to have a C-shaped infinity pool outside, running almost all the way around the venue. Now it's dry and filled with exotic-looking plants with larger-than-life leaves and trailing tendrils. The club's main attraction is that there's always an interesting crowd, a good mix of BEE and reverse-BEE millionaires, bohemians, sports celebrities, tourists and race car drivers.

'Hey,' she greets Keke, 'this place is packed! I thought we were only meeting at nine-thirty.'

She waves off the woman. 'I decided to come early, to network.'

'So that's what the kids are calling it nowadays?'

Keke smiles, and Kirsten grabs the still-warm barstool, which is more of a post-modernist statement than an actual chair.

'Seriously, she's a good contact to have. Grinds for the Nancies.'

'Yuck,' says Kirsten, 'and I thought my life was bad.'

'She's clearly a masochist.'

'Those masochists. Handy to have around.'

Keke orders them a couple of beers, hits the 'tip' button twice, and the barman delivers them with a wink in her direction. Her account will be debited with the balance by the KFID system as she leaves.

'So, why are you early? I thought Marmalade was taking you out tonight. What happened, did he stand you up? No petrol in Zim again? No water? No aeroplane stairs?'

'It would have been better if he had.'

'Oh, shit. Sorry. Another fight?'

'Argh... I'm so sick of hearing about my own problems. Fuck it. What are we here to celebrate?'

'Well... can I tell you a secret?' asks Keke, eyes a-sparkle.

'Hello,' says Kirsten, 'who else would you tell?'

'You can't tell anyone, not even Marmalade.'

Won't be the first time. Kirsten nods.

'I'm just about to break this big story. It's huge. I'd love to say that it's been weeks of hard journo-ing but actually it just fell into my lap. All I had to do was fact-check.'

'In other words, all your Friend With Benefits had to do was fact-check.'

'Yeah-bo.'

'Hey? Who did it come from? Why would someone just hand over a story to you? And why you?'

'I don't know. The gods of the fuck-circus that is journalism decided to smile down on me. Why do whistleblowers toot their flutes? Justice? Revenge? It arrived in my SkyBox with no note and no author. Just the picture of a little green rabbit that disappeared as soon as I opened it.'

'Bizarre,' says Kirsten.

'I know already. But listen to this. You know that Slow-Age super-expensive beauty-salon-slash-plastic-surgery clinic in Saxonwold? Tabula Rasa. They were the first spa in SA to have a Lixair—vitamin air—chamber. They made headlines a while ago with their FOXO gene therapy? The one with all-white everything? Like, you get blinded when you go in there?'

'Heard of it. Never been. My freelance salary doesn't stretch that far.'

'Lucky for you. All that white was hiding something very dark indeed.'

'Let me guess. They were exchanging their wrinkled flesh-and-blood clients for smooth-skinned Quinbots?'

'Worse,' says Kekeletso.

'Ha,' says Kirsten. 'What?'

'They were buying *discarded embryos* from dodgy fertility clinics, spinning them for their stem cells, then injecting them into their clients' *faces.*'

Kirsten stops smiling. 'No,' she says.

'That's what I thought. No way it could be true, but this report came from someone who had worked there. Had infiltrated the system and had proof of hundreds of transactions. Pics, video, everything.'

'That is so fucked up. Horrible. I wish you had never told me. I wish it wasn't true.'

'Sorry,' says Keke. 'I had to tell someone. I've been sitting on it for days waiting for all the facts to check out.'

'What kind of world are we living in?' asks Kirsten.

'One where at least there is someone willing to out those bastards. If something like this had happened fifty years ago we wouldn't have had a cooking clue. May The Net bless Truthers everywhere.'

'To Truthers!' says Kirsten, raising her drink. 'Also, ha ha.'

'Huh?'

'Don't you think it's funny? The name? Tabula Rasa means "clean slate", doesn't it? Like, come in all aged and wrinkled and shit and leave with a face like a clean slate.'

'And a brain to go with it,' Keke adds.

'Except now it's going to be revealed as a black clinic.'

'Poetry!'

'You're right, it is funny. Ha!'

'Or would be, if it wasn't so fucked up.'

'Yes,' Keke pulls a face, 'well. You know what they say.'

'Tell me. What do they say?'

'If you don't laugh, you cry.'

'Story of my life. Well, congratulations. That's one big fucking story. I sense some kind of award for journalistic excellence on the horizon. Huzzah!'

'I wish I could take the credit. Oh, Kitty... there's something else,' says Keke, looking hesitant.

'What's up?'

'I found something else. It's something about you. About your parents.' Keke rubs her lips, rings for another round. 'You're not going to like it.'

*

Seth is gliding to electro-house swampo-phonic with a drunk woman in a kimono on the superglass dance-floor. It is easier to dance if you don't look down: five hundred floors up, the vertigo from looking down sucks the rhythm from your feet. Usually he loves the mixed crowd at the SkyBar but he feels off-balance tonight. The drinks don't taste as good; the women aren't as pretty as usual. It's too crowded. He tried taking more coke earlier but it seems like a waste with this mood. Usually he would have already banged this girl in the plant pool, or in the unisex bathroom, but tonight it doesn't feel worth the bother. This makes him feel worse. Is he getting old? Is grinding in a corporate environment leaching him of his personality? What's next? Wearing a suit and tie? A nametag? A hearing aid? Joining the Fontus D&D club? Facebook? Getting married? Viagra? He shivers involuntarily. The sooner he can get his job there done and move on, the better.

He gives up on having a good time, abandons his drink, shrugs off the kimono and goes to get his jacket and gun from the security counter. While he manoeuvres through the warm bodies that block him he inadvertently gets close to the bar. As he's making his way forward he feels a surge, an electric current zip through his body. It shocks him into standing up straight. He is surrounded—touching so many creeps at the same time—and he looks about to see if anyone else felt it, but no one around him registers any kind of surprise.

The fuck was that?

*

Kirsten is doubled over. Keke grabs her arm.

'Are you okay?'

'Christ,' she whispers, 'what the fuck?'

'What?'

'I just had the weirdest feeling.'

'Your synaes-stuff?'

Slowly she starts to straighten, hands on hips. 'Fucking hell. I don't think so. More like getting the electric chair. You didn't feel anything?'

Keke shakes her head.

'I must have touched something.' She looks around for anything that may have shocked her. 'It's so crowded in here, maybe it was just some kind of sensory overload.'

Keke looks unconvinced. 'Good god, woman, the more I get to know you, the stranger you become.'

'It's nothing. I'm okay. Hit me,' she says to Keke. 'I can take it.'

'You weren't adopted,' says Keke.

'What?' says Kirsten, cupping her ear.

'You weren't adopted!' shouts Keke.

'That doesn't make any sense.'

'I know,' says Keke. 'But my FWB knows his stuff and there is no record of your parents adopting you, or of you being put up for adoption. He's the best hacker I know. If Marko didn't find anything, believe me, there is nothing to find.'

Kirsten can't think of anything to say.

'It wasn't easy, either. I did some of the digging myself. Since the last orphanage closed in 2016 it's tricky to get information... enough red tape to strangle all the bureaucrats on the planet. It's as if, now that adoption doesn't happen anymore, it's a closed chapter in SA history.'

'I guess that makes sense. Now that babies are... hard to come by, no one wants to think of a time when there were hundreds of them growing up in nasty institutions.'

'Another legacy of the HI-Vax. No more AIDS orphan babies.'

'And of the fertility crisis. No more babies, full stop.' Pain flashes across Kirsten's face.

'Sorry, I know this must be difficult for you.'

'It's not. I mean, of course it is, but for different reasons. So you're sure? No record of an adoption?'

'Actually, no record of you being born. At all.'

Kirsten had guessed the birth certificate was a fake. She laughs despite herself.

'So, what? You're saying I don't exist? I'm a ghost? No wonder I feel hollow. It's all starting to make sense now!'

'Not quite a ghost, but there's definitely something odd about the way you came into the world. We just need to work out what happened. I mean, if that's what you want. You could just forget about the autopsy report. Go back to living your normal life. It's probably the sensible thing to do.'

'Impossible. Besides, it's never been *normal*. I need to find out the truth.'

Keke downs the last of her drink.

'I was hoping you'd say that.'

*

Seth looks at the clockologram on his bedroom wall for what feels like the hundredth time since getting into bed. Agitated, he wonders if he should get a sleeping pill but he's already had two TranX so another downer would probably be a bad idea, especially on top of everything else he's had today. A rock lyric comes into his head.

'Sandy,' he says to the open room.

'Yes, Seth,' purrs the apartment voice.

'Play the song 'Slumber is For Corpses'.'

Three beats later the song comes onto the sound system.

He closes his eyes and listens for a while, then reaches over for the sleeping pills, taps one into his palm. *Fuck it*, he thinks, and swallows it dry. He feels immensely dissatisfied with life in general. His QOL score was sitting at 32 out of a possible 100.

He logged on to the Alba network when he arrived home to see if there were any messages, but there was no green rabbit. He looked for a chatterbot in the quantum philosophy circuit but didn't find one interesting enough. He watched half an hour of a really bad ultra-reality programme about the Underground Games: NinjaJitsu and Punch-Rugby, before giving up on the day and going to bed. He has been alone for so long, but has never gotten used to the feeling. On nights like this his life gapes before him, one big, empty gash. He is a prime number, and prime numbers are always lonely.

The animated graphic novel on his Tile fails to interest him, and he doesn't feel up to gaming, so he just lies back and watches the red hologram digits click over and over. 00:00. He can't even be bothered to jerk off.

*

They leave the SkyBar at around midnight. Kirsten knows by the look in Keke's eyes that she's on her way to a booty call.

'Watch yourself,' Keke says, strapping her helmet on and inflating it. She flings her leg over her sleek e-motorbike, releases the kickstand, and revs the engine. Kirsten waves as Keke takes off with a roar.

Standing in the monochrome rectangular box of the almost empty, poorly lit parking basement, Kirsten feels restless, cocky, horny, and not at all in the mood to go home. If she were single she'd go back to the bar, pick up some unsuspecting man and show him her talents.

She misses that, sometimes, the thrill of sleeping with someone for the first time. The feeling of a stranger's lips on hers—lips that have nothing to do with love or affection. The first undressing, the first nipple-in-mouth, pulling of hair, and then the heady relief of that first swollen thrust. Just thinking about it, Kirsten feels her breathing deepen, and a general throbbing in the lower half of her body. James is a generous lover, but he doesn't have the same nagging libido she does. Add thirteen years of old-fashioned monogamy to that and it's always tempting on nights like this, with booze in her blood, to accept one of the many advances made to her. After all, no one would have to know, so no one would be hurt. She has never cheated on James, but at times like this, angry with him, angry with the world, she feels a hard, rebellious recklessness, a sharp chipstone in her fist.

The idea of meeting someone new at the bar, someone who doesn't know any of her problems, is tempting. She could pretend to be a different person. Be someone lighter: someone who didn't think as much. Make up a fake name, live one of those parallel lives that loiter in her subconscious, if only for a few hours. Shake some yellow stars of adrenaline into her bloodstream. Have dirty sex.

But she won't do it, wouldn't be able to live with the haunting guilt. Kirsten may have a dozen flaws, but she is not a cheater. Cursed at birth with honesty and loyalty, she's not dissimilar to a Labrador, as Keke likes to say.

All relationships have their rocky roads. She reminds herself to think with her brain, and her heart, and takes a definitive step in the direction of the late-night bus stop.

In the distance a silhouette steps out from behind a car and Kirsten jumps.

Jesus! She scrabbles for her mace.

The figure slowly approaches her and her beer-clumsy fingers can't find the mace so she decides to run. The parking basement, however, is in virtual darkness apart from the exit, and the creep now stands between her and the light. Kirsten squints, shields her eyes, tries to see the face of the stranger.

'Hello?' She pushes her voice deeper, tries to seem strong and confident. The figure slows, but keeps moving towards her, gliding silently, also cautious. With a zinging in her head, Kirsten realises this is the person who has been following her all night. She sweats, feverish with fright.

'Don't be scared,' says a woman with a wobbly voice.

'What do you want?' shouts Kirsten, an edge to her tone. She imagines herself waking up the next morning in a bath of dirty ice, with untidy green stitches (Seaweed Sutures) where her kidneys used to be. But that kind of stuff doesn't happen anymore. They print organs now.

'I have something for you.'

Kirsten can make out her face, cheek-boned but androgynous, with a matching haircut. Skeletal figure hidden in unflattering clothes: mom-cut jeans and a tracksuit top flecked with dog hair. No makeup on her dry lips or darting eyes. Clenched hands.

'Stay away from me!' shouts Kirsten. 'Stay away!'

'I have something for you,' the woman says again.

Jesus Christ. What? A knife? An injection? A cold pad of chloroform to hold to my mouth?

'I'm not here to hurt you,' she says, scuttling up close in dirty sneakers. She has body odour: dried figs and BBQ sauce. The stink smacks Kirsten in the face: it's a giant grey curtain, poised to smother. The woman has some sticky white sleep in her eyes. Kirsten is repelled, nauseated.

'I'm here to warn you.' Her eyes flash from beneath her blunt-cut fringe. 'There are people, people that want to hurt us.'

'Us?'

'You, and me, and the other four.'

'Six people?'

'Seven! Seven! One is dead already!'

Oh boy.

'He was first on the list. He sang a song. Music man. Now he is dead. We were too late. Now I am warning you.'

Kirsten tries to step around her, but she blocks her way.

'I didn't believe it either when she told me,' she rambles, 'but she said I had to find you! Had to warn you. Had to give you the list.'

The woman takes her hand, and the feel of her clammy fingers makes Kirsten cringe. The woman presses a cold object into her palm and closes her fingers over it. A new wave of BBQ BO washes over Kirsten and she almost gags.

'There is real danger. Don't go to the police, they are in on it! They are pawns. Don't tell anyone. Don't trust anyone. Like dominoes we'll fall,' she says, softly clicking her fingers. *Click, click, click.* 'Dominoes.' She clicks seven times. 'Don't trust anyone! Not even the people you love.'

Kirsten's heart bangs, her watch alerts her to a spike in blood pressure. The woman turns and scurries away. After a few steps she turns and whispers, 'Be careful, Kate.'

'My name is Kirsten!'

'Yes,' says the woman. 'Your Kirsten is my Betty, Kate. Betty-Barbara. Kirsten-Kate.'

Kirsten looks down, opening her hand to reveal a small silver key.

*

'Thank Christ!' says Kirsten as she catches sight of James. Spooked by the delusional woman in the basement, she called and asked him to fetch her, and has been waiting for him in a bright, 24-hour teashop around the corner from the bar. She gets up too quickly to hug him and sends her cup and saucer stuttering to the floor where they crack and break apart in slow motion. They move awkwardly to pick up the pieces.

'I'm sorry,' he says, mid-crouch, eyes on the floor.

'Me too,' she says. 'Well, sorry that we fought, anyway.'

'Yes,' he says.

She's too strung out to catch any kind of public transport, so they walk home. The pavement trips them up, but it's a small price to pay. Kirsten tells him about Keke's latest discovery: that there's no record of her birth.

'That's impossible,' James says. 'There must be. Just because she can't find proof... Look, I got your pills for you.' He takes a plastic bottle of little yellow tablets (Lemon Zest) out of his manbag and hands it to her. After bumping him the prescription from the inVitro offices she has forgotten about it.

'Thanks.'

He stops her, takes her by her elbows. 'Kitty, are you okay?'

'That... that stupid woman in the basement scared me,' she says, childlike, vulnerable.

'Creeps like that should be locked up,' he says, anger grating his voice. 'Instead of, instead of going around... frightening people. We should report her.'

Kirsten knows she shouldn't tell him about the silver key but it's glowing hot in her pocket, in her brain. They are walking over a bridge when she takes it out and shows it to him.

'I know I should get rid of it,' she says, 'but something in me says I should keep it. I mean, I *want* to get rid of it...' She feels silly. 'I don't know.'

'I do,' says James. He grabs the key out of her hand and throws it over the bridge. It glints against the dark sky then is lost forever. Not even a sound as it lands: seconds, metres, storeys, away. Swallowed by the night. Kirsten is shocked by her empty, moon-white palm.

'It's for the best,' James says, and marches on.

JOURNAL ENTRY 9

10 December 1987

Westville

In the news: *During a police raid on shacks in the Port Elizabeth area, they meet heavy resistance from the residents. The police drive a Casspir over the shack, killing four. Ireland is reeling from the Enniskillen Remembrance Day bombing.*

What I'm listening to: *Faith! By George Michael*

What I'm reading: *Kaleidoscope by Danielle Steele. I needed something light because the only time I have to read is when I'm half asleep and breastfeeding! The story is about three sisters who are separated by fate. I'm hoping they'll be reunited.*

What I'm watching: *3 Men and a Baby. Tom Selleck is gorgeous and hilarious.*

Life keeps surprising me. After 18 hours in labour (an early labour and a very long 18 hours!) Sam Chapman (2.6kg) was born at 8:45. Ten minutes later – surprise! – A little girl arrived too. We have named her Kate (2.2kg).

We were totally shocked but actually my belly had been so big that everyone in shopping malls etc. kept asking if it was twins so we did have some kind of warning. P left the hospital once I fell asleep so that he could go get 'emergency supplies'. It took us months to do up the nursery and here he is, having to double it up in a day!

Sam latched immediately but Kate was too hungry to try—she just screamed!—So P gave her a bottle to get her blood sugar level stable. They are so tiny; the nurses are keeping them in the warming drawers that look like Tupperwares. Pink tummies and tiny little toes that I want to kiss. I am exhausted and sore; all I want to do is hold my babies and sleep. Very tired, and relieved that we are all safe.

SHINING & SLIPPERY WITH SWEAT

9

Johannesburg, 2021

Seth saunters into the Yellow printer room.

'Oh, hi Fiona.' He smiles at the curly-haired woman and acts surprised, as if he didn't know she was in there. She blushes at him knowing her name. Seth brushes skilfully past her.

'Hi.' She smiles, holding her locket to her lips, warming the silver with her breath. They both watch the printer for a few seconds, as if willing it to print faster. She unconsciously pumps her high heels, as if warming up for a race.

'Our printer's being repaired,' he says. 'It's a dinosaur of a thing: still uses toner. That's why I'm in Yellow.'

'Okey-dokey,' she says.

'Not all bad, though,' he says, 'getting to see you.'

She guffaws. After a while, hand on hip, she says, 'This won't do, you know. I know what you're trying to do.' Her freckles fade against the rose of her cheeks.

'Really?' he says, 'and what is that?'

'Trying to find out Yellow's secrets.'

He moves closer to her. 'Ah, so you *do* have secrets.'

'We do,' she says, 'and we're going to win this quarter.' Her large breasts rise and fall under her unfashionable paisley blouse.

'You don't have a chance,' he says, rubbing his hands together. 'Red is so far ahead, there's no way Yellow can catch up.'

'But you're wrong,' she says in mock-seriousness. 'We were just saving ourselves. We've got something massive planned. It'll sell thousands of units.'

'It'll need to,' says Seth. The printer stops then, as if to flag the end of their conversation.

She gathers up the A4 prints and holds them to her chest, pretending they are top-secret documents, even though Seth knows that they are just her latest holiday snaps: Bali.

'Are you coming to the teambuilding on Friday?' she asks. 'I heard that we're going to go on a 4D-maze tetrick treasure hunt.'

I'd rather stick a fork in my eye.

'Sure,' he says. 'Well, if you're going.'

'Yes! Yes, I'm going.'

'Then I'll be there,' he says.

'Great!'

'Great.' He smiles, almost winking.

He turns to face the printer and presses *print* on his Tile. The printer hums, then starts spitting out pages. She gives him a royal wave and walks away. He waits for a few moments, reading the moronic posters on the wall, then heads back to his office, leaving the blank pages in the printer tray.

*

Betty checks the locks on her door for the fifth time. They're locked, but checking them makes her feel safer. She has to do things that make her feel safer.

She sits in front of her blank homescreen but realises the remote isn't working. Betty shakes the remote around a little, tries again. Then she opens up the back and makes sure the batteries are in place. Takes them out, puts them back in. Still the glass stays clear. Betty gets up to check its connections and sees it's unplugged. She picks up the plug and moves it towards the wall but stops when she reads an orange sticker covering the electricity outlet and switch: 'Don't watch TV.' It's in her handwriting.

Yes, television is not good for me. She should really get rid of the screen, but it was expensive and she abhors waste. The voices are the reason she can't watch any more. They tell her to do things. Soap opera stars, talk show hosts, newsreaders. They tell her that creeps are trying to kill her, blow up her building, decimate the country. They make her write letters to people, telling them that they are in danger. Politicians, local celebrities, airlines.

The police have been here before. They were rough until she showed them the doctor's note she keeps in her bra. The paper is leathery, now. The voices speak directly to her. 'Barbara,' (for they have recently taken to calling her Barbara), 'the next bus you take will be wired with a car-bomb with your name on it.' That's when she stopped taking the bus. The communal taxi and individual cab drivers are also not to be trusted. They could take you anywhere and you'd never be seen again.

Disappear. She clicks her fingers. Just like that. *Click, click.* She has started walking, then running everywhere. She gets to the grind shining and slippery with sweat. She is losing a lot of weight. The running has done it. Also, food is a problem. She can't run with all her groceries so she has to shop every day. She doesn't like shopping: too many people. Her psychologist says to try online shopping. Everyone's doing it, but that will mean giving strangers her address and the hours she will be home. Even if the shop people are harmless, the information could be intercepted.

When she finally builds up supplies she ends up throwing them away. The fridge door looks suspicious: as if someone else has opened it. An intruder. She tries to work out exactly which food they have contaminated but can never stop at one item. Once the pineberry yoghurt has been binned, the cheddar looks suspect, after that, the pawpaw, the black bread, the SoySpread, the feta. The precious, innocent-looking eggs, the vegetarian hotdogs, the green mango atchar, the leftover basmati, until it is all discarded and sealed tightly in a black plastic bag. The dumping of each individual item causes her pain; she so hates to fritter. This happens once a week.

Sometimes she needs to check the cupboards, too. Sometimes it's not just the open things in the fridge that may have been tainted. She'll get an idea, a name, in her head, and those things will have to go too. Last week it was Bilchen—pictures in her head of factorybots polluting the processed food then sealing them in neat little parcels, ready to eat. It is as if someone is shouting at her: Bilchen! Bilchen! Like a branded panic attack. Then she has to check every box and packet in her cupboard and toss everything with the Bilchen logo. Not much is left over.

She chooses a lonely tin of chickpeas, checks the label, and eases it open with an old appliance. She polishes a fork with her tracksuit top and eats directly out of the can. Canned food is relatively safe. She reaches for the kosher salt pebbles, but before she starts grinding it she sees the top is loose. She pictures arsenic, cyanide, a sprinkling of a strain of deadly virus, and puts it back without using it. Washes her hands twice and sprays them with hand sanitiser.

She takes the chickpea can with her and walks around her flat, checking all the windows. She touches the locks as she goes, counting them. Mid-count she hears a noise. A scraping, a whirring. Is someone trying to get in? Is the front door locked? Icy sweat.

There is a high-pitched squeal at her heels and Betty jumps in fright. Her beagle scurries away from her with hurt in her eyes.

'Oh, I'm sorry,' she says, moving to hug and pet her. 'I'm so sorry my girl. There's a good girl, there's a good girl.' The words soothe her.

Sometimes if she talks loudly enough to herself she can drown out the voices. Not in public, though. She shouldn't talk to herself in public. She doesn't like being in public anymore. Sometimes she has to show people the note; she doesn't like that, the look in their eyes.

Squatting on the ground, she feeds the dog some chickpeas. She'll start the counting again.

Outside the door to her apartment, there is humming. A large man in overalls is polishing the parquet corridor.

JOURNAL ENTRY 9

12 December 1987

Westville

In the news: *A group of police officers is fired upon by freedom fighters from a moving car in <u>Soweto</u>; two police officers are killed and four injured. In Melbourne, Australia, they are attempting to understand the Queen Street Massacre: why 22-year-old Frank Vitkovic killed 8 people in a post office building before jumping from the eleventh floor. Microsoft releases Windows 2.0.*

What I'm listening to: *U2's 'Where the Streets have no Name'*

What I'm reading: *'Tommyknockers' by Stephen King.*

What I'm watching: *Flowers in the Attic. I've read the book before, but now that we have babies we just found it too creepy, P had to turn it off!*

We brought the twins home this week. They keep us very busy but not-busy at the same time. Sometimes when they are both sleeping, P & I just sit in the lounge and wonder what to do. Other times they are both crying at the same time and we feel totally overwhelmed.

P has a pair of red DIY noise-cancelling headphones (that he uses when he does drilling etc.) which have come in very handy at bath-time!

I feel so attached to them that I want to be with them all the time. When we settle them down at night for their longer sleep I don't want to leave the nursery. Once I'm out I feel relieved that I have some time to myself but miss them immediately. Sometimes when I'm not with them I catch myself looking at photos of them. Crazy!

We are totally in survival mode, sleeping when we can, showering IF we can, eating takeaways when we run out of 2-minutes noodles. I feel so consumed by the feeding and caring that I feel like I hardly exist. Or at least, the person I was before, hardly exists. I am just a vessel. A milk machine. As for P and I—we are like ships passing in the night.

We keep the babies next to our bed at night so that I don't have to get up to feed them every 2 hours. Then if they cry I just reach over and pop them in bed with us and snuggle while they feed. I feel very protective of them. Tiger mother.

It's almost Christmas and I think it will be, like, the happiest Christmas ever.

A SWARM, A SMACK

10

Johannesburg, 2021

The ragged tooth shark swims straight towards her, his dull eyes apparently unseeing in water the colour of an overcast sky. Serrated teeth hang out at all angles, as if he has long given up hunting. Her pulse quickens as he approaches, her finger on the trigger. He glides quickly with little effort. The water is murkier than she had hoped. Kirsten fires away. Just before it reaches her—a severed arm's length away—the shark turns to avoid the tempered glass of the tank. Superglass.

She gets a few shots of his profile: a vast muscle-and-cartilage body wrapped in slate sandpaper. Her head throbbing, she flicks through the thumbnails on the screen of her camera, making sure she has enough that are in sharp focus.

The lighting is tricky because she can't use her flash; it will bounce off the glass. She is shooting in MultiFocus 3D to get more drama out of the looming shark. The shots are certainly dramatic, but shooting in MF3D always gives her a headache.

She sits for a moment, watches the dancing blue light of the water (Aqua Shimmer) paint her arms and hands. The pressure in her head makes her feel as though the silicone-framed glass is going to give way and knock everyone over in a tidal wave of exotic fish, eels, and strangling seaweed.

She has a long gulp of CinnaCola from the can her assistant hands her. She has been at it for ages and she still isn't sure if she had the shot. She powers up her Tile and looks at the pictures in subpixel HR. The pictures she had of the Leafy Sea Dragon, the Blanket Octopus and the Sea Wasp jellyfish are fantastic. The Blanket Octo looks like a silk scarf underwater: a billowing maroon cape. She can watch it for hours.

The Sea Wasp is almost invisible: smoke caught in a bubble underwater, with elegant silver tentacles and enough deadly venom to kill up to sixty humans. If you get stung by this jellyfish in the sea, says the digital projection on the glass, it causes you such intense pain and shock you won't make it to the shore. A group of jellyfish is called a swarm or a smack. Such grace in its movement: hypnotic. She makes a mental note to do a jellyfish project in the future.

Her assistant offers her a ganache-glazed kronut but she, for once, declines. She doesn't feel great. A bit dizzy, nauseous. It had been a long morning and she still has to shoot the model. Her eyes are strained and she's battling to concentrate on the photos, so she closes the window and looks around the aquarium for a moment.

It's deliciously cool and quiet inside; even the children whisper. The cobalt luminescence ripples over the floor and the visitors, making everyone seem calm. It has a clean taste: ice and fresh mint, with a hint of citrus.

Who would have thought an aquarium would work in Jozi? It was an impromptu idea of some BEE-kitten who had more investors than sense. There are so many things up against the project: the water shortage, the protesting fish-hippies, the transport costs. Can you imagine the logistics of trucking sharks, dolphins and other endangered fish from some sleepy coastal town to Johannesburg? It was a joke. Until it wasn't anymore, and now it's AQUASCAPE: a gushing money-spinner, a veritable pot of liquid gold. She looks around at the illuminated faces of the kids and their parental units, and feels a twinge. In drought-blasted South Africa it does feel magical to see so much water. She had always loved water—rivers, lakes, waterfalls, oceans—and swimming. She often wonders why she lived inland. Perhaps one day they can retire to the Cape Republic.

As a teenager she read an article in the New York Times about the 'loneliest whale in the world'. It was about an animal that looked like a whale and sounded like a whale, but her call was slightly off, which meant that even though she called and called, no other whales could hear her.

The people who found her named her 52 Hertz. Her tone was *bassa profunda*, just a notch higher than the lowest note on a tuba, and it became deeper over time. She kept swimming, kept calling, but the entire ocean was dark, cold and deaf to her. *That's me*, Kirsten had thought at the time. *That is the whale version of me.*

Her news tickertape lights up with a fresh story. She clicks it and is taken to page six of Echo.news, the local online newspaper for which she does odd jobs. It's a satirical cartoon of the NANC politician who was caught with a secret pool. He is standing in court with a sheepish smile, dressed in nothing more than soggy grey underpants, with a yellow duck-shaped inflatable tube around his waist. The prosecutor has a whistle around her neck and the judge is sitting on a lifeguard chair, the ones you used to get in public pools. Kirsten moves her cursor to close the window when she spots a headline that draws her in.

WOMAN FOUND DEAD IN BRAAMFONTEIN FLAT.

This has always been a secret fear of Kirsten's: ending up old and alone, slipping in the shower/accidentally electrocuting herself/choking to death on a toaster waffle, only to be found weeks later by the building's rodent-control man. She scans the article to see how ancient this woman was and how exactly she kicked the bucket, so she can at all costs avoid the same sorry end.

But it turns out the woman is precisely Kirsten's age, and

it's a suspected suicide. 'Betty Weil's body,' it read, 'was found yesterday by her mental health doctor who had grown concerned when Miss Weil had missed several appointments. She was found in the kitchen where she had died after apparently gassing herself. Miss Weil had a history of mental illness, most notably paranoid schizophrenia.' A little more info on her history follows, and then the usual disclaimer to seek help if needed. Lawsuits are sticky now that suicide is trending. The small black-and-white picture accompanying the article shows a laughing young woman with long dark hair, obviously before her illness took hold of her. Something makes Kirsten look twice. She reads the article again. Betty. It can't be.

Not the mad woman in the parking lot. She had to have been in her forties, at least, and didn't look anything like this photograph. Kirsten puts her fingers over the woman's long hair, giving her a helmet-cut.

Your Kirsten is my Betty.

'Fucking hell,' Kirsten says, speed-dialling Keke.

'I'm busy,' Keke answers, noise and static in the background.

'Where are you?'

'The Gladiator Arena, in Roma. Well, fake Roma, anyway. Roman Rustenburg. Dusty as hell but some fine ass here in gladiator get-up. Skin all bronzed and shit. Failed Amusement Park turned film set for the second instalment of the *Mad Maximus* thrillogy.'

'You do lead a charmed life,' says Kirsten.

'What's up?' asks Keke.

'That mad woman I told you about, the one who stalked me in the basement the other night?'

'Yebo?'

'She's in the paper today.'

'Arrested? Admitted to an asylum? Elected as a minister?'

'Dead.'

'Who wrote the article?'

'What?'

'Which journo wrote that article? Was it from Echo?'

Kirsten scrolls and sees the name of the journalist.

'Echo, yes. Mpumi Dladla.'

'Ha! He's a hack. He probably didn't even investigate. Most likely lifted a police report.'

'Do you have his number?'

'Of course I do.'

*

Fiona's moans, though stifled, are getting louder. Seth cups her mouth with his hand, smudging her lipstick and butting the back of her head up against the gun-metal grey locker door in the stationery room, which makes her groan even more. It started innocently enough, or so she had thought. She was there to pick out some new pens, e-paper and stickernotes for her desk. She had been looking forward to it all week: Fiona Botes had an almost unhealthy love of stationery. It was so old fashioned—romantic, really—to use real pens on real paper.

She had been inspecting the different kinds of yellow pens on offer in anticipation, when Seth strode in and locked the door, startling her. He had used her temporary breathlessness to advance on her. Not a word exchanged, he had put his hand behind her head and kissed her slowly, making sure at every stage that she wanted more. As the kiss grew deeper, she pulled her stomach in as his hand slid over her smooth pink shirt, her generous breasts. Seth used just the right amount of teasing, and the right amount of pressure. He pushed her against the closed door of a locker, trapping her body between the heat of his body and the cool metal. His mouth didn't leave hers as his hand travelled down, lifting her knee-length tweed skirt and stroked her through her panties. At first slowly, in lazy circles, then faster and harder as he felt her grow wet. Her arms, holding the door behind her, became stiff; she stopped groaning, held her breath, and her whole body became rigid before the orgasm took her. He held her up as her knees almost buckled—her entire being felt as if it was buckling—and tears sprang to her eyes.

Fiona Botes has not had many orgasms in her life, and the ones she has never seem quite satisfactory. Her girlfriends tell her that she has to DIY before she can show a man how to do it for her, but she doesn't like thinking about that. It seems smutty. Besides, she believes a man should intuitively know what to do with her parts; she certainly doesn't. Never has Fiona imagined that an orgasm could feel like this. And so quickly! Fully clothed! She is in shock. Intoxicated. What surprises her even more is that she finds herself unbuckling him. This gorgeous, tall man, in the stationery room, with her! She couldn't have dreamt up a better fantasy if she had tried.

*

Kirsten feels a twinge in her abdomen. *Maybe I'm ovulating.* She checks the OvO app on her watch: 36 hours to go, it says. At least she'd hasn't laid this week. She takes the escalator to the second floor of the pastel green art deco building (Pistachio ice cream), where the journalists, editors, copy editors and layout artists buzz around in the open-plan offices of Echo.news like a drone-swarm.

They moved to this downtown building when their original offices in ChinaCity/Sandton were firebombed a few years ago by a group of Christian extremists called The Resurrectors. Previously infamous for their mission to ban The Net, the group had since taken to terrorising anyone who 'disrespected Jesus'. The newspaper had published a column by a cocky, jaded journo in which he criticised each major religion in turn, and from which could extrapolated that he found anyone of religious persuasion a bit dim-witted. A line about rising-from-the-dead Jesus being a huggable zombie particularly inflamed the group and the next day—*poof!*—the Echo.news building was razed. The Lord doth smite cocky columnists. No one was hurt—how very Christian of them—and because Echo doesn't put out a hard copy, the newspaper business goes on as usual, operating remotely from the employees' individual lounges and tennis courts until this new building is found.

The Resurrectors have also recently taken to threatening fertility doctors, SurroSisters, and bombing IVF clinics. They call fertility treatment 'devil's work,' surrogates 'SurroSluts,' and the resulting embryos—very unimaginatively, in Kirsten's mind—'devil spawn.' They published a piece on FreeSpeech.za outlining their thinking, backing them up with archaic biblical verses. Kirsten tried to hate-read it once, to make fun, but all the exclamation marks had hurt her eyes.

Firebombing the Echo.news building is one thing, but a public outcry follows about their disrespect for the SurroSisters. Without professional surrogates, South Africa's birth rate will be through the floor. Singe fertile women who volunteer to assist infertile couples are afforded special treatment in almost every facet of their lives: free accommodation, travel, medical treatment. Each SurroSis has their own bodyguard, and their own car. Fashion houses dress them, jewellers loan them diamonds, brands nearly trip over themselves to place their products in their hands. They wear 'SS' badges in public so they can be easily identified and shown the proper respect: the opposite of a scarlet letter.

When Kirsten reaches the top of the escalator at the Echo offices, no one takes any notice of her, so she walks up to the closest table and asks where she can find Mpumi. She is directed to the untidiest desk in the place where she casts around for familiar faces but sees no one she recognises. Mpumi is on the phone, and typing at the same time, so she smiles at him and gestures that she'll wait. It's obviously a personal call, because he wraps it up quickly and calls the person on the other side of the line a 'chop'.

'Hi,' she ventures, but he holds up a silencing finger at her and finishes typing his sentence with his other hand. He reads it again, makes an adjustment, makes another adjustment, then smashes the *save* key.

He looks up at her and blinks, as if to clear his head of the previous conversation. Mpumi is super groomed and dressed in 1950s Sophiatown chic. Retrosexual. Kirsten thrusts an extra-large, double-shot cappuccino at him, believing from experience that you couldn't go wrong with that in a news office. He crinkles his nose.

'Sweet, darling, but I don't do caffeine. Or sugar... or moo-milk.'

Kirsten swaps his for hers. He fiddles with his bowtie.

'Half-caff, stevia, soymilk.'

He takes it from her, flips off the plastic top, and takes a small sip.

'So you *are* an angel. I thought so, when you walked in. All fiery-haired and horny and shit, with the light behind you. Are you here for the Feminazi interview?'

'No,' she says. 'I just need five minutes.'

'What can I do for you?'

Kirsten sits on an old, bashed-up office chair, pulls it closer.

'That article of yours on the tickertape this morning...'

'The monkey that they've programmed to talk? My sources swear it's true.'

'No, the woman. The woman that committed suicide.'

'Ah,' he says, 'you a relative? We haven't been able to find any relatives, nor could the cops, so we went ahead and named her. Not a friend or frenemy in sight. If you're—'

'No,' interrupts Kirsten. 'I just have a question, about how she died.'

'Straight up-and-down a suicide, m'lady.'

'You're sure?'

'No sign of forced entry. In fact, the windows and doors were locked from the inside. The super had to get in by smashing a window—the lady had, like, ten different locks on the front door.' He snorts. 'Well, it's ironic, isn't it? Locking the baddies out before you stick your head in the oven.'

'When do you think she died?'

He looks down at the masses of paper spread on his desk and, after a few moments, locates a blue file.

'It's a finely tuned arrangement.' He smiles at her, gesturing at the mess. 'It's the only way I find anything.'

Keke is right: it's a copy of the police file.

He flips through a few pages then stops, pointing to a

detail Kirsten can't see. 'Estimated TOD was the evening before.'

'But then how did they find her so quickly?'

'She hadn't been showing up at her shrink's appointments, had been avoiding her calls. It looked like she hadn't left the place in a week.'

'Is there anything else you can tell me?'

His phone rings, but he mutes the tune. 'Not much else to tell. Suicide is contagious now, didn't you know? Bitch went schizo and offed herself. All in a day's grind in this crazy-ass city. Believe me, I've seen worse. A lot worse. In fact, I remember thinking, how considerate of her to take a clean way out.'

'What do you mean?'

'Well, you know, she could have jumped out of the window, slit her wrists, put a shotgun to her head. Can you imagine having to clean that shit up?'

The pictures of her wax doll parents come back to her. Dark red holes, weeping.

'Never thought of it that way.'

'Yeah, well, they're mostly selfish bastards, Suiciders. We used to call them suicide victims but, ha! Hardly. Men are the worst, always the messiest. Pigs. They seem to like the drama of leaving blood and bits behind. Leave their mark, like a dog pissing on a tree. Women are more considerate. Usually do it with more grace: pills, asphyxiation, walking into rivers.'

'But she *was* a victim,' says Kirsten. 'I mean, she was ill... she couldn't help it.'

He purses his lips to show that he doesn't agree. His phone rings again.

'Anything else I can help you with? I have a 6pm deadline and I don't have any of my facts checked yet.'

She gets up to leave, binning her coffee cup. Caffeine dulls her synaesthesia, so it feels as if she is moving in monochrome. She still can't believe normal people see the world this way. Flat.

'Was there anything weird about it? Anything that you thought was strange?'

He uses the back of a pencil to scratch his scalp. Shakes his head, but then stops, narrows his eyes. 'There was one thing... I wanted to put it into the article but Ed said it was unnecessary. He didn't want it to sound like we were making fun of the lady.'

'What was it?'

'It was something the shrink said to the cops. I didn't interview her personally but she said that the woman had out-of-control paranoid delusions. She heard voices talking to her and telling her to do shit. But she also had this idea that she had been microchipped, I don't know, by aliens or Illuminati or something. She had a lump on the back of her neck—had it for as long as she could remember—and she started to believe that it was a tracking chip. Thought someone was monitoring her. Maybe she watched too many nineties movies. But it's cool, you know, in a way, that's why I wanted to put it in the article. I mean they say they want more readers but I had to pull the most interesting part. Ed can be a bastard.'

'So what you're saying is that she really was crackers, and she really did kill herself.'

'Yes, ma'am. Oh, and one other thing...'

Cheeky shit, calling her 'ma'am' as if she is twice his age. 'Yes?'

'There were dog bowls—and dog hair—but no dog food, and, well... no dog.'

She stares at him. His outfit is now desaturated of colour. She snaps a pic of him with her locket.

'You look like you stepped out of a fifties Drum magazine cover. I like your style. Thanks for your help.'

'You're Kirsten Lovell, aren't you?'

She is surprised, and nods.

'I've just recognised you. I loved your photo essay on Somali pirates. It was really cool. Bang tidy work. Epic stuff.'

That was years ago, how could he know it is hers? The essay is from a time when she had been young and irresponsible, doing dangerous work to try to fill The Black Hole. It hadn't worked, but she won some awards. It advanced her career, made her semi-famous in the journo circuit.

'You a freelancer now?' he asks.

She nods. 'Now I have the flexibility to panic about my job insecurity at any time.'

It's an old joke. He smiles, holds up the coffee cup in thanks and farewell.

*

He waits until he sees the escalator swallow her then dials a number. 'She came.'

He doesn't know why the cop wants to know this, but that is the deal, in exchange for a copy of the police report. Mouton is a cop, after all, Mpumi reasons, trying to assuage his guilt. It's not like he's a psychopath.

*

Seth is reading the news while he waits for The Weasel to go to lunch. A headline about a woman committing suicide catches his eye. So young, so alone. He feels a jab. He knows better than to think it's compassion; it's just his own mortality raising its head to give him a nudge. *That could be you, dying alone in your apartment. Not suicide, never suicide, but people die all the time, and you could be next. Freak accidents, dehydration, murder. And who would miss you?*

The Weasel leaves his desk at 1pm every day, on the dot, and goes downstairs to the American-styled health diner. He has a cheese fauxburger, which is less delicious than it sounds, and certainly not anything vaguely sexual, which is what Seth first thinks when he overhears Wesley's order and almost chokes to death on his whole-wheat carob-chip doughnut. Choking, falling, earthquake. No one would miss him.

The Fauxburger is a shamwich: the diner's healthy take on the old classic, with a full-grain rye roll, cottage cheese, masses of micro-greens and sprouts, a black bean and wild mushroom schmeat patty, topped with a black tomato-chilli salsa, and sweet potato wedges on the side. Since meat and fish have become so expensive, many sheeple have switched to meat alternatives. Not before, not to save massacring animals, or to spare thousands of cows/pigs/chickens their sorry battery lives, but when steaks start to cost a week's wage. Enter the age of carnaphobia. Then all of a sudden soya loses its bland taste; vegetarianism becomes mainstream and schmeat steaks and Portobello burgers become the food of choice to bring to Saturday braais. Hairy men snapping their tongs and discussing the merits of citrus versus balsamic marinades over their fire-warmed tins of lager.

Seth still eats steak—ostrich, duck, venison, or any GMO version thereof. His favourite is still real beefsteak, AKA cow-meat, bovine oblivion. Medium rare: he likes it a little bloody. It's not that he doesn't have empathy for the animals. He just believes humans are top of the food chain. You don't see a leopard crying over its prey.

After The Weasel eats his sad burger, wipes his too-full lips with the old-school red-and-white checked linen napkin, he goes to the bathroom, presumably to wash his hands. Then he opens the communal drinks fridge and gets himself a CinnaCola, which sits on his desk for the rest of the afternoon. Seth has never seen Weasel drink the stuff—after all, he would know what's in it—but there it is, every day, sweating on his desk at 1:30 sharp. Seth no longer takes lunch breaks because it's the only time he can escape his manager's beady eyes. He uses this time very carefully.

JOURNAL ENTRY

January 24th, 1988

Westville

In the news: *6 African National Congress guerrillas are injured in a car bomb explosion in Bulawayo, Zimbabwe.*

What I'm listening to: *Johnny Cash is Coming to Town*

What I'm reading: Dr Spock's *The Common Sense Book of Baby and Child Care*

What I'm watching: *Good Morning Vietnam*

P loves the babies so much. He is good at comforting them. He sings in a really deep voice—these silly made-up songs—and makes these funny faces and then they stop fussing and laugh. Sometimes they laugh at the same time and that's the funniest thing, then we all laugh together.

CORPSE FINGERS STROKE HER NECK

11

Johannesburg, 2021

Kirsten watches Keke pull into her building's entrance in a wide arc and is reminded why she has so many suitors of both genders: her punk hairstyles, roaring bike, deep, easy laugh and fuck-you fashion. It's a hot little package.

'Sorry I'm late.' She deflates her helmet and hugs Kirsten. Keke smells like leather and something more feminine. Hair product? Little violet shiny balls float in the air around them.

'No problem. It's probably my punctuality karma finally

burning my ass.' Kirsten had, herself, been twenty minutes late.

'There was a breaking story and I was five minutes away so I had to pop in.'

'Anything interesting?'

'Not really. Just a little shoot-out between the AfriNazis and the Panthers. Some scratches, some crocodile tears, no fatalities.'

'Oh my God, *racism*. It's so 2016.'

The two groups were extreme right and left wings, white and black respectively. No one took them too seriously; in a nation that is now indifferent to skin colour, their bizarre antics leave everyone shaking their frowns.

'Just some punks looking for an excuse to spill blood.'

'Too many video games.'

'I blame hip hop. No, *marabi*.'

'I blame sugar. And processed food.'

'Hyperconnectivity.'

'The Net.'

'GMO produce.'

'ADHD.'

'Neglectful parental units.'

'Lack of corporal punishment in schools.'

'Boredom. There's nothing to rebel against anymore! We're a nanny state and it's a very gentle, easy-going nanny, with no tattoos or inappropriate piercings.'

'Although she must have a very high libido.'

'Ha!' laughs Keke. 'This nanny likes to screw!'

'And get screwed,' adds Kirsten. 'It's a mutual arrangement. And also: polyamorous.'

'Hey,' says Keke. 'Don't knock polyamory. It's the way of the future.'

Inside Kekeletso's Braamfontein apartment, the door automatically locks behind them.

'Too early for wine?' asks Keke, glancing at the clock on the wall. 12:55. A giant Elvis Presley poster looks down at them.

'I don't understand the question,' says Kirsten.

Keke smiles and grabs a bottle of Coffeeberry Verdant-Pino. Two glasses. Kirsten instinctively reaches for a nearby empty Tethys bottle, fills it up with grey water from the waterbank (Liquid Smoke), and goes around watering Keke's sad-looking houseplants. Using her father's pocketknife, which she now always keeps handy, she snips a few dead leaves off the aspidistra on the lounge coffee table and sends them down the communal compost chute.

'It's not that I don't love them, you know.' (That's what she always says.) 'It's just that I'm never home.'

After binning a long-dead and crumbling plant a year before, Kirsten had suggested keeping succulents instead as they wouldn't need as much care, but Keke said she had read somewhere that thorns were bad for your sex life. 'Feng Shui or some shit. What is it with you and plants, anyway?'

Kirsten had shrugged: 'I don't know. I just like looking after them.'

Keke had pulled a 'you're sad!' face, and Kirsten had thrown something at her.

'If you knew how amazing they were, you wouldn't perpetuate mass murder against them like you do.' This is her pet hate. Her mother had been just as bad. Her teenhood had been strewn with dead chrysanthemums. 'Besides the whole filters-the-air-we-breathe thing, do you know that there is a flower that turns red when it grows over landmines?'

'Okay Miss Greenfingers.' Keke had sighed. 'I get it, no more needless slaughter of our plant-friends.'

'If you're like this with plants I'd hate to imagine you being responsible for something with actual feelings. Ever consider getting a pet?'

Keke had almost choked. 'No!'

'Good.'

'So, what's the emergency?' Kirsten commandeers the bottle and passes Keke a glass of wine, who in turn opens a packet of chilli-salted beetroot chips and empties them into a bowl, which may have needed a bit of a wipe beforehand. The shape of their taste is unusual: spinning flat discs, like frisbees, but not as rigid. Rubber. Quite uniform, earthy, with little spikes of salt and a halo of warmth from the chilli.

'Something came for you today, through The Office.'

This isn't unusual. Keke and Kirsten office-share in the same building in the CBD. As card-carrying members, or colloquially: 'Nomadders,' they are allowed unlimited access to everything they might possibly need in an office environment, from receptionists, couriers, IT support, boardrooms, carpooling and bad filter coffee to 4D scanner/printers. A steady stream of people is always coming and going, as well as a 24/7 cleaning team to make sure that each new client gets a sparkling office. They charge by the hour, but the longer you stay, the better the rate. They even have a (legendary) annual end-of-year office party.

Keke knows someone at The Desk who keeps a premium office free for her when he can, at no extra cost. It is one of the few with a fridge and a concealed safe where she can keep some of her grind paraphernalia and clean underwear without having to drag it around town on her bike. It also has a dry shower and a SleePod.

'Through The Office?'

Kirsten thinks it must be something she ordered online and had since forgotten. New lenses for her camera? Prickly-Pear Verjuice? Sex toy? Bulk box of pregnancy test strips?

Keke produces a small white envelope that looks a bit worse for wear.

'That's it?'

'Yip. Isn't it wonderful?'

Kirsten takes it from Keke's hands and examines it. The address is scratched on, as if the penman-or-woman was in a hurry. She doesn't recognise the handwriting. Two colourful stamps are glued on the front: an illustration of the president wearing too much lipstick, and an extinct fish. The post office stamp obscures both of the pouting images. No return address.

'I mean,' says Keke, 'when is the last time you saw an actual letter? In the—you know—the post! In an envelope! It has stamps and everything.'

Kirsten uses her pocketknife to slit open the envelope. She takes out the note, and as she does so a key drops into her lap. She picks it up and inspects it, recognises it; feels corpse fingers stroke her neck. Hands it to Keke.

'It's the same one,' she says. 'The same one James threw over the bridge that night...'

'It's a wafer-key,' says Keke. 'For a safety deposit box. This part,' she says, touching the head, 'contains some kind of circuit, to allow access. So, for example, the wafer will get you into the bank and into the safety deposit box room. Then the key itself is used to unlock the box.'

Kirsten opens the note and sees more of the scrawl: DOOMSDAY.

'The fuck?' Keke comes around to read it over her shoulder.

'Who's it from?' she asks.

Kirsten studies the signature. 'A ghost.'

*

At exactly 1pm Seth watches The Weasel make his way down to the Fontus diner. Seth waits five minutes. In that time, three different sheeple stop outside his office to say hi and ask how he is. He recognises the same vacant look in their eyes as the employees he sees around the campus: scoffing ultrabran muffins, playing squash, jogging, waiting for the decaffee to percolate. Staring, expressionless, as if a zombie had eaten their brains. And then as soon as they register him (eyebrow ring, Smudged eyes, faux-hawk, hoodie) they snap to attention and greet him effusively. Their smiles become wide and full of white teeth, but it never reaches their eyes.

Once the coast is clear, he slips into the filing room, which is really just a giant computer in the middle of the room full of whirring fans. He's not allowed access to this room but the door is sometimes left ajar. There are clearly people in the world less paranoid than him. Ribbons in different shades of blue are tied to the fan skeletons, giving the feeling that the room is some kind of stage design for a scene out of Atlantis, or an experiential advert for Aquascape.

He closes the door and sits backwards on the swivel chair, starts to work on the machine. The security on the files he wants to look at is ironclad. There will be a chink, there always is, but as he looks around he realises that it will take him months to hack. He smacks the side of the flatscreen.

'Fuck a monkey,' he says.

'Excuse me?'

Seth spins around. Weasel.

'Oh,' says Seth. *Fuck!*

With all the white noise of the fans he hasn't heard Wesley come in. He quickly uses a shortcut to close his windows. Has The Weasel left this door open on purpose: a test?

'This is a limited-access room,' says Weasel, 'you're not allowed in here.'

'I didn't know,' says Seth.

'It was in your Fontus Welcome Pack,' says Wesley.

Seth gives him a blank look. 'I needed to find something.' It wasn't a lie.

'Look,' starts Wesley, rubbing his beard and drumming his fingers on his chin. 'I'm going to have to report this... incident. They're not gonna like it. They're not gonna like it one bit. We're talking a warning, or a disciplinary meeting at best. You'd better come in tomorrow wearing that suit I've been asking you about.'

'Are you kidding?' asks Seth.

The Weasel starts guffawing. Seth looks on in astonishment.

'Of course I am, Mr Maths!' he snorts, whacking Seth on the back. 'You genius-types sure lack a sense of humour. Ha! Ha!' He steers Seth out of the room with a firm hand and makes sure he closes the door behind him. It beeps twice to signal that it's locked.

'Beep-beep!' says Wesley, and guffaws again.

*

Kirsten reads the letter out to Keke:

KIRSTEN/KATE—

I know you didn't believe me when we spoke. Am sending you extra keys. THEY ARE WATCHING YOU. DO NOT LET ANYONE TAKE THEM FROM YOU. Take care of yourself. Do it for your mother. Despite this mess, the list is proof that she loved you.

DOOMSDAY is the key. God help the Taken Ones if you don't get this. ACT NOW. B/B

Keke lets out a loud wolf whistle. 'No prize for guessing which particular delusional schizophrenic sent this.'

Kirsten replays their interaction in her head: the shadows in the basement, the shock, the foetid warning, James throwing the key off the bridge.

'I guess sometimes it pays to be paranoid,' says Keke.

'What do you mean?' asks Kirsten, dry-mouthed.

'Well, just that, you know, she knew you wouldn't keep the first key.'

'She said keys. She said I'm sending you extra keys, plural.' She shakes the envelope even though she knows it's empty.

'Maybe she didn't get around to sending the other one,' reasons Keke, 'you know, before she stuck her head in the oven.'

'I don't understand,' says Kirsten.

'I'll explain it to you,' says Keke, taking the letter to the compost chute. 'This lunatic lady didn't know fantasy from reality, and she for some reason decided to drag you into it.' She is about to throw the note away when Kirsten jumps up.

'Don't you dare,' she says, snatching it away.

'Listen, Cat. She was a delusional schizophrenic. She killed herself. Surely that's the end of this conversation?'

'Not necessarily.'

'You have got to be joking. They're watching you? *Dooms*day?'

Kirsten thought Keke understood her Black Hole but clearly she doesn't.

'She is dead, Keke. She said that they would kill her, and now she's dead. She believed in this enough to track me down. Approach me. She wasn't even leaving her flat to see her shrink anymore, but she came to see me. I think I at least owe it to her to see whatever this key unlocks.'

Out of the corner of her eye, she sees a familiar blue-and-white striped jersey (Cobalt & Cream). It doesn't make any sense to her. It takes her a few moments to catch on. That's James's jersey. It should be on James, or at home. Their home. She walks towards it, picks it up, smells it. Marmalade.

'What is this doing here?'

'Kitty,' says Keke, 'I was going to tell you. I just wanted to give you the letter first.'

'Fine, then, I have the letter.'

'James was here last night.'

'What?'

'He's worried about you.'

'Why? What is there to worry about?' She knows the question is disingenuous.

'He says that you've been having a rough time. Obsessing about your parents—'

'He used the word 'obsessing'?'

'Said you're not sleeping. That you haven't been feeling well. Haven't been yourself. In denial about all of the above.'

'What did he want you to do about it?'

'He asked me to keep an eye on you. He said he knows you tell me things that you don't tell him.'

'He wants you to spy on me? Tell him what I tell you?'

'He wants me to make sure you're okay.'

'Make sure I don't stick my head in an oven too?'

'Well, yes. I guess that would be first prize. And he asked me to... discourage... you, from investigating any of this... what-what. Your parents. The crazy lady. He just wants what's best for you. You guys have been together for what? Eleven years?'

'Thirteen.'

'A lifetime. He said you're pushing him away. And he's worried that you might do something... risky.'

'Fuck.' She sighs. 'Am I out of control? I don't feel out of control.'

'That's what you said when you went off chasing pirates.'

'Which I won awards for. Which launched my career.'

'Kitty, no one respects you as a photojournalist more than I do. No one. That story was cosmic. You deserved every award you got. But you almost died.'

'Well, that's an exaggeration.'

'Cat, you almost *died*.'

'Okay, but that was different. I was young. Reckless.'

'So you're less reckless now?' Keke laughs.

'Hello? Yes! I'm practically a housewife. I mean, look at me.'

'The day you become anything close to a housewife I will personally deliver you to the Somalis.'

'Keke, I have a fucking OvO app on my watch. I can tell you the actual minute that I ovulate.'

'Marmalade is right, you *are* out of control. What's next? Hosting crafternoons?'

'Ha,' says Kirsten.

'Look, lady, I told your better half I'd watch over you, and I will. But I'm behind you all the way with finding out about your parents.' Keke opens the freezer and brings out the bright red box that she keeps as a staple especially for Kirsten. She pops some waffles into the toaster and pushes down the lever.

'So, what do we do next?'

JOURNAL ENTRY

27 January 1988

Westville

In the news: *Guerrillas open fire on a police vehicle in Soweto and injure three policemen and a civilian. The first reviews are in for Andrew Lloyd Webber's musical 'The Phantom of the Opera' which debuted last night on Broadway.*

What I'm listening to: *Pop Goes the World (the babies like it!) Men Without Hats*

What I'm reading: *Bill Cosby's 'Fatherhood'—hilarious.*

What I'm watching: *The Running Man with Arnold Schwarzenegger*

P went to the nursery today and bought us a few trees and plants. He's trying to make the house as homely as possible for us.

I hope he is not missing his old life (his wife).

I've never really been interested in gardening but we worked a bit together today—I just planted some flowers and watered, really—and I enjoyed it. (Petunias? Pansies?) I think I'll spend some more time in the garden. It's a nice break from taking care of the twins.

They are doing really well. Me, less so. In the beginning I didn't mind the sleep deprivation too much but I think it's building up now. It is starting to impact on my mood, and my memory. And my day-to-day functioning: I do ridiculous things like put the teabag canister in the fridge. The other day I answered the front door with my shirt unbuttoned! I don't know who was more embarrassed, me or the neighbour! My God I would do anything for a full night's sleep. Amazing what we take for granted! Sometimes I just get one of the twins to sleep and the other one starts crying and wakes up the other, then the other way around, and I just want to sink to the floor and cry.

They are both good eaters. Thank God. Sometimes I feel like I'm a walking, talking (leaking!) boob. Sam is a frowny, focused feeder, who goes in with closed eyes and gets the job done. Kate, always hungry, starts off quickly but then takes her time. She stares at me with her big slate-grey eyes and I hope that she can feel how much I love her.

They have very distinct personalities, even at this age. Sam is serious and independent and seems to always be thinking about something, working something out in his head. I'd love to know what babies think about. And Kate is always smiling and likes being with people. They seem to get on with each other, too, which is great. Hope it carries on that way!

Sometimes strangers stop us to look at the babies, say how cute they are, ask who is the 'oldest', say they look like me, or if P is with us, that they look like him.

I tell myself every day how lucky I am. I look in the mirror, at my pale skin and the dark circles under my eyes, and smile. I've learned to put on a good smile.

A GOOD VIEW, TOO

12

Johannesburg, 2021

Seth is sipping a coffeeberry shot at his local barista when an Echo.news story flickers on his tickertape. He clicks to listen to the audio version, which automatically streams to his earbuttons.

In breaking news, William Soraya, South Africa's gold medallist sprinter and media darling was this morning severely injured in a skycar accident. Soraya, known as 'Bad Bill,' who is no stranger to adrenaline pursuits (or front-page news), was flying the new Volantor StreetLegal plug-in hybrid car as a publicity stunt for the corporate, who are 'deeply distressed' about the accident, and have begun an intensive investigation.

'We have tested and re-tested this new model and were 100% certain that it was safe to fly. We have no idea what could have gone wrong, but we will find the reason behind this terrible tragedy,' said Volantor spokesperson Mohale Mhleka.

Despite the low number of uptake, the fatalities due to skycars and hover-cars are numerous and on the rise. Various groups are lobbying for the skycar to be banned, including a 2 000-strong protest outside the Union Buildings this morning, with a further 6 000 citizens adding their presence online.

'Look, it's something we're going to have to get right,' said Minister of Transport Solly Ngubane. 'We mustn't shy away from technology. We must embrace progress. When motorcars were first introduced there were also a great deal of accidents. This episode was unfortunate. We have to take a hard lesson from this, look forward and make this mode of transport the safest we possibly can.' In the mean time, Ngubane has promised a task team to launch an official enquiry, and committed to flying his own Volantor every day for a month, to prove his faith in the product.

'Last year Soraya made news for breaking the national record for both the 100m and 200m sprint, as well as for his notorious partying, womanising, and more than one incident of road rage. He was also accused of 'resping' or 'respirocyting': injecting robotic red blood cells to improve his performance, but was cleared of the charge after undergoing vigorous testing. Ironically, he may now undergo respirocyte treatment in order to speed up his healing.

Soraya is in the ICU of an undisclosed private hospital. He has broken bones, including both tibulae or shin-bones, and internal bleeding; his spinal cord is swollen, but intact. His PR manager says that his condition is serious, but stable. As the minister said today: 'The hearts and minds of South Africans everywhere are with William Soraya, and we wish him a speedy recovery'.

Fuck, thinks Seth. He had always kind of identified with Soraya. They were the same age. They lived a similar lifestyle, although Seth preferred the shadows to the limelight. He gets that fluttering cold feeling again, almost like a premonition that a similar fate awaits him. He shakes himself out of it. He has got to pull himself together, up his game. Put his plan on fast-forward. He sends Fiona a bump. Acts cooler than he feels.

SD> What are you wearing?

FB>> LOL! Naughty. *blush*

SD> Send me a pic.

FB>> NO!!

SD> I want 2CU.

FB>> In meeting, in meetings all day. Yawnerz!

SD> Take 1 under the table. No 1 will eva know.

If he can get prudish Fiona to sext him it will be a very good sign. It would mean that—apart from getting to see her knickers—she is, to a certain extent, under his spell.

FB>> LOL I can't!! Very NB meeting. Boss is presenting w/Serious Face.

SD> Killing me.

She goes quiet for a while, and he thinks she's probably put her phone away to concentrate on the meeting. He pictures her, sitting up straight, blushing slightly, just-sharpened pencil at the ready, nodding sagely at her fellow colleagues. But he's wrong, and his Tile buzzes with an image.

Yes please, he thinks, picking it up and sitting back into his chair, admiring it. A chocolate brown lace affair. Teal trimmings. Excellent. A good view, too: she would've had to open her legs wide to take it. Despite not finding her particularly attractive, he feels a twinge in his pants and moves to adjust himself.

Thundercats are go.

*

Kirsten is at her apartment, touching up the aquarium pictures, when James comes home. She is relieved to have a break; her eyes feel scratchy, overworked. She saves the huge 4DHD RAW TIFF file that she has been working on and is about to shut down when she feels a warm hand on her back, then another on her chest. She looks up, smiling, but the smile is wasted on James.

His mouth is on hers; he snaps the cover of her Tile down. His hand moves to her right breast; her nipples harden. She begins to stand, but he puts his arms underneath her and picks her up, carries her to bed. Throws her down. She laughs, reaches to unbutton him, but he stops her, pushes her back. She can tell he is angry with her. There is rare passion in his face, but it's shadowed with anger. This is going to be bossy sex, one of her favourites.

He looks at her while he takes off his belt, as if he is going to spank her with it, but then lets it drop to the floor. Kirsten feels heat trickling inside her thighs, her stomach. Her hand travels to her open zip to touch herself but James bats it away. He wants to do all the work. He pushes up her shirt and guzzles the tops of her breasts, above her bra, then yanks the lace down and sucks her erect nipples. She feels his teeth, his hot mouth on her skin, closes her eyes, groans as the warmth builds.

He pulls off her jeans, her white cotton panties. She wants him to lick her, would do anything for him to put his warm tongue on her, knows she would come in a second if he did. But, no, this is her punishment, and he is showing her who's boss. He grabs her around the waist and turns her around, so that she is on her knees, facing away from him.

She wants him inside her so badly that she wants to shout, but holds it in. Agony, bliss. He slaps her butt, gently, then harder, sending orange vibrations (Sunset Sex) through her pelvis. She almost comes, but he stops in time. She wants to beg, but doesn't. The cresting becomes unbearable. A whimper. She bites her own shoulder.

James, relenting, enters her from behind. She comes immediately, her spine curling, her muscles contracting around him. Feels as though the bed is swallowing her. Before she finishes he begins thrusting into her spasms and she cries out, her body half crumpled. He grunts, breathes deeply, thrusts harder, deeper. Put his hands on her. Again her body is seized, stiff and then soft, as she melts into the next rolling orgasm.

*

FB>> Hey, good news.

It was a bump from Fiona.

SD> All yr meetings hve been called off & U free 2C me?

FB>> LOL, no, been promoted.

Seth smiles. Just as planned, but it feels good that everything is on track.

SD> See? U shld send me pics more often. Promoted 2 what?

FB>> Head/Marketing at Waters. Hydra. Eeeeek!!

SD> Wow. Well done, sexy thing. Mind-5.

FB>> Sooooo happy.

SD> Meet me in the red stationery room in 10min 2 celebrate?

FB>> *blush*

SD> I'll make it worth your while.

A moment's silence.

FB>> CU in 5.

*

Afterwards, Kirsten still tingling with pleasure, they

spoon, naked, on their bed. She sighs. It's not often she feels sated like this. He rubs her neck, her back, her waist. His hands tell her that the anger is gone and now there is only tenderness. God, in this moment she feels so connected to him. Nothing else matters but his warm hands on her, the damp bedclothes, their nestled feet. If only the moment could last forever.

JOURNAL ENTRY

3 February 1988

Westville

In the news: *I don't know. When I look at P's newspaper the words all swim before me.*

Not watching, reading or listening to anything. Have the concentration span of a gnat. When will the babies sleep through the night?!

Need. To. Sleep.

But now there is more than just sleep deprivation. There is a darkness.

A nothingness. Am being swallowed whole.

MESSIAH MAGIC

13

Johannesburg, 2021

Kirsten waits for James to leave for the paediatric clinic in Alexandra before she pulls out the envelope from Betty/Barbara. While he tries to save the world she'll try to, well, save herself. She flattens out the note on the desk in front of her and tries to decipher it.

Doomsday. D-day. Apocalypse. Armageddon. End-of-the-world. She's never been good at this hellfire-and-brimstone thing. While everyone else in the classroom was learning about the cheerful trio of Christ, Mohammed and Buddha, she had been staring out of the window, wondering why no one else saw what she saw, felt what she felt.

A school religious counsellor once tried to tell her that her Black Hole was the absence of Jesus's light, God's love, and if she were to take the righteous steps and be saved then it would disappear, just like that. Messiah Magic.

Kirsten's eyes had rolled so far back in her head she almost lost them completely. Later, with his warm hand on her back, he had instructed her to stay behind after class, with a look in his eyes that told her that if she did her life would never be the same. His handprint still tingling on her skin, she had been first out the door when the bell rang.

She holds the note to the light, hoping to find a clue. Turns it over and over in her hands. Suddenly she feels ridiculous, trying to make sense of a demented woman's ramblings. She looks at her Tile. Her Echo.news tickertape flashes with new stories. A man gunned down fellow shoppers in a Boksburg mall, killing five people and injuring three. A(nother) municipal worker strike, as if our streets don't stink enough.

The usual spate of muggings and hijackings, some fatal, some just inconvenient. A flaming crucifixion in Sandton Square, courtesy of The Resurrectors. Funny, that they call themselves that, when they do the opposite. Jesus's light, my foot. They also cover the small spat that Keke told her about the day before, exaggerated by graphic pictures of gaping knife wounds, and a convicted rapist taking the government to the Constitutional Court for 'enrolling' him in a Crim Colony, or PLC.

When the government instituted the Penal Labour Camps the rest of the world was horrified. *Concentration camps for criminals!* Shouted the international headlines.

New Apartheid for SA! and *Underground Crim Colonies!* It was in the beginning of the New ANC rule—when they still had balls—and they were dead-set on implementing the programme despite the international pressure not to.

They move prisoners from their crowded, dirty cells to various high-security farms and mines throughout the country where they set them to grind. They learn skills and earn wages, with which they pay their food and board, and have mandatory saving schemes that will be released to them, with interest, at the end of their sentences. The money that is saved by emptying the prisons go to prisoner rehabilitation and university fees.

Crime stats are down and all in all it is a neat move; the conviction rates are still low, but at least the captured criminals are in some way paying their debt to society. The then-defunct 'reclaimed' farms have been revived and South Africa has reverted to being a mass exporter of goods. The general public is still divided on the matter, but the initial outrage seems to have dissipated, along with the trade deficit.

Kirsten scrolls down. Thabile Siceka, the health minister, is in Sweden to receive some kind of award. South Africa has had some pretty dodgy health ministers in the past, including HIV-denialists who promised that a beetroot and olive oil salsa would cure even the direst case of Aids. Siceka doesn't have to excel at her job to be the best minister to date, but excel she has.

It is well known that she had a tough start in life. Both her parents and her grandparents died of Aids, and she had to leave school at eleven to look after her younger siblings.

When the HI-Vax was in development she pushed it through every stumbling block. She raised funds when they were needed, flew in experts, sped up the testing phase. The vaccine could have taken twenty years to get into public circulation; Siceka had it out in four. She took HIV/Aids from being the Africa's biggest killer—apart from mosquitoes—to being as easy to avoid as MMR.

The Nancies do have some strong ministers, but as a whole their leadership just doesn't stand up to the pressures of the country. Too many poor people, poor for too long, too few rich people, and a wide, painful gap in between. Add to the mix deficient service delivery, economy-crippling strikes, the panic of the water shortage and relentless violent crime and it's no wonder that creeps are ready to pull out an AK47 at any asshole who says the wrong thing. South Africans are frustrated, and it is erupting in every facet of life. Clearly she is not the only one with a hollow where her heart should be. Where is the Messiah Magic when you need it?

JOURNAL ENTRY

13 February 1988

Westville

In the news: --- *I don't care.*

Something strange is happening to me. A twisting inside. I have everything I want, a wonderful husband, a nice home, two precious little babies, but I have this weird feeling of dread and sadness. When I wake up in the morning I don't want to get out of bed. I'm exhausted and just want to sleep all day. When I do get up I am like a zombie. Sometimes P gets home and I'm sitting in front of the TV in my sweaty pyjamas, not even watching, not really, and the kids are screaming from their room. He gets angry with me but he tries not to show it, tries to be understanding. When he is angry like that he doesn't talk to me. Doesn't want to show his feelings. In this terrible stony silence he fixes the babies up, changes them, feeds them, finishes the ironing. I should care more, but there is something wrong with me.

He doesn't understand. The days are just too long.

I've lost my appetite, no food seems appealing anymore. I exist on endless cups of tea. Tea sometimes makes me feel better. Not sure if it's the actual tea or if it's just something to look forward to: a treat, to break up the day yawning ahead of me. And biscuits, if there are. A hot mug of tea and a biscuit—like a little steaming beacon of hope. If there is a (rare) moment in the day that I have my hands free, the first thing I do, instead of doing the washing or cleaning the kitchen, is have a cup of tea.

There is no energy for anything that is not completely vital: Washing my hair seems an insurmountable task. The thought of lifting my arms for that long just seems exhausting.

P hugs me and tells me that he loves me, but that I need to 'snap out of it', for the babies. Doesn't he know that if I could, I would? Does he think I WANT to be like this?

I feel like nothing matters anymore. Don't see the point in anything. Overwhelmed.

Maybe I am being punished for breaking up P's marriage. Devastation wreaks devastation. Only myself to blame.

Sometimes I find myself wishing that we had never had the twins. They are so dear, they truly are, and I love them with my entire being but sometimes I just resent their existence. Wish we could go back in time when it was just P and me, and we went out to concerts and dinners, and sleep and sex came so easily. Sometimes when the babies are being demanding I want to pinch them. Hard, so it leaves a mark. Or just smack them when they won't stop crying. I picture the welt my hand would leave behind on their pale thighs. Of course I don't ever hurt them, won't ever.

But these dark thoughts smear my soul. Make me feel so terrible. Terrible mother.

Being washed away by despair.

The flowers I planted are dead. They were violas.

TEAMBUILDING

14

Johannesburg, 2021

Fiona and Seth lie naked in their hotel bed. They are on their backs, gazing at the ceiling, allowing the air conditioner to cool their pink skin. It's a Friday afternoon and they're supposed to be at teambuilding, but instead they're at the third hotel on their list: The Five-Leafed Clover. They have decided to try out all the top hotels in Jo'burg; they have thirty-six to go.

Fiona loves hotels. She likes to arrive at the concierge, hot, breathless, and get a room for an hour, or an afternoon. She likes leaving the room a tangled, stained mess, steal the stationery, and flounce out of the entrance a few hours later, flashing the eyes of a woman clearly satisfied.

Seth expected her to be the opposite: shy of checking in,

sure to make the bed before they left, straightening towels on her way out, but she has surprised him, and herself. She giggles, mid-strip, and says things like 'Goodness, what has happened to me?' or, more specifically, 'What have you done to me?'

She still wears polka dot silk blouses, but underneath she has exchanged her practical undies for the expensive lingerie Seth buys her, or she now buys herself. She still has the innocent freckles and the easy-blush cheeks but she won't hesitate to go down on him in his office, as long as the door is locked and the camera cloaked.

Seth holds her hand, which is wrapped around the locket she always wears. Lockets are back in style; even some forward-fashion men wear them, but Seth gets the feeling Fiona has been wearing hers long before they started trending again.

'What's in the locket?' he asks. They are used for so many purposes nowadays: pills, flash drives, patches, pedometers, mirrors, cameras, keys, IDs, phones.

'It's a vintage one,' she says, 'just holds a couple of pictures.'

'Let me see,' he says, peeling her fingers back.

'No!'

'Why not? What are you hiding?'

Fiona giggles. 'Nothing.'

'You are,' he says, kissing her nose. 'What is it? A photo

of your ex? Your KGB files? Your real identity?'

She laughs some more. 'No, silly.'

She relents and lets him open the locket. Two cats stare back at him.

'That's Khaleesi.' She points. 'And that's Killmouski. I have a third one now, but I don't have his photo in here.'

'Kevin?' he asks. She smacks him, laughs, kisses him. He closes the locket and lays it back down to rest just above her cleavage.

'Lucky kitties,' he says, resisting a dirtier phrase.

She smiles at him. He thinks: *I've got you.*

'Although,' she starts.

'Mmm?' he murmurs.

'Talking about spies... I'm sure it's nothing... I don't want to talk... but when I was looking at the composition reports, just as a matter of interest, 'cos I'm trying to learn everything there is to know about the Waters, I saw that this month's Hydra reading was exactly the same as last month's, and as the month before. I mean, I know nothing about science...'

Seth lifts his head, acting interested, but not too interested. 'Isn't that normal?' This was just the pillow talk he was hoping for. 'I mean, it's supposed to remain stable.'

'Relatively stable, yes, but these reports are carbon copies of each other! As if someone in the lab is too lazy to test the sample and is just copying the exact same data every month. I mean, if I was too lazy to do the readings then I would just tweak them slightly month to month.'

'And the others?'

'Tethys and Anahita have fewer samples, fewer readings, but their reports vary slightly. You know, January magnesium 3.13, February it's 3.11. It just doesn't make any sense.'

'Strange, indeed,' Seth says, moving onto his side to face her, stroking her stomach. 'I think you'd better investigate.'

Fiona scoffs. 'Yeah, right, little Fiona Botes against the megacorp that is Fontus.'

Seth's hand moves down to stroke her, and she stops laughing. 'It's probably nothing.' She inhales. 'An admin error.' She feels the blood rush away from her head: no more talking shop now.

'Yes,' agrees Seth, 'probably.' He shifts his body down; she opens her legs.

Maybe she would just check it out.

EVERY PERFECT BONE

15

Johannesburg, 2021

An attractive platinum-haired woman sits on a park bench at a children's playground in uptown ChinaCity/Sandton. You can see that she is wealthy. She's laser-tanned, wearing SaSirro top to bottom, some understated white gold jewellery, and has a smooth, unworried forehead, but that's not what gives her wealth away. She is watching the ultimate status symbol: her white-ponytailed son, playing in the sandpit next to the jungle gym. He holds a dirty grey bunny—a stuffed animal—under one arm as he builds a sandcastle with the other. The toy clearly goes everywhere with the boy.

The perfectly made-up woman may look like a bored, stay-at-home mother, but in fact she is on her office lunch break. She was top of her class every year at Stellenbosch University and was fluent in 26 languages by the time she was twenty-one. She didn't finish her degree: she was poached by the top legal attorney firm eight months before she graduated, won over by a huge salary and the promise that she would make partner by twenty-five, which she did.

She opens her handbag, takes out a pill, pops it into her mouth and washes it down with a gulp of Anahita, saying a silent prayer for whichever drug company it is that makes TranX. She should know the name—she can tell you the capital city, currency and political state of nearly every country in the world—but today she can't picture the label on the box of capsules in her head. She wonders if she is burnt out; she definitely feels it.

Her son begins a tentative conversation with another little boy in the sandbox. Always the charmer. Her heart contracts; she loves him fiercely, every square millimetre of his skin, every pale hair, every perfect bone, she loves. The scent of his little-boy skin. His cow-licked crown. She has such dreams for him, wonders what he will be like at ten, sixteen, thirty. She never thought she'd feel this way about another person. She'd grown up feeling aloof, alone, her parents blaming it on her stellar IQ, but when her son was born that sad bubble burst. It hasn't taken away her anxiety or depression, but it has given her quiet, exquisite moments of joy she hadn't before imagined possible.

Satisfied that her son is playing happily, she opens her lunchbox. She takes home 14 million rand a year but she still packs her own lunch every day. Today it is a mango, pepper leaf and coriander salad, humble edamame with pink Maldon salt, and a goose carpaccio and kale poppy-seed bagel.

She takes a few bites of the bagel, enjoying the texture of the expensive meat, the tingling of the mustard. Soon there is a slight tickling at the back of her throat. She tries to swallow the irritation but it lingers. Trying to stay calm, she opens her bagel and inspects the contents, assuring herself that she had personally made the sandwich, there is no place for contamination, but the itch becomes stronger, furring over her tongue too.

She drops the bagel, starts to hyperventilate, presses the panic button on her locket. It sends a request for a heli-vac and a record of her medical history, including her severe peanut allergy, to the nearest hospital. Her airways are closing now and she clutches her throat, desperate to keep it open. She searches for her EpiPen, but when she can't see it, looks for a straw, a ballpoint, anything she can force down her throat to keep breathing, but her hands are shaking too much and she loses control over her fingers.

She stands up, lurches forward, waves blindly trying to attract someone's attention. Her vision becomes patchy; there are sparks and smoke clouds blotting out her son. She tries to call him, tries to call anyone for help, but it's too late for that. One arm outstretched towards her son, she sinks to her knees on the grass, then, blue-faced, topples over.

A woman's gasp rings out, and concerned strangers come to surround her. Ambulances are called, CPR is administered, but the woman dies within the minute. A white-haired toddler is held back, not kicking and screaming as you'd expect, but dumb with shock.

The strangers stand distraught, arms by their sides, not knowing what to do next. Just terrible. What a tragedy. They begin framing the story in their minds, to tell spouses and friends later. They think of how to word it in their respective status updates. Where is the ambulance? They have children to mind, places to be. One of the bystanders, a large man with a scarred arm, gives up on finding a pulse and walks away. Furtively, he strokes the soft stuffed rabbit he has hidden under his jacket. He retrieves his dog, a beagle, whose lead he tied to a swing post moments earlier, and ambles off. Chopping of the sky can be heard in the distance: the heli-vac approaching. It forms the intro to the song that starts in his head. He hums along—Pink Floyd?—and doesn't look back.

*

Fiona is on top of a cliff, ready to tumble. She holds back her curls with one hand, breathes hard, feels all her muscles contract, is paralysed, and then she topples. She flies through the air, through warm air, sultry water, then lands, is laid down, her blood turned to syrup. Seth comes with her, gasps with her then holds her until she stops twitching.

They lie clutching each other on the floor of the Fontus recreational cloakroom. They've been playing lasertag. Down to her last life, her nerves on edge, she screamed into her mask as someone in the shadows tackled her to the floor and dragged her into the cloakroom.

She knew it was him, knows the feeling of his hands on her. He zipped her out of the body-hugging suit, out of her clothes, and took her roughly against one of the dressing room tables, watched her body spasm in the reflection of the mirror.

'This is becoming a bad habit,' she says.

'I find that this kind of teambuilding is right up my alley.'

Fiona giggles. She can feel his gaze on her. She opens her eyes, self-conscious at his staring. Covers up her still-hard nipples.

'You're not going to spoil the moment, are you? By confessing how you really feel about me?' She is half-joking, half-pleading. *Please God, tell me you're falling in love with me.*

He laughs, a low bark, says, 'That's the last thing you need to worry about.'

While Fiona showers, Seth pulls on his clothes and adjusts his hair.

'I'm heading off,' he calls through the half-open shower door.

'Okey dokey, pig-in-a-pokey,' she sings. 'See you later!'

On his way out, Seth pockets her Fontus access card.

JOURNAL ENTRY 9

29 March 1988

Westville

In the news: --- *Something about an ANC rep being assassinated in Paris. Not sure, just heard something about it on the radio.*

After staying in bed for three (?) days, P showered me (washed my hair, tenderly), dressed me, and hauled me off to a shrink. After an hour or so of talking she explained to P & I that it looks like I have something called Post Partum Depression - PPD. I knew about Baby Blues—most women feel some kind of down after giving birth (hormone crash, exhaustion, disillusionment, etc.) but this is different.

Just admitting the terrible thoughts I have been having (only when P was out of the room) helped me. Judy (the shrink) asked me lots of questions and we went through a checklist of symptoms. Just knowing the symptoms exist on a piece of paper made me feel slightly better — definitely less guilty. Other mothers also feel this way? It was like a huge raven that had been sitting on my shoulder shook his feathers and flew away.

She gave me some pills and I need to go back to see her a few times a week until I'm better. Before the session I had so little energy that I felt like I didn't even care about getting better anymore. Now I feel like I would do anything to feel better. P kept glancing over at me on the way home, not sure if it was because he was worried or relieved.

HELLO, PRETTIES

16

Johannesburg, 2021

Fiona jumps out of the communal taxi with a skip in her step. She has ordered lingerie online and the nondescript parcel has been delivered to her at work. It has burnt a hole in her desk drawer the whole afternoon. She hasn't been this excited to open a package since she won a stationery extravaganza basket a few years ago. At five o'clock she grabbed it and ran to catch a lift home.

She opens the door to her flat and her three cats rush to trip her.

'Hello, pretties,' she says, and they meow back at her. She stumbles in, looking for a place to put down her parcel while trying not to step on any of the cats.

In her bedroom she opens the box and spends time admiring the silk and satin. She can feel the excitement build in her pelvis. A hum, a zing. She strips down in front of her full-length mirror. The sun is setting and the light coming through the window bronzes her body. She touches her nipples. She takes the first set, an ivory satin push-up bra ribbed with black lace, and small matching panties, and puts them on. In her mind, the bra makes her cleavage look like a swimsuit model's.

She stands and admires her reflection, moves to see the different angles. She runs her fingers over the softness of the material, over the bra then over the panties. Her fingers trace her buttocks and the triangle of her front. She feels swollen from the afternoon of anticipation. She touches herself, hesitantly at first, but as she feels the pleasure build she lies down on her bed and lets her hand take over.

Afterwards, she lies in the light of dusk, listening to her pounding heart and enjoying the full body tingle that she had before only associated with sex with Seth. It's dark when she hears a noise in the front of the house. She grips the bed. It must be one of the cats, she thinks, but hurries to put her dressing gown on. She would investigate, to put her mind at rest. Chide the cats for giving her a heart attack. But then she hears something else, something like slow footsteps, and knows that there is a stranger in her house.

SUB ROSA

17

Johannesburg, 2021

KL> I found it.

Kirsten bumps Keke.

KK>> God? Jesus? Yourself? The Meaning/Life?

KL> No, asshole. Doomsday.

KK>> Intriguing. Let's say our final g-byes & go.

KL> Too far to drive on your bike. Limpopo. Comm taxi?

I can get away by 1.

KK>> Sure. Meet u at Malema rank/town? Can lock up there.

*

Seth is busy with a taste diagram of CinnaCola. Each taste has a specific shape, made up of how each of its flavours hits certain zones on your palate and nose. CinnaCola, for instance, has a complex, multi-layered flavour repertoire, so the diagram is very much 3D, with spikes on certain levels and rounded notes on others.

This isn't dissimilar to the grind he did at Pharmax. There he would map out the delivery system of the drugs he created, making sure that the hits and the mellows were in the right place, conveying the best possible high and softest downer he could. Fizzy drinks aren't all that different. Apart from the aromas, you also have to map the fizz, the refreshment factor, and the sugar-and-caffeine buzz.

He's almost finished, and it's looking good, if he doesn't say so himself. It'll make a good abstract artwork for the red boardroom. Tomorrow he'll work on variations, ideas of how to 'up the feel-good factor', and 'maximise the full-palate experience' in CinnaCola-speak. It's only 2pm but he feels as if he's done enough grind for the day. He stands up, bracing himself for Wesley's disappointed expression, but realises he's not in.

He glances both ways down the passage, as if to cross the road, then enters his manager's office, closing the door behind him with a soft click. He swoops behind the desk, smacks a few keys, checks the projection. Checks the desk drawers. They are clean, tidy, disturbingly organised, apart from one item of contraband: a rogue packet of Bilchen BlackSalt. Nothing how an office desk drawer should look. No expired snack bars, Scotch hipflasks or decade-old packets of cigarettes. Also, nothing to help his mission.

The computer asks for a password. Seth tries the Weasel's wife's name, the kids, the pet dachshund. Their birthdays. The date of their wedding anniversary. Access denied. Out of frustration he tries 'fauxburger'. Denied. It was worth a try. He walks down to the Waters section, where Fiona now works. He circumvents her office and gets to the elevator, presses the button for the labs. Stepping inside the silver room, he takes off his red lanyard and stuffs it in his pocket. Puts Fiona's new blue one on. Tries to not look suspicious as he exits the lift and holds Fiona's access card up to the Lab entrance.

The Laboratory is a huge, glass-walled warehouse filled with an army of white-coated nerds. Transparent doors lead to the adjacent factory, giving the impression that it is one huge—busy—hall of glass. He has his own lab coat on, so blends in to a certain degree, but still feels as if there is a brightly lit, candy-coloured Las Vegas-style arrow hanging above his head, pointing out his intruder status.

He grabs a mask and sprays on some insta-gloves. He puts his head down and walks towards the back of the hall, taking mental notes as he goes. There are floating graphs in the air: 3D liquid displays, animated spinning cheese-wheel pie charts, shivering towers of calcium versus magnesium. Infographic heaven.

The other activities surrounding him are UV sterilisation, water ozonation, deionization, reverse osmosis, water softening, and blow moulding of the superglass bottles. A ticking banner overhead informs him that this plant produces a hundred thousand litres of water per hour. He needs to get a sample, which means he needs to get into the factory. He doesn't know if Fiona's access card is authorised but he knows he may not get another opportunity to try it. He holds the card up to the glass door—

The building's alarm goes off, high volume, as if it's right in his head. *Fuck!* He swings around, expecting to see security guards with handcuffs, ready to cart him to the Red Jail. He wouldn't be surprised if they had cheerful, colour-coded cells in the bowels of this building.

He hurriedly makes his way back to the lab entrance, but the white ants follow him. Looking over his shoulder, he sees masked faces and blank eyes, looking in his direction. He rushes out, trying to escape them, pulls off his own mask so that he can breathe. Gets to the elevator and pushes the button over and over, looks for stairs and takes them. Whips off Fiona's lanyard.

He runs up the three flights to the Colours' offices, steps into the corridor and starts to head in the direction of the building's main exit. Sweating, breathing hard, he wonders if he'll make it before being shot with one of the guards' stun guns. All of a sudden there is the chaos of people going in the opposite direction to him, as if choreographed.

For once, the Reds, Yellows, Greens and Blues mix madly and without prejudice. Like vibrating atoms threatening to spill out of the building. As if the building is going to spew this multi-coloured mess onto its perfect pavements. *Rainbow Vomit,* thinks Seth, surprised by the strange phrase. The workers seem puzzled that he is walking against the flow. A worker bee flying in the wrong direction. Then, a firm hand on his back, and he turns around, expecting to see a guard, but it's Wesley, smiling from ear to ear in all his fat-lipped glory.

'Seth!' he says, rosy cheeks aglow.

'I was just on my way—' Seth says, motioning vaguely.

'No, no,' laughs The Weasel, still holding onto him tightly, 'you're going the wrong way. That wasn't a *fire* alarm, it was a *gala* alarm.'

Seth has no idea what he means, but allows Wesley to steer him into the stream of Fontus employees. The swarm seems excited. They gather in the main boardroom, a massive space filled with glass screens, holograms, cascading AVs, stocked fridges. People hand out drinks to their colleagues, joking about catching Yellow team members drinking Green drinks, and vice versa. The only cross-product consumption allowed is water: everyone is authorised to drink any of the waters, guilt-free. There is animated murmuring and smiling, a sea of expectant faces.

As a rule, public gatherings make Seth uncomfortable. It makes him feel as if he is buying into something, an automatic victim of groupthink, a forced Kool-Aid enema. A (black) sheeple. Now, especially on edge, perspiring, he manoeuvres himself into a corner and swallows a TranX.

He tries to spot Fiona but can't see her. Didn't see her

yesterday, either. The crowd peels away from a tall, handsome man striding in, like Moses parting the sea. Everyone falls silent. He is wearing a sharp black suit—expensive—and just-greying beard and hair. The shoulders-waist ratio of a superhero.

Seth recognises him immediately from the Alba brief: Christopher Walden, founder and CEO of Fontus, one of the richest men in South Africa, and general do-gooder. Like a politician, he has the knack of getting good deeds in the media at every opportunity.

'Good afternoon, my favourite employees.' He beams. His white teeth are a spotlight on the tittering crowd. Given his appearance, you almost expect him to talk in a broad American accent, but his delivery is Joburg Private School. He cues his assistant, who presses a button on a remote control. Images of an informal settlement come up on the scattered screens: a Mexican wave of blue skies and tin roofs. They are the usual images used to manipulate: dry-skinned, snot-crusted toddlers, skinny-ribbed dogs, litter bunting on wilting fences.

'This is a suburb in Thembalihle, just forty kilometres away from here. These people are in dire need of our help. They can hardly afford staples like water, bread and maize. It came to my attention yesterday that a couple staying there had been trying for five years to have a child. Finally, they were granted their miracle.' He pauses and the picture of a sunny baby comes up on the main projection. The infant's petroleum-jellied dimples elicit a chorus of coos.

'This is Lerato. She was hospitalised yesterday with cholera symptoms. I don't need to tell you how dangerous cholera is for a small child. It happened after the mother mixed her formula with grey water, from the tap.'

The crowd shakes its head, clicks its tongue.

'She was desperate. She had run out of money for food. It was her only option.' He pauses to let his employees feel the weight of it. 'But we're not going to stand around and let this happen!' he says. 'There are buses downstairs, waiting for you. We're off to visit Lerato's neighbourhood to deliver care packages. Food, paraffin, blankets, and water!' The room erupts into applause and cheering.

'Are you ready, Fontus?' he shouts. There is a ripple of affirmation. Walden's eyes glitter.

'I didn't hear you! I said, are you ready, Fontus?'

The room shouts 'Yes!'

'Go Fontus!' he yells, fist in the air.

'Go-o-o-o-o Fontus!' the room yells back, and everyone starts moving out.

*

Kirsten had brought them cold-pressed coffeeberry juices, cream-caff for her, to dull her synaesthesia for the trip in the communal taxi: black double-caff, extra stevia for Keke. Two vanilla-bean xylitol kronuts the size of saucers.

'Okay, lady, spill.' Keke says, once they are squashed in at the front. 'Where are we going and how did you find it?'

'How does our generation find any wisdom of great

substance and worth?'

'Er... Google?'

'Yebo.'

They are stuck in traffic. Nowadays this is unusual, but still seems to happen to Kirsten when she is in a rush to get somewhere. She sticks her head out the window to glimpse of what is causing the delay. A line of obedient vehicles snakes ahead of them.

'It couldn't have been easy, with all the doomsday prophets around, promising that every day is our last. The Suiciders, the Rapture kids, the Resurrectors.'

'I've never understood the whole "The End is Near" crowd,' says Kirsten, sitting back down.

'I know,' says Keke. 'You hate it when people state the obvious.'

'Exactly. Of course the end is near! As soon as there is a beginning the end is near.'

'I hope that coffee of yours is full-caff. You need a cup of optimism.'

'I don't mean it in a macabre way,' says Kirsten.

'Is there another way?'

'Yes! I mean it in a... I don't know, a Zen way. All beginnings have ends and that's the circle of life.'

'So what's your point?'

'I don't have a point. All I'm saying is that it's ironic. Life is really short and the creeps going around with their shouty-shirts telling you "The End is Near" are wasting their time.'

'Got you. Really they should listen to their own message and get a life. Literally.'

'Exactly.'

'So there were hundreds of silly results for "Doomsday"?'

'Thousands! So I ended up Googling *her* instead: the deranged lady.'

The driver enjoys pumping the pedals. The combi pitches forward, then stops dead, pitches forward, in an awkward dance of accelerator and brake. He speaks at volume to no one in particular. The passenger next to Keke is wearing a bad weave and singing along to the punk-gospel in her diamanté earbuttons, flashing a gold front tooth. They have to talk over her vibrato. Despite Kirsten's dulled senses, all the stimulation around her is disorientating. Finally they see the reason for the gridlock: a red-light brigade dominating the highway.

'Someone should tell them that this is supposed to be the fast lane,' mumbles Kirsten, and gets a dirty look from a fellow passenger. The red-lights signal it is a SurroSis and her entourage, and are to be respected at all costs and inconvenience. The driver touches his hat and then his heart, and they finally nudge past.

'She may have been schizo, but she was also, well…

gifted.'

Keke shoots her a look of thinly veiled patience.

'Seriously, she had what they called "advanced intelligence".'

'Who called it that?'

'Her colleagues, at Propag8—where we're going. She ran the whole project. She was a bio-what? A biohorticulturist.'

Keke takes the straw out of her mouth, frowns. 'Propag8 sounds familiar.'

'It's a seed sanctuary bank in an old sandstone quarry. Like Svalbard on Spitsbergen, but a local, more indigenous version. They nicknamed it The Doomsday Vault.'

'Doomsday. Ha.'

'Vavilov built the first one. A botanist-geneticist in the 1930s, he grew up poor and hungry, so became obsessed with ending famine. The seeds even survived the Siege of Leningrad. And Hitler. Although not all the guards did.'

'Starved to death surrounded by edible seeds?' says Keke.

'Clearly better people than you or I.'

'And Vavilov? Became a rich and famous hero?'

'*Nyet*. He died in prison.'

'Hitler?'

'Stalin.'

'Jesus.'

'Are we just saying names out loud now?'

Keke cackles.

'What about your coco-loco lady?'

'According to her colleagues, she was the best in her field, some kind of genetic genius. She was no garage genome-hacker; she invented all kinds of disease- and pest-resistant crops. Got a 99 million-rand grant for her work on revolutionising vertical farming. Contributed to amazing brainswarming sessions when she open-sourced her ideas for cheap, organic biofuel and designs for living buildings. And she was ambitious. I mean, Propag8 was her idea. She was guarding against Doomsday.'

They travel for a while in silence.

'So her paranoia worked for her, to a certain degree.'

Kirsten shrugs. 'Maybe it used to, anyway.'

They disembark ten kilometres south of Bela-Bela. A local cab drives them from their stop on the main road along the dusty way to the slick exterior of the Propag8 building.

The design of the sandstone façade looks sunken into the ground, giving the idea that half of its face is under the earth. It's the same colour as the surrounding sand and rocks, which makes it blend into the landscape, despite it being the only building on the horizon.

It reminds Kirsten of Shelley's poem *Ozymandias*, and it makes her smile. Doomsday, and *'Nothing beside remains.'* The architect obviously had a sense of humour.

Keke moves to ring the bell but the smoked glass doors slide open before she touches the button. The inside is huge, cavernous, bare. There is a figure eight in the floor mosaic; Kirsten realises that it's an infinity sign. The only colour is a row of what must be a hundred different succulents in African clay pots along the dark glass front.

The receptionist looks up, ready to help them, but Keke motions that they've got it, and subtly moves Kirsten towards the large stainless steel door at the opposite side of the expanse. As they get to within two meters of it, the light on the doorway switches from red to green with a beep (Cashmere Cherry to Spring Leaf) and they hear the mechanism on the other side unlocking. The heavy doors glide open, revealing a high-tech elevator with confusing buttons. Instead of a neat ladder of floors, one on top of the other, they are set out in a complicated 3D diagram in the shape of a lotus flower.

'Lotus flower?' says Keke. 'Was she some kind of yogi?'

'Lotus seeds are viable for a thousand years,' says Kirsten. She had read it while researching the vault on The Net.

Fifty-two stops to choose from, and they are clueless. Keke pushes the stud closest to her. They start as the elevator moves sideways. When the doors open again, it's into a dark corridor. They step out, and the light above them flickers on. Keke does a quick dance, *Caipoera*-style, and more lights come on. Kirsten considers the whole seed bank in utter darkness, apart from this little cell of light.

There is another door across the passage. Kirsten steps towards it and holds up her key. The light stays red, and the door locked. They step back into the elevator and study the plan etched into its wall.

'Do you remember anything else from what you read about her work here?'

Kirsten racks her brain, tries to use Google on her watch, but there is no signal. She moves closer to the map and one of the buttons automatically lights up. Sub Rosa, it says, floor 36. She opens her hand to look at the key. The doors close and this time they move downwards, into the depths of the old mine.

When the door clicks open they enter a space that would look like a bank deposit box room if it weren't for the floor-to-ceiling animated wallpaper. Huge rose buds and blooms (Rusted Carmine) caress the walls, as if alive. Kirsten tries to take a photo with her locket but it's blocked. It feels as if she is looking through pink mist. She should have doubled the caff in her coffee.

Keke takes the key from her and approaches the wall of safety deposit boxes. It does its now familiar magic trick and a box on the right, just below eye-level, shows a blue light. Keke pushes it in, and it slides out like a drawer, the size of a shoebox. Inside is another box, with a keyhole, which Keke unlocks.

'It's like pass-the-parcel,' whispers Keke.

'Pass the what?'

'Oh,' says Keke, 'Never mind.' They both peer into the box, wary, as if something could jump out and bite their fingers.

'It's empty,' says Kirsten.

As an act of desperation, she puts her whole hand into the box and rummages around, just so that she would have no doubt in her mind that the box is definitely, absolutely, 100% empty. But it isn't.

'Hey,' she says. The far side feels different. Not textured metal, but plastic. She gets her fingernails underneath the corner and rips it off, bringing it out of the box and into view. It's a small plastic bag, like a sandwich bag, but four-ply and heat-sealed.

*

On the way home, a white minivan comes into view, then disappears, then appears again. It looks like another communal taxi, but without the trappings: no dents or scratches, no eccentric bumper stickers, furry steering wheel or hula-girl hanging from the rear-view mirror. Instead: clean paintwork, tinted windows. Something about it bothers Kirsten.

'I know I sound crackers but... is that van... following us?' Kirsten frowns.

'Please don't start,' says Keke.

'Seriously,' says Kirsten. 'They've been behind us for the last ten minutes.'

Keke looks over at the vehicle, then turns back around and plays on her phone. The white minibus weaves aggressively and gets too close to the taxi. Kirsten starts to panic.

'They know we have it. They're trying to stop us.'

'Stop it,' growls Keke, but as her eyes go back to her screen their taxi is knocked sideways. The minivan swerves away then back to hit them again, causing the passengers to scream and the driver to grab his hat, fling it down, concentrate on keeping the vehicle on the road.

Metal screeches as the van pushes hard against the taxi, trying to force it into the guardrails. The taxi driver keeps his head, accelerates, takes back the road. Keke pushes Kirsten down and covers her. They are smashed again, harder, and they veer off the road, onto the shoulder. Their driver steers hard to not go over the rails, then overcorrects and crashes into a bakkie, almost rolls the vehicle.

They sway on two wheels, then land safely back on the tarmac. The white minivan speeds off. Cars all around swerve and hoot, people shout. Inside the taxi: silence, the caustic smell of burning brakes. Broken glass glitters.

JOURNAL ENTRY 7

15 April 1988

Westville

In the news: *A bomb explodes prematurely outside* Pretoria's *Sterland cinema killing the carrier and injuring a bystander. The passengers of plane-jacked Kuwait Airways Flight 422 are still being held as hostages — it's been 11 days — the Lebanese guerrillas are demanding the release of 17 Shi'ite Muslim bombers being held by Kuwait.*

What I'm listening to: *Chalk Mark in a Rainstorm* — Joni Mitchell

What I'm reading: *Margaret Atwood's 'The Handmaid's Tale' — I feel like this book is speaking directly to me, making me question my life.*

What I'm watching: *Beetlejuice*

My shrink says that it's good to write my feelings down so here I go: the ugly truth. I don't think the pills are helping. I love the babies more than life itself. I do, honestly, it's like they are physically connected to my heart. I can't imagine life without them.

But I also feel trapped. Isolated. I'm so young and here I am washing and cleaning and changing nappies while I should be out in the world, making friends and money and just LIVING. I feel like I am stuck in a life – that sometimes feels like a living hell of pee and poo and vomit – that I didn't choose.

I miss home and my family, even though we don't get on that well. I'm sad that they haven't come to visit the babies. I love P. Sometimes I think that he must regret marrying me; I can't imagine how he finds me attractive when I am such a stretch-marked baggy-eyed zombie. Other times I think, I am so pretty and young (on the inside!), I should be out there dating a whole lot of different men, be taken to new restaurants and getting flowers and goodnight kisses.

I don't want to eat because eating binds you to this earth in some way and I want to be free. I can see my clothes hanging off my body and it feels good to have an outward expression of the way I'm feeling inside.

I feel like I have wasted my life, that there is nothing to live for. Even though I know it's not true, that is how I feel, and that's why it's so difficult to get up in the mornings. And then when I do get up the babies cry and cry and I just feel like jumping out of a window.

The sticky love for the twins is push-pull: sometimes I'll be holding one of them and swaying and they'll melt into me and I think that the moment couldn't be more perfect. In the next minute something will happen: I'll slip on spilled milk, the washing machine will pack up, Kate will vomit on my clean top, Sam will start screaming, then they'll both be screaming and the kitchen will flood and I'll realise we're out of breakfast cereal and I can't stand it so my mind just floats away.

On these days I have the urge to just run away. To leave P and the twins. Not to be a coward, but to be brave, to save my life. I get anxious in the car on these days because my body and mind want to push that accelerator as far as it will go and just go anywhere that isn't here. Another province. Another country. Or even into the side of a bridge. But then I pull over and breathe and try to listen to my heart, which is connected to the babies, the sweet babies, my beautiful Sam and Kate, and it tells me to stay.

BORROWED SCRUBS

18

Johannesburg, 2021

The man dressed as a nurse puts his latex-covered fingers on William Soraya's wrist, feels his pulse. It is slow and steady. There is no need to do it: the athlete is hooked up to all kinds of monitoring equipment. He fusses about the room, rearranging giant bouquets of flowers and baskets of fruit and candy. He admires the medal—Soraya's first Olympic gold—on the bedside table. Its placement seems a desperate plea: *You were once the fastest man in the world, you can beat this. Please wake up.*

The nurse takes what looks like a pen out of his pocket, clicks it as if he is about to write on Soraya's chart, and spikes the tube of the IV with it. It is slow-acting enough to give him the ninety seconds he will need to leave the hospital. No alarms will go off while he is still here. He takes the medal and slips it into his trouser pocket as he moves. It is cold against his thigh.

It's a bitterbright feeling for him, leaving while his mark is still breathing. Doesn't feel right, especially after the accident he engineered hasn't proved to be fatal. Still, there will be others. He walks down the passage as quickly as he can without alerting anyone. He breathes hot air into his medimask, requisite for any doctor, nurse, patient or visitor in the hospital. It's large and covers most of his face, which is most fortunate. Hospitals are one of the easiest places to kill people. His borrowed scrubs cover his other distinguishing characteristics, apart from his generous build, and height. But no one will say: there was a nurse in there with a burnt arm.

PIRANHAS

19

Johannesburg, 2021

Seth gets home at midnight. He'd been drinking at TommyKnockers and is a bit unsteady on his feet. A cab dropped him off, courtesy of Rolo. Upstairs on the 17th floor, he punches in the code—52Hz—and his retina unlocks his front door. It clicks open, and Sandy greets him. He shows the speaker his middle finger. He checks all the security screens, sees the place is empty.

Knowing he's had too much to drink, he shrugs, pours a few fingers of vodka into a tumbler with ice. Takes it to his Tile to check for messages. He's been checking throughout the day to see if Fiona tried to get hold of him, but *nada*.

All he sees is update after update about William Soraya's death in hospital. He tries to block the story in his feed but it keeps on coming up on his screen, as if to haunt him, as if to say: this could have been you. You think you're indestructible; so did Soraya. Now he's lying on a slab with multiple organ failure, because that's what happens to people like you.

Not being able to get hold of Fiona adds to his anxiety. He doesn't know where she lives, doesn't know who her friends and family are, which makes it impossible to get hold of her if she doesn't come to work, and doesn't answer her phone. It nags at him: Fiona isn't the kind of girl to screen calls or not come to the grind for two days in row. He takes her Fontus access card out of his hoodie pocket, looks at it. His guilt accentuates her clear blue eyes, the salmon of her cheeks. No one has mentioned her absence at work. Piranhas.

He turns on the Tile, takes a slug of vodka. The green rabbit flashes; FlowerGrrl bumped him earlier in the evening.

FlowerGrrl>Hey SD, what's/hold-up? Thought u'd hve Fontus in bag by now.

He knows she's kidding, but feels the pressure nonetheless. He's been there for weeks without much progress. He'd figured Fiona would be his ticket, but she's gone MIA. His drinking tonight has had a purpose: to wipe out any inclination that he is worried about her. It hasn't worked. The more he drinks, the more it becomes clear that, for the first time in his life, he cares about someone else.

He replies to FlowerGrrl:

SD>> Making headway, shld hve s/thing soon.

Without washing his face or brushing his teeth, and still in his jacket, he gets into bed with his slippery glass of vodka. Takes a bottle of pills from the pocket, pops two, washes them down with the spirit. Spreads a throw untidily over his body, and falls asleep with the lights on.

Outside the building, a large man is walking his dog. The dog pauses to sniff the innards of a pothole. The man uses the time to look at the entrance of the building, get an idea of the security system. Backs up, looks up to the corner apartment of the 17th floor where a light is still on. Having seen enough, he makes a kissing noise: pulls the protesting beagle along, firmly, but not unkindly.

*

Kirsten's watch rings; it's Marmalade. Oh shit, she thinks, looking at the time, then at the two empty bottles of wine on Keke's desk. The clockologram clicks in disapproval. She touches her earbutton to answer the call.

'Hi, sorry I'm late,' she says, her voice gruff. Gives Keke the grimace of a schoolgirl in trouble.

'And you haven't called,' he says.

'And I haven't called. Sorry.'

'I was worried about you.'

'Sorry.'

'When are you coming home? I made dinner. Four hours ago.'

'Ah, sorry! I didn't know. You should have told me.' She stands up, throws two empty sauce-stained Styrofoam shamburger clamshells in the bin.

'I wanted to surprise you. Do something nice for you.'

'I'm really sorry. I'm with Kex.'

Keke gives her a soft kick in the shins.

She winces and hops up and down. 'At The Office. We're working on a... story.'

'Well, wake me when you get home.'

'It'll be late.'

'Wake me, Kitty. I miss you.'

He ends the call. They never say 'I Love You.' They agreed long ago that that the phrase is overused and trite. They won't reduce their relationship to a cliché. What they have is deeper.

'How much trouble are in you in?' asks Keke.

'He cooked dinner for me: a surprise.'

Keke looks at the time on her phone. 'Ouch.'

'He wanted to do something nice for me.'

'Double-ouch.'

'So where were we?' Kirsten asks, but Keke is looking at her strangely.

'What?'

'Since when do you lie to James?'

'What? I didn't. I don't.'

'We're working on a "story"?'

'Well,' says Kirsten, 'we are, kind of. Aren't we?'

Keke pouts, not convinced.

'You're the one that says everyone has a story. Maybe this is mine. And, believe me, the less James knows, the better.'

They go back to solving the puzzle they have been working on all night: trying to make sense of the code that is in the plastic envelope they found in the seed bank. It is a list of barcodes that, when scanned, are numbers, 18 digits to a line.

100380199121808891

104140199171209891

20290199142117891

20201199161408891

101250199160217891

201250199160217891

1010199112016891

They all start with either 10 or 20, all contain the numbers 1991 in the same position near the middle, and end in 891. The more wine Kirsten drinks, the more the numbers glow with their colours. It is distracting. For this reason, she has never been good at maths.

'I don't know how much longer I can look at this,' she says, rubbing her neck, which is tender from the car accident. 'Are you sure you don't know any maths-geniuses-code-crackers?'

Keke shakes her head. 'Nope.'

They have tried everything they can think of, from simple alphabet a=1 algorithms to squares and prime numbers, and all the search engines they can think of. Kirsten is playing with Keke's Beckoning Cat. If you push its belly-button its USB port comes out the other side, like a stunted tail. A secret porthole of information.

Maneki Neko, she thinks: *Japanese Lucky Cat. Brings good fortune to owners.* She gives the hard plastic a squeeze, puts it back on Keke's desk.

'Look, we've had a hectic day and we're not getting anywhere tonight.' Keke sighs, standing up. 'Why don't you go home to Marmalade and make up?'

Kirsten starts to protest but Keke is right.

'Besides,' says Keke, putting on her leather jacket. 'I need to get laid.'

*

As soon as Kirsten opens the front door she smells roast chicken, her favourite. James had left a plate for her on the kitchen counter: a succulent thigh, butter-roast potatoes, candied golden beetroot. She peels the cling wrap away and starts to eat the chicken with her fingers. It is exactly right, the taste: an undulating curve with a few small points bouncing off it, finishing in a wavering line. She's exhausted; it feels like more than just tiredness. Deathargy.

Her body is cold when she climbs in next to James, and she's unsure of whether to wake him. She moves closer to him, barely spoons him, trying to gauge how lightly he is sleeping.

'Thank you,' she whispers, 'the potatoes were perfect.'

He grunts, turns around, pulls her towards him in a full-body hug. A warm, sleepy hand slides under her pyjama top, rubbing her back, then settles under her panties, on the arch of her hip. She moves against his hand, slowly, rhythmically, but stops when she realises he is asleep.

A few hours later Kirsten wakes with a start. Colours swirl in her head: green, grey, brown, yellow. 7891. She knows the colour combination so well, but where from? Pine Tree, Ash, Polished Meranti, English Mustard. Somehow she knows it's part of her. Then she gets it. She bumps Keke, even though it's past 2am:

KD> The colours are backwards!

Surprisingly, or not, Keke responds.

KK>> Wot R U doing? LSD?

KD> It should be yellow/brown/grey/green.

KK>> U need to be institutionalised. Good night & good luck.

KD> Not 7891, but 1987, the year I was born. Think the whole sequence is backwards. It says 60217891, that's my birthdate, backwards. 6 December 1987. It features twice in the list, 5th and 6th lines. It must mean something. I knew the colours but it was hard to see when they were backwards.

KK>> What about the other numbers?

KD> No idea.

KD> Yet.

TOY CHASE

20

Johannesburg, 2021

Despite a late night, Seth is in the office early. In theory he is trying to tweak his 3D mathematical model animation of the CinnaCola taste experience, but his head is pounding and Fiona's pass is burning a hole in his pocket. He gulps down his anxiety with a few pills and leaves his office, heads towards the Waters wing of the building. He walks past Fiona's office and does a double take as he sees her sitting at her desk. Relief like a splash of water on his face.

'Fiona!' he says.

The brunette at the desk looks up at him, puzzled.

'Hello?'

It's not Fiona. Similar looking, thinner, more attractive.

'Oh,' says Seth, taking a step back and looking at the new name on the door. 'Do you know where Fiona is?'

'I don't know a Fiona,' the usurper says, mechanical smile, cherry red lipstick, and a whiff of Stepford. 'Can I help you with something?' She is being super polite: she wants him to leave.

'This is her office,' Seth says, incredulous.

She blinks at him, stops smiling. 'Not anymore.'

Despite Seth's better judgment he strides up to the main reception. The receptionist looks alarmed.

'Fiona Botes,' he says, 'she's been away from the grind, and I was wondering if you knew where she was.'

The man fingers his hair, taps on his tablet, looks cheerfully confused.

'No record of a Fiona working here,' he says.

Seth wants to pull him by his effeminate tie, punch him in the face. He does everything in his power to keep calm. He shouldn't be here asking questions, calling attention to himself.

'Check again,' he says.

The man taps a bit more then patches the HR infobot on his earbutton. 'Botes,' he says, 'Fiona.' After a moment he ends the call. 'It appears that Ms Botes is on a business trip. Asia. She's not expected back any time soon.'

'Asia?' mumbles Seth, 'Is that the best you can do?'

At the look in Seth's eyes, the receptionist takes a step back, despite the counter separating them. His eyes dart to the army of security guards. Seth retreats. He has five, maybe ten minutes before someone with clout realises he needs to be taken care of.

He runs to the Waters wing and uses Fiona's access card to get into the lab, hurries to put on a mask. Once he gets into the factory it's easy to disappear between the giant vessels of water, darting between gauges, graphs, clicking dials. Fiona had told him that the tap at the end of all the barrels and valves, just before the bottling, is where the sample test tubes are filled.

Seth removes the test sample of Anahita, replacing it with a virgin tube, and slips the sample into his pocket. Then he walks over to the Tethys section, and the Hydra section, and does the same there. Cameras are everywhere.

Once he is out of the lab he bins his mask, runs up the stairs, towards his office to grab his Tile, but immediately feels as if someone is following him. He picks up his pace. As he's about to turn into his office he sees them: three security guards armed to the max, ready to pounce. Dobermans with a rabbit in their sights. Just before they grab him, The Weasel steps in their way.

'No, no,' he's saying. 'I'm telling you there has been a mistake.'

Hurting an innocent Fontus employee would have consequences.

'On whose orders?' Weasel's demanding, the back of his white-collared shirt straining, struggling with the mountainous men as they try to reach around him, but Seth is just out of their grasp.

He darts into his office and locks the door. Grabs his backpack and jumps out of the window, onto the narrow balcony. Sprints towards the back of the building and runs down the perforated metal stairs of the fire escape. Once he hits the grass, he hijacks a CinnaCola golf cart, floors it, mows through a gazebo, sending trays of breakfast hors d'oevres and flutes of Buck's Fizz flying. A waiter in a tux stands frozen, open-jawed. Seth swerves and narrowly misses the corner of the squash courts.

He can hear them behind him now, in turbo-carts with flashing lights. They motor past the swimming pool, a strip of restaurants, a mini touch-rugby field. It's like playing cops and robbers in Toyland. He can see the exit, but at the speed they're approaching they'll be able to stop him before he reaches it. A bullet zings past his head. Another hits his cart. Toy chase, but real guns, real bullets.

A small bang and his cart spins and tumbles, rolling over itself and throwing Seth out. He stands, re-orients himself, notices his head is bleeding. Feels for the test samples to make sure they're not broken. The three guards are out of their vehicle and pointing their weapons at him with practised aims. A trio of testosterone. More guards will be on their way. Seth doesn't have a choice: he reaches to his ankle holster and pulls out his gun. They all begin to shout orders at him, drowning each other out.

'Put down your weapon!' yells the one with the blond crew cut.

'You put your fucking weapons down!' shouts Seth, flicking off the safety catch. No one moves.

'I am warning you, Mister Denicker, we will use force against you if you don't come with us.'

'We just want to talk,' pipes the other one.

Seth walks backwards, towards the exit. The men stiffen their arms, each one wanting to take the shot. Frustrated wannabes with itchy fingers: dangerous.

'You have families, children,' he shouts at them. 'I have fuck-all. No one. Nothing. You've got the most to lose.' They keep their sights trained on him. Then, slowly, the youngest of the three lowers his gun. The crew cut shouts at him, swears, but the man slides his gun back into his hip holster, backs away.

'You two: you're ready to widow your wives over fucking bottled water?'

They don't say anything but keep advancing while he inches closer to the exit. Seth has no choice: he squeezes the trigger and puts a bullet in crew cut's leg. The man lets out a shocked noise, falls to the floor, lifts his gun at Seth, pulls the trigger, misses, and misses again. Now empty, the felled man's gun clicks impotently in Seth's direction, and he roars in frustration. Specks of saliva in the sunlight. The other man doesn't know what to do. He appears shocked by the blood and doesn't seem to want to shoot or be shot. His gun is still raised but it's at an unconvincing angle.

'Tell them to open the exit,' says Seth.

'No!' shouts the crew cut, his arms out at his side as if to hold back the other man. Seth points his gun at the uninjured man's thigh.

'Wait!' shouts the man, 'wait,' and he throws his weapon forward, onto the grass, and speaks into the crackle of his radio.

'We have the suspect in hand. Call off back-up and open exits. Repeat: suspect is apprehended, all clear.' An acknowledgement sputters back.

Seth collects the abandoned gun. 'Give me your access card,' he says, and the man does so. He wonders what in particular this man has to live for.

Thirty seconds later Seth walks out of the Fontus grounds and the colourful throngs of morning tuk-tuk and taxi traffic swallow him up. Until now he hasn't been convinced that Fontus had something to hide.

RED FINGERPRINTS

21

Johannesburg, 2021

Kirsten takes her eyes off her screen to think, and sees the file she has been keeping on her mother. Opens it, looks through the morbid illustrations, the pricked paper dolls, the onion-skin birth certificate, sees the colours. She thinks that's the end of the file but then she sees the magazine cutting again, the one she found framed in storage. Cute baby, but not her. The date on the back says 1991.

She puts away the file and Googles the year 1991. She searches South African pages: South African cricket was unsanctioned, political violence continued, Nadine Gordimer won the Nobel Prize for literature. 1991: Yellow, brown, brown, yellow. Not a nicely coloured year at all. She can't imagine it being a very happy year for anyone.

The birth dates, if that's what they are, thinks Kirsten, are all around the same time. From 1986 to 1988: a year or two apart at most. So that's seven people, born around similar dates. Then the other set of dates all contained 1991. Her watch rings, making her jump. She turns on her TileCam and answers the call.

'Hi,' she smiles, happy to see Keke, but Keke doesn't return it.

'Listen, you're in trouble.'

'What?'

'You should leave your house.'

'Now who's paranoid?' Kirsten laughs.

'As soon as you can, Cat. The list, it's a... kind of a... poisoned chain letter. It's not just a list. It's a hitlist.'

'Slow down, Keke. You look manic. Too much caffeine?'

'I'm not fucking around, Kirsten, you need to listen to me. It's a *hitlist*. You are *on it*.'

'Seriously, you need to calm down.'

'Someone wants you dead. You need to leave your apartment.'

'You're not making any sense. Why would anyone want to kill *me*?'

'Marko… he came up with this mad algorithm and matched the birthdates with recently dead people. As in, the last few weeks, days. The people born in those years, the numbers at the end of the lines, they're dead. One, two, three, four, they're all dead, in that order. The schizo was number three. William Soraya was second. Before him, a musician in the bath.'

Panic reaches for her: serpentine plumes of yellow smoke (Sick Leaf). Betty/Barbara had said something about a music man.

'A musician, in the bath?' she asks.

'He was drowned.'

'In the *bath?*'

'Oh, for Christ's sake!' screams Keke. 'Just leave the fucking house already!'

'But you're not making any sense!'

'Listen to me, Kitty. Number four, a woman in a park. Dead. You're number five. You're next on the list.'

'I'm next on the list.'

'You or the other person with your birthdate. You're five or six.'

'Wait, you're saying that the crazy lady was right?'

'We don't have time to talk about it now. Go to a police station. I'll meet you there.'

'Okay.'

'Okay?'

'Wait. No. She said no cops, Betty/Barbara said no cops.'

'Well then just get out of there. They know where you live. Two of them were killed in their own homes. Get out and go somewhere public.'

'But you said... number four was killed in a park?'

'Jesus Christ, Kitty, I'm about to strangle you myself.'

'Okay. Okay. I'll go somewhere safe.' Even if this is some stupid misunderstanding. It doesn't matter. Even if it is just to prevent Keke from having a heart attack.

'Okay,' she says, 'I'm leaving.'

As she stands, a thought almost knocks her over.

'What about the chip?' she whispers.

'What?'

'The microchip. The crazy lady said she had a tracker chip in her head.'

A recent trend had been that overprotective mothers had them implanted in their children's necks, but it had only became legal a few years ago. Kirsten's hands fly up to her head. She tries to search her scalp but her hair gets in the way.

'A tracker? That's impossible, right?'

'No. I don't know. I just want you to get out of there.'

'But if you're right about the list, then Betty/Barbara was right, and she told me about the chip. Which means that they'll find me wherever I am. I'm not safe anywhere.'

'Yes,' says Keke, 'if she was right.'

'But you're saying she *was* right.'

'I don't know what I'm saying!'

'Holy fuck, Keke!'

'A chip is implausible, but even if it's true… So there's a chip in your head. What could you do about it anyway?'

'Hold on,' Kirsten says, and runs to the bathroom cupboard. Grabs James's hair clippers. She sits in front of her screen and sweeps the zinging shaver from the base of her neck all the way to her forehead. Keke lets out a sound of shock: an almost-sob. Masses of red hair fall to the wooden floor as Kirsten finishes the job. The buzzing stops, and Kirsten is bald. She tries again, palpating her scalp to feel for anything strange.

'Those things can… move,' says Keke, emotional, 'it could be anywhere.'

Kirsten's fingers freeze at the back of her head. Just lower than halfway down is a thickness, a form. She gulps. She didn't believe it existed until this moment. Now there it is, under her finger.

'I think I found it. Now what?'

Keke looks at her with plates for eyes. They both know the answer.

'Let me phone James,' says Keke, 'let him do it for you. He'll have the right... instruments.'

'Do you honestly think he is going to believe any of this?' shouts Kirsten. 'That I'm on a hitlist and have a fucking tracker in my head? I need to get it out *now*. Now!'

She runs to the spare room and starts to search through James's things. It's the room they use to store her camera equipment and his medical gear and its suitably messy. She doesn't find a scalpel.

As she's raiding, a white envelope falls out of a back pocket of his doctor's bag. At first she ignores it, focused on the search, but then she sees the envelope has her name on it, and her address. This apartment's address. She remembers now a day not so long ago when she had walked in on him in here. He had jumped.

'You gave me a fright,' he said, tucking a white piece of paper into his doctor's bag.

'Sorry,' she said, lifting a lens off the windowsill. 'Just wanted to get this.'

She hasn't given the interaction a second thought, except maybe to observe that they were being overly polite to each other: never a good sign for a relationship.

She pockets the envelope and keeps looking for something sharp until she had gone through every satchel. Then she remembers the pocketknife in her handbag. She speeds back to her desk, brings it out, flicks open the glint.

'No!' whispers Keke, covering her eyes, 'you can't!'

Kirsten grabs a bottle of vodka and some surgical cotton wool. She wipes down the blade and the back of her head. Brings the knife up to her shorn skull, feels for the lump, takes a breath. She chickens out, puts the knife down and has a large mouthful of vodka, then another one, and tries again. This time she draws blood, splitting the skin just above the thing. She waits until the cut is finished before she shouts in pain. Keke is covering her eyes but shouts in sympathy. Kirsten tries to get it out but her fingers are shaking and greasy with blood. She gives up, wipes them on her jeans.

'Tweezers!' says Keke.

Despite tears in her eyes, Kirsten finds a pair in her make-up bag, douses them, and starts to root around in the wound. Every movement of the sharp metal in the gash sends bright orange currents of pain down her neck, down her spine. She feels all the blood drain from her head, as if she's about to faint, but then she gets a grip on what she hopes is the chip and pulls it out. She holds the tweezers up to the camera, and there, in its sticky grasp, is a tiny microchip in a glass capsule. A treacherous grain of rice. Warm liquid runs down Kirsten's neck, between her shoulder blades. She is swaying in her chair. She holds the cotton wool up to the wound to staunch the bleeding, then rips open a platelet-plaster and sticks it onto the wound.

'Have some more vodka,' says Keke, but Kirsten feels too dizzy, wants to keep her head.

'I found this,' says Kirsten, her speech slurred by shock and spirits. The envelope is stamped with red fingerprints. She tries to open it with her stuttering hands. Gives up. 'I don't know where to go.'

'Go anywhere, just get out of there!'

'I need to warn the other people on the list.'

JOURNAL ENTRY

2 July 1988

Westville

In the news: A car bomb explodes near the gate of Ellis Park stadium in Johannesburg. Two people are killed and 37 injured. Bombs, bombs, bombs. What kind of world have we brought the twins into?

What I'm listening to: *Tracy Chapman. Fell for her after watching a bootleg VHS of her amazing performance at the Nelson Mandela 70^h birthday celebration concert at Wembley Stadium. Talkin' about a Revolution!*

What I'm reading: *'Radical Gardening: Politics, Idealism and Rebellion in the Garden (George McKay).*

What I'm watching: *Who Framed Roger Rabbit?*

I don't know if it's the pills or the sessions with my shrink or just the fact that the twins are sleeping through the night but I feel SO MUCH BETTER! I feel almost like myself again. It is like coming up for air after a long, deep dive in some cold black lake.

P hired a domestic worker / nanny to help me with the kids. She comes in on Tuesdays and Thursdays and does all the washing and cleaning (usually with one of the twins strapped to her back!) It gives me time and space to just 'be.' Who knew you needed time for that? But I do. I work in the garden and read books and then I feel ready to be a mom again. I no longer feel as though I am being consumed.

I feel better, I look better, I even put on a new dress the other day and took the kids for a walk. I am hungry again and it feels good to cook and eat.

P is so happy he is spoiling me. Buying me clothes and a nice necklace, and we even got a babysitter the other night and went to dinner like we used to. I had a sirloin and a baked potato with sour cream and P just watched me eat as if he had never seen anyone eat steak before.

My shrink says I'll have good days and bad days while I'm getting better and soon the good days will outnumber the bad days. I think that is starting to happen.

I planted some new flowers – arums this time – they flower beautifully in winter instead of dying like some other annuals. Also planted some other things. P says I've got green fingers now. I laughed. It felt good.

TSOTSI

22

Johannesburg, 2021

Seth is in a communal taxi heading towards his apartment. His fellow passengers give him a wide berth as he tries to stem the flow of blood from his forehead. He is lucky the driver let him on. A pearl-clutcher wearing thick glasses clicks her tongue at him and calls him a *tsotsi* under her breath. He bumps Alba.

SD> In some trouble here, position at F compromised.

FlowerGrrl>> What do u need?

SD> Security check & bugsweep ASAP at my place. I'll remotely disable my BM-retina access.

FlowerGrrl>> Motioned, will contact u when it's confirmed clean. You need a bodyguard?

SD> Ha. Since when does Alba hve budget 4 bodyguards?

FlowerGrrl>> Worried about u. It can b arranged.

SD> I'll b fine.

FlowerGrrl>> Famous last words.

SD> Hopefully not LAST words.

FlowerGrrl>> ROFLZ! Danger suits you. Never knew u had/sense/humour.

SD> Funny. Also, I'll need someone/labs, I'll b bringing in samples.

FlowerGrrl>> Excellent. Will have someone here ASAP.

Seth's head stops bleeding.

*

Kirsten's head stops bleeding. She switches on the shower and doesn't wait for the water to get warm before she blasts her face, neck and back, then quickly towels off, leaving a Pollock of red and pink behind (Blood Marble). She throws on some fresh clothes: black, and steps into her dark trainers. Grabs her bag but leaves her Tile behind. Just as she is out the door she remembers the envelope and goes to fetch it, stuffs it in her bag along with a clean plaster and the pocketknife. She doesn't have time to think, she just moves.

HER ABDUCTOR'S HANDWRITING

23

Johannesburg, 2021

Kirsten puts her watch up to the screen so the ATM can scan it. She draws her daily limit of ten thousand rand, hoping it will keep her going for the next few days. The machine thanks her for her business and ejects 20 perfumed five hundred rand notes. The cash is bulky but she can't leave a credit trail. She checks over her shoulder for anything suspicious but everyone seems to be going about their regular lives without a clue of what hers has become.

She catches a communal taxi to Mbali Mall in Hyde Park.

She can't think of anywhere safe to go but when the taxi driver stops outside the shopping centre for another passenger, Kirsten jumps out, leaving the microchip hidden in the fold of the seat.

Usually she hates malls, but for now the soulless space and dazzling lights seem like a good idea. Polished floors, store staff too tired to smile and shopzombies bleached by the artificial light. The killer wouldn't pump her full of bullets in front of all these people, will he? Still, she is cautious, keeps her head down and walks along the shop fronts, gazing at the window displays without seeing anything. She grabs a mask off a rotating display and uses it to cover her face.

*

Seth is walking, to kill time and get some air, and is twenty minutes away from home. Tuk-tuks and bike-cabs hoot at him as they pass, offering him a ride. Alba had just confirmed that their bugsweep has entered his apartment, so by the time he gets there it should have been given the all clear. It is just a precaution: so far as he is aware, no one at Fontus knows his address, but he was born with a healthy sense of paranoia and it has kept him alive and (relatively) unscathed up until now. What the fuck is going on at Fontus that they would remove Fiona and set armed security guards on him? Numbers stream through his head as he thinks of the files he had accessed there, the graphs, the summaries, all seemingly in order. What is it that they're so desperate to hide? He will find out soon enough: he needs to get the samples to Alba HQ.

*

Her adrenaline flagging, Kirsten looks for a place to sit but is accosted by a Quinbot, AKA Stepford Wife. Despite her side-stepping it, the mannequinbot sidles up to her.

'Hello *Kirsten*,' it says. 'How are you? Isn't it a wonderful day?'

'Jesus,' says Kirsten into her mask. 'Really?'

'I'm sorry. Hello *Jesus*. How are you? Isn't it a wonderful day?'

'Leave me alone,' says Kirsten.

'Jesus, would you like to try on this SaSirro alpha-cut dress? It has a built-in corset that will accentuate your lovely body shape.'

'No.'

'The shimmer in the hemline adds grace to your movement, and—'

'No, thank you, not interested.'

'Jesus, if you look at the detail, you'll see—'

'Stop calling me Jesus.'

'I have scanned your measurements. You have a lovely body shape. This is how the dress would look on you.'

The Stepford Wife grows a little taller, her bust shrinks by a cup, and her waist grows by a few centimetres. Her abs get softer, and her calves become more pronounced. Her hair is reeled into her scalp. Kirsten picks up her pace, but the bot keeps up.

'Leave me alone,' she says. 'Scram.' She looks around to see who is watching.

'It has a built-in corset that will—'

'Fuck off!' she shouts, causing some nearby shopzombies to look at her. The bot stops and reverses. Its wide lipstick-smile doesn't falter.

'Thank you for your time,' says the bot. 'It's always lovely to see you.'

'Fucking bots,' mutters Kirsten, jogging away. The last thing she needs is to cause a scene.

'Don't be a stranger!' it calls out after her.

Mannequinbots are always getting abused: fondled, defaced, hacked, taken for trolley rides that invariably end up in some kind of accident, shoved into garbage removal chutes, stolen, decapitated. Kirsten has little sympathy.

She finds a hoverbench outside a Talking Tees shop. It seems to be a politically themed store; usually they're more light-hearted. The four shirts in the window tell her, via rather basic animations, to 'Beware The Net,' 'Boycott Bilchen,' 'Ban the SkyCar,' and 'Pray for Peace in Palestine.' She prefers the more light-hearted shirts, ones with beautiful, evolving illustrations, and ones that tell you jokes. The problem with the joke-shirts, though, is that you have to walk past the person before you hear the punchline.

She opens the letter she found in James's case. Her name

is scrawled on the outside of the envelope.

Dear Kirsten, it says, in her abductor's handwriting. *When you find out the truth you won't believe that we loved you, but we did, in our own way. It's terrible to want to tell you the truth, because it puts you in danger, but the truth will out, I can feel it bleeding out of me already, and it's better if you are warned. Your foster father, my pretend-husband of thirty years, heard us talking on the phone just now and—*

Maybe he thinks they'll spare him, but I know differently—

I don't have long—I know they'll be here any minute—who is to say no one else has confessed... I can't be the only one who feels like this. Festering, about to burst.

The details aren't important. Please know we truly believed we were doing the right thing.

This is important: What you must know is that I have now compromised the cell and if you don't move now you will be removed from the programme—killed.

My God, what have we done?

Once you are safe, contact ED MILLER in Melville. He is my life partner & soulmate. We've been together for 26 years. He doesn't know anything about GP, I spared him that much, but has a packet of info for you. Everything you need to know about why you were taken. You need to read this to understand why we did what we did.

You need to get rid of the tracking microchip (embedded in your scalp). You need to move countries. Just get on a plane, fly anywhere, for now. You need to do this without letting the police know. And you need to do this immediately. They will eliminate everyone in our cell, all seven children that were taken. Enclosed is a list of the others. I am sending this and a duplicate to the only other person I (shouldn't but do) know in the programme, Betty Weil (Barbara). I have given her your address. You can't trust anyone in the GP, but I had to take the chance. Warn them too, if you can.

Kirsten, one of them is your twin brother.

I'm sorry. Truly. We chose you because you were special. You were all special. God forgive me, and God help you. RUN.

Kirsten's brain stumbles. All she can see on the page are the words 'taken,' 'twin brother,' and 'RUN.' Kirsten's watch rings, snapping her out of her shock. It's Keke.

'Hey Cat,' she says, 'how are you doing? Hey, never mind. You're alive. That's the most important thing.'

'Yes,' says Kirsten, lowering her mask. 'I guess so. I'm inside—'

'Whoah! Don't tell me where you are.'

'Of course. I'll buy a 'sposie.'

'Good.'

'You got anything for me?'

'Ready for your rather interesting day to get a bit

more… interesting?'

'Impossible.'

'What?' says Keke.

'What?' says Kirsten.

'What do you know?' she asks.

'I need a moment,' says Kirsten, trying to think straight. 'You go first.'

'So FWB Hackerboy Genius found the other person on the list.'

'Where is he? Joburg? Do you have an address?'

'How did you know it was a he? And get this, you were right, he was born at the same clinic as you.'

'I know,' says Kirsten.

'Wait, what?'

'Just carry on,' says Kirsten.

'While Marko was hacking into some illegal tax shit to find his address, I checked the other names on the list and they—you—were all born at the same clinic.'

'What kind of clinic was this?'

'That's exactly what I thought, so I looked into it, and according to Google and the National Health Authority it never *existed*.'

'It never existed.'

'Correct.'

'So... I was born to a mother without a uterus in a clinic that never existed.'

'Er... correct,' says Keke. 'In other words—'

'In other words,' says Kirsten, 'she was not my mother and that is not my real birth certificate.'

'It looks like it, yes.'

'I was kidnapped,' Kirsten finally whispers. Snatched. Abducted.

Keke is talking again; Kirsten tries to tune in.

'... but I have a feeling this is just the beginning. It's clear that someone will do anything to keep whatever this is, a secret. Get that disposable phone and we can meet up. We can look for this guy together.'

Seven people on the list, all with forged birth certificates. The first four on the list: dead. Five, six, seven alive: orange, pink, green (Grapefruit Skin, Baby Toe Pink, Camouflage).

'Kitty Cat? Hello?'

'No, it's too dangerous. Stay where you are and keep looking.'

'Will you at least phone James? I'd feel much better if he was with you.' James hid the letter from her. Kirsten ignores the question. 'You'll bump me this guy's co-ordinates?'

'Yebo. Watch yourself!'

For a moment the danger fades and the realisation glitters before her: She has a twin. Unbelievable. But hadn't a small, lonely part of her known all along? 'RUN' the letter says. *Fuck. Fuck running away.* She is going to find her twin.

*

Seth hasn't received anything from Alba, so he waits outside, sure he'll get the go-ahead soon. He still has a few bullets left in his gun, which is cold but reassuring against his palm. He keeps his head down, his hood up. Slips into the camouflage of pedestrian traffic, but the creep is headed straight in his direction.

He feigns nonchalance, flicks off his safety. The person is getting closer, closer, and Seth's finger travels to the trigger. When the person is a metre away Seth finally looks up and is ready to fire.

There is a blast of light, and his mind scrambles to work out what has just happened. Has he been shot? Has he shot? He doesn't remember pulling the trigger. But no one is hurt and there is a shock of a beautiful woman in front of him: a haunted look and a shaved head.

'Seth Denicker?' she says, breathless.

'Who are you?' They've never met but he feels as if he knows her. Kirsten's body is vibrating. This man's face, his presence, shakes her, she feels like she's touched a live wire. There's an immediate electric psychic connection.

Seth is paralysed by the magnetic field of this familiar stranger.

'I'm...' she starts. Could it really be true? But she knew it was, without a doubt. Every bit of her could see it, taste it, feel it.

You are my parallel life, she wants to say. *I have always felt your existence echo in mine.*

She pulls off her face mask.

'I'm your twin sister.'

JOURNAL ENTRY 9

6 December 1988

Westville

In the news: *A limpet mine explodes in at the Department of Home Affairs in Brakpan. Bangladesh is devastated after the cyclone of December 2 – 5 million homeless and thousands dead.*

What I'm listening to: *Patti Smith's Dream of Life.*

What I'm reading: *Keith Kirsten's South African Gardening Manual*

What I'm watching: *Die Hard. I love Bruce Willis!*

The garden is absolutely exploding with colour. P says he can't believe it's the same garden. I'm so proud of it. Durban weather is the best: heat to get things growing and blooming, and lots of rain to keep it going. Allamanda, Bougainvillea, Mandevilla,

Plumbago. Now I understand the saying 'riot of colour'. The babies and I spend some time in it every single day.

But besides the garden, there was a big celebration today! The twins turned ONE! We took them to Mike's Kitchen and they both had a free 'kids meal' – a vienna and some chips with tomato sauce and then an upside-down ice-cream cone with a clown's face on it. Kate has such a sweet tooth and loves ice cream so that was her favourite part. She said 'green, green' (even though the ice cream was white). The waiters sang happy birthday to them and gave them red balloons with ribbons (which Sam promptly popped with his teeth). It was so cute, he had this shocked look and he looked at us, not sure if he wanted to laugh or cry.

It was a wonderful day. While the kids were eating P put his hand over mine and gave me this searching look, as if to see where that awful vacant person is, and I smiled back as brightly as I could. That part of me is pushed deep inside and I'll do whatever it takes to keep it there.

A LITTLE LESS CONVERSATION

24

Johannesburg, 2021

Seth scrubs his scalp with his knuckles. It is obvious that this woman is insane, you can tell at a glance: head shorn, blood-stained. Of course, his head has been bleeding too, but... that wild look in her eyes. She does seem eerily familiar. No, not familiar, but similar. Looking into her flecked irises is like looking through a mirror into some parallel universe.

'You what?'

'Your sister. Twin. I think.'

'You *think*?'

'This is also new to me. I still don't know what happened to us or what is going on, but I know that we're both in danger.'

'Look, lady...' He puts his hand up and takes a step back.

'I know! I know that I sound crackers. That's what I thought about the woman who warned me, but then she turned up dead.'

'Who's dead?'

'It's not important. What you have to know is that there is a... list... and the people on the list are being killed, in order, and we are next.'

Too many teenage summer horror movies.

'Bullshit,' he says, and then, 'by who?'

Kirsten takes the piece of paper out of her bag, hands it to Seth, who makes sure their hands don't touch. Looks down, looks at her.

'Lotto ticket?'

'They're barcodes. Of people. Look at five and six. That's us—see our birth date? Everyone above us on this list has been murdered.'

'What happened in 1991?'

'I don't know yet.'

'Where on the list is the woman, the one that approached you?'

'Number four.'

'So then I am five and you are six?'

'So you believe me?'

'No, but I'm naturally paranoid and I like patterns, and when I hear that someone is trying to kill me I pay attention.'

Seth's rational side knows the story is far-fetched, but what if this is really his twin? His flesh-and-blood sister? Standing here with her feels right. There is an unmistakable connection. Against his better judgment he flicks the safety back on.

Kirsten looks at his face, wants to touch it, but all of a sudden he grabs her arms and throws her to the ground. As she opens her eyes a body crashes down onto the pavement next to her, where she was standing. In slow motion she watches black oil spread towards her, and just before it reaches her, Seth pulls her away from it and to her feet.

The dead man on the ground is young, twenty-something, black-clad with waxed spiky hair and smudged eyes. He lies with his mouth open towards the sky, a leg bent at an awkward angle. Seth bends over the warm body and searches his pockets. Kirsten wants to ask him what he is doing but her voice doesn't seem to be working. Seth doesn't find a wallet. He sees the glint of a locket, and looks inside: the smallest green rabbit glows at him.

'Fuck,' he says, 'fuck!' He rips off the locket, pockets it, grabs Kirsten's hand, and they peel off into a charcoal alley.

A few blocks south, out-of-breath Kirsten manages to flag a cab. Before they get into the car, Seth makes a point of checking the cab driver's licence.

'You're good at it,' puffs Kirsten as they climb inside.

'Good at what?'

'Being paranoid.'

'Ha.'

Kirsten gives the driver the address of The Office.

'I wouldn't have—' She motions to the driver. 'checked.'

'Ja, well, it comes naturally.'

'Being paranoid comes naturally?'

'Yip.'

'Bad childhood?'

'Is any childhood not bad?'

Kirsten hesitates. 'I'd like to think so.'

'Yours?' he asks.

'Actually, to be honest, I don't remember a lot of my childhood, especially early on.'

'Me neither. Our brains are programmed to forget bad stuff.'

'So you're a glass-half-empty kind of guy.'

He shrugs. 'Depends what's in the glass.'

Kirsten fidgets, plays with the ring on her finger, desperate to tell him about the microchip, knowing that every minute it stays in his head is a minute's advantage they've lost, but she has to weigh up the consequences. *Just another half hour, till I can show him some proof. Till then I need him to stick around.* Instead she tells him about Keke.

Seth watches Kirsten talk, recognises himself in the anxious motions of her hands, the spinning of the ring on her finger. He feels impelled to do the same, but denies the urge. He pops a pill instead. She watches him do this, and without thinking, reaches for her own pills. She keeps forgetting to take them. She snaps the cap off the bottle, but before she can take one he grabs it out of her hand.

'What is this?' he demands.

She is shocked. 'Um,' she says, 'a prenatal supplement.'

Seth studies the label: *Dr Van der Heever*, it says, *PN supp 1 per day*.

'Prenatal?' he asks, 'so, you're...'

'Yes. Well, no. Been trying for a long time. No dice.'

'Where did you get this from?'

'Take it easy,' she says, 'my boyfriend filled it for me.

He's a doctor.'

'I hate doctors,' says Seth.

'So do I. Ironically.'

Seth pockets the pills. Kirsten lets him.

'How long have you known this guy?'

'James?' She laughs. 'Forever.'

'How long?'

'Thirteen years longer than I've known you.'

Betty/Barbara said to not trust even the people you love. And James hid the letter from her. She doesn't know what it means, and she wishes Marmalade is with them, but there was a little tapping, a little whirring in her brain, warning her to be careful.

They arrive at The Office and take the stairs to stay out of view. Kirsten leads Seth to Keke's regular office.

'Keke!' she shouts, glancing around. The room doesn't look right: it's in its normal mess but it doesn't have the right colour. It feels like cold water is rushing over her body.

'Has someone been here?' Seth frowns at the open drawers and floor white with paper.

'It's difficult to say. It is usually—messy—but something doesn't taste right.'

'Excuse me?'

Kirsten checks the safe; it's empty. Keke's Tile is gone.

'Maybe something spooked her and she ran for it,' says Kirsten, more to reassure herself than anything else. 'Maybe she's hiding out, waiting for to hear from us.'

She dials Keke's number, and they both jump when a disembodied voice starts singing from underneath the desk. Elvis Presley: *A Little Less Conversation*. Kirsten scrabbles around on the floor, and she finds Keke's phone.

'Fuck,' she says again. Keke would leave a lot of things behind in a hurry, but never her phone. 'They've taken her.'

All her contacts. More importantly: her SugarApp.

Seth scrunches up his face. 'Elvis? Really?'

While she is on the floor she spots the Beckoning Cat flash drive. Thank God. They don't know it is a drive. She holds it up to Seth, pushes its belly to reveal the tail. 'They left her flash drive.'

He takes it from her, plugs it into his Tile.

Kirsten uses her pocketknife to unlock the fridge. As soon as she opens the door, she sees Keke's insulin kit and there is another wave of cold water. She shuts her eyelids against the glow of the refrigerator, wishing the insulin away, but it's there again when she opens them. She puts it on the desk in front of Seth.

'We've got seven hours to find her.'

'Hey?'

'Seven hours to go,' she says, 'before Keke... gets really sick without her insulin.' She says 'really sick' but what she means is: 'die'—she just can't say it out loud.

'She's diabetic?' he asks.

Kirsten doesn't answer. She sits back down on the floor and closes her eyes for a while. After a few minutes Seth is kneeling in front of her. He touches her gently on the shoulder.

'Kirsten?' I think we've got something.'

THE SEVEN THAT WERE TAKEN

25

Johannesburg, 2021

There are two folders on Keke's *Maneki Neko* flash drive. The first one is called 'The Seven That Were Taken' and has seven old, scanned and archived newspaper articles, dated from 1991. The second folder—'RIP'—contains four recent PDFs from Echo.news.

They start with the folder called RIP. Kirsten recognises the first article immediately. She read it a week or so before at her shoot at the aquarium, about Betty/Barbara being found dead in her flat.

'This is—was—her,' says Kirsten. 'The crazy woman

who gave me the key.'

'The key?' asks Seth.

'The key that opened the safety deposit box at the seed bank that had the list in it. Look at the date of her birth, the colours are backwards.'

Seth frowns at her. 'You are truly odd.'

'Look,' she says, and shows him that Betty/Barbara's date of birth is backwards in the third line of numbers on the list.

'So the one date is our birth date,' he says. 'What is the other?'

They open the next article. It's about a well-known composer, found dead in his bathtub, by his lover. Seth frowns.

'I remember this story from a couple of days ago.'

Drowned, it says, apparent suicide, or accident, although the lover wouldn't accept it, said they had everything to live for. They were about to be garried: a trip to Paris planned for spring, after an intimate wedding in Paternoster. On finding the blue body, the lover smashed up the apartment, destroying any evidence that may have existed. He swore foul play: Blanco's most prized possession is missing: an antique ivory piano key from a Roger Williams piano. It was his proposal gift. The lover required sedation, and was not being treated as a suspect. The musician is dead, their future washed away in a few inches of waxy grey liquid (Cold Dishwater).

'It could have been suicide,' says Seth.

'He was first on the list.'

Seth hesitates then opens the next document. A picture of a blond woman laughing into the camera comes up on screen. *Top executive dies in front of toddler son.* The story is about a high-flier corporate who accidentally ingested peanut matter—the source unknown—and went into anaphylactic shock and died in the kids' park down the road from her office. The people at the park had tried to resuscitate her but her airways were swollen closed and CPR wasn't successful. The white-haired child was first taken in by the paramedics, then the policewoman on the case, and eventually collected by the husband who had unplugged on the golf course and had heard about his wife's death on the radio on the way home from the pub. The fourth article was Soraya's organ failure. He had felt a connection to Soraya. Coincidence?

They move on to the second folder; there is a picture of an awkward little boy, a toddler, dressed in a brown suit, sitting on a piano stool in front of a baby grand. *Baby Beethoven kidnapped,* reads the headline.

'The drowned composer,' says Kirsten.

Seth opens the other archived articles: they are all stories of abduction. *Toddler missing,* about a too-blond two-year-old who can speak four different languages. The executive.

Has anyone seen Betty Schoeman? A mug shot of a not-pretty baby dressed in old-fashioned clothes, frowning at the camera. Betty/Barbara.

Child abducted from nursery school, reads another, about Jeremy Bond, a two-year-old snatched from a crèche playground just minutes before his parents arrive to collect him.

Seth reads the fifth one:

Saturday Star, July 1991

Toddler kidnapped while father shops

Tragedy struck in the friendly city today in the unlikeliest of places. Young Ben Jacobz (14 months old) escaped his pram in a department store at Green Acres Mall, Port Elizabeth. 'He was always so fast,' his mother told us, unable to keep from crying. 'He started crawling at eight months, was walking by ten. He would just tear around the place like the Duracell bunny.'

Baby Ben managed to toddle out of the store while his father was standing in the queue to pay for some clothes for him. 'It happened all the time,' says Mrs Jacobz, 'his uncle used to call him Now-You. Now you see him, now you don't.'

'We even tried one of those terrible things,' said Mr Jacobz. 'Those toddler leashes, but he would [...] throw a tantrum. He hated it.'

As soon as the boy's father spotted the empty pram he left the queue and started looking for him. 'I wasn't too worried yet,' he said, 'Ben did it all the time and we always found him.' But then he saw a strange woman outside the entrance of the store pick the baby up. 'I started shouting at her, and at Ben, but she didn't look at me and hurried off [...] and disappeared into the crowd. I started running after them, and that's when the guards tackled me.' Mr Jacobz was unknowingly still holding store merchandise when he ran out of the door, setting the alarm off. The security guards, not aware of the kidnapping, saw him 'make a run for it' and apprehended him. When he could finally explain the situation the baby was gone.

The police have launched an extensive search. They ask that the public keep a look out for anything suspicious.

'We're sure they'll find him and bring him home,' said Mrs Jacobz. It was then Mr Jacobz broke down weeping.

That must be William Soraya. Ben/Bill. They open the last PDF.

The Observer, 21 May 1991

Snatched

Twin tragedy hits small Durban suburb

After a gruelling 48-hour search in uncharacteristically cold weather for the missing Chapman toddlers of Westville, KZN, the South African Police called off the operation as of 2 AM.. Brown-eyed twins Samuel and Kate (3) were last seen in the front garden of their parents' home before Mrs Anne Chapman moved inside to answer a telemarketing phone call on the landline. Less than a minute later the children had, according to their mother, 'vanished'.

The search party combed the area, as well as a nearby river where Mrs Chapman purportedly used to take the children to swim and picnic. Anne Chapman, having a record of PPD or post-partum depression, is being questioned despite the divers not finding anything incriminating. Mr Patrick Chapman is standing by his wife, stating they are both 'extremely anxious' to find the twins. In a strained voice, on camera, he urged anyone with information to come forward. The SAP, faced with a dearth of any kind of evidence and an already-cold trail, promised they would keep looking, but don't seem to hold out much hope of finding the children, dead or alive.

Kirsten and Seth stand pale under the fluorescent light in the office, looking at each other, speaking aloud as they process the jolt of information.

'Holy fuck,' they say at the same time.

'Samuel and Kate,' says Kirsten. 'The mad woman—Betty/Barbara—called me Kate.'

'Samuel and Kate, abducted at three, become Seth and Kirsten.'

'Moved to a different province, and split up.'

Kirsten shakes her head. It doesn't make any sense.

'Wait, it says 'brown-eyed.' She looks into Seth's blue-green eyes that mirror hers (Sound of the Sea).

'They must have had our irises lasered. Strōma'd the

brown out. It's easy enough to do.'

She thinks of her biological parents, the Chapmans, and feels overwhelmed. What they must have gone through. What she and Seth must have gone through. There is an extreme feeling of loss for the life she should have had, the life that was taken from her, and here he is now, standing in front of her: the missing piece of her puzzle.

'The Black Hole,' she says. 'It finally makes sense.'

He blinks at her. She has the feeling he understands; maybe he feels The Black Hole too but has filled it with other things.

'I was always—disconnected—with my father,' he says. 'Never met my mother. Never felt he really wanted me around, didn't understand why they had me in the first place.'

'Exactly,' says Kirsten. 'But why abduct a child you don't want? Surely a creep so desperate for a baby would, I don't know, love the child more?'

Seth is silent.

'It doesn't add up,' says Kirsten. 'It's too much to take in. I don't have the mental bandwidth to cope with this.' She moves to run her hands through her hair but feels her prickly scalp instead, the plaster on the back of her head. Realises she's been holding the knife all along and puts it on the desk. He glances at it and narrows his eyes.

'Whose knife is that?' he asks.

'This?' she says, 'It was my father's—well, whoever he was—the man who pretended to be my father for twenty-eight years. Why? What's wrong? Why are you freaking out?'

'Who was your father? What did he do?'

'Who was my father? I don't know. He was a research guy, a lab guy, a grindaholic who ignored his wife and daughter to read a lot of scientific literature. I still don't actually know what he *did*. Will you please tell me why you are getting so freaked out by the knife?'

'You're not quite Nancy Drew, huh?'

'What?'

'Did you even think to look up that insignia?'

'No. Why would I? And who the fuck is Nancy Drew? I'm a fucking photographer, not a member of the Hawks. All this—' She motions around her. '—this fuck-circus, is new to me, okay?'

He stares at her, then scans the insignia of the pocketknife and does an image-match search. Nothing comes up.

'You recognise it, the logo, I can see.'

'Yes, I recognise it,' says Seth. 'But... it's impossible. An urban legend, a myth. It's not supposed to exist.'

'I don't understand.'

Seth points at the diamond-shaped insignia. He traces an angular 'G' in the left of the diamond and a 'P' in the right.

'The guys at Alba are going to flip out when I show this to them.'

Kirsten looks at the knife, looks at him. She sees him smile for the first time.

'GP,' he says. 'It's the fucking Genesis Project.'

NON-LIZARDS

26

Johannesburg, 2021

'Okay,' says Kirsten, 'there's no easy way to say this, so, well, here goes: I need to cut a microchip out of the back of your head.'

'Wow,' says Seth, 'just as I was beginning to think we were getting on.'

'The crazy lady—'

'Now you're speaking about yourself in the third person.'

'The *other* crazy lady, Betty/Barbara, said she knew they were tracking her because she could feel the microchip in her head. And the killer—killers—whoever is trying to kill us, knows where we live. Knew that lady who took her toddler to that park.'

'Look,' says Seth, shaking his head, 'that just can't be true. Technology for trackers didn't even exist when we were kids. Wait, is that why the back of your head was bleeding? You tried to look for a fucking microchip?'

'Not tried, I found it!'

'Show me,' he says.

'I planted it in a taxi. It could be anywhere.'

He looks around the office, rolling glassy eyes. She's known all along he won't believe her.

'Next you'll be telling me to wear a tinfoil hat.'

'Actually, that's probably not a bad idea.'

'Ha,' he says.

'I'm not fucking with you.'

'Okay, but you're not cutting it out with that thing. I know someone.'

'We don't have time to fuck around!' shouts Kirsten.

'Look,' he says, 'I need to go to Alba. That is not negotiable. They'll be able to remove the chip. Analyse it. Then we need to get bullets, and get you a weapon.'

'What the hell is Alba? What about Keke?'

'We can only find your friend when we have more information. The chip is the only thing we have at the moment.'

A thought strikes Kirsten.

'Hackerboy Genius,' she says. 'Keke's contact. His number will be on her phone. He can get into anything: it's how we found you.'

'You think he'll know something?'

'He'll know more than what's on this drive,' says Kirsten. 'She asked him to dig.'

Seth shoves his Tile into his backpack.

'We'll call him on the way.'

'What is the Genesis Project?' asks Kirsten as they head down the fire escape stairs, towards the basement.

Seth shakes his head. 'There's not a lot to tell. I mean, there have been rumours for years, but I don't think anyone actually believed them.'

Kirsten thinks of her father: heavy, steel-framed glasses, dulled by time. Big hands, badly tailored trousers, egg-yolk stains on his ties. She finds it difficult to imagine that he was involved in any kind of covert movement. *Unless he was good, unless he was very, very good.*

'It's a bit like The Singularity – never gonna happen, but still as scary as shit.' He shoots a glance at Kirsten, as if to size her up, as if to see if he can trust her. 'When I started at Alba—'

'You still haven't told me what that is.'

He stops on the sixth landing. The caged light next to his head flickers, a loose connection.

'Alba is a bit like *Fight Club*. The first rule of Alba is: never talk about Alba.'

'Fight Club?'

'Have you *ever* read a book? Do you know that inquisitive mice grow more neurons?'

The only book she has ever read cover to cover is the collector's edition of *Hansel & Gretel* that James gave her. The cruel coincidence is not lost on her.

'Besides, we're probably going to die tonight,' says Kirsten, 'I'm thinking all rules are off.'

'Well, ja, that's the second rule.'

'Ha.'

'Seriously,' he says, holding her arm, 'no one is allowed to know, do you understand?'

They start moving again.

'Alba is a crowdfunded underground organisation: a rogue group of engineers, scientists, biologists, geneticists…

We experiment with biotechnology, but mostly we investigate others that do the same thing.'

'You're a biopunk?'

'Technically I'm a chemgineer, but, yes, biohacker, biopunk, hacktivist... basically we're high-tech Truthers.'

'You uncover stuff.'

Seth nods. 'We're a technoprogressive movement that advocates open access to genetic information. We play around with DNA—only in a clean way—but our aim, the reason we exist, is to infiltrate and expose what we call black clinics—megacorps who use biotech in an uncool way.'

'Like?'

'We look for anything dodgy: any way the company might be ethically dubious, illegally practising, or trying to exercise any kind of social control.'

'That plastic surgery place—in Saxonwold. Tabula Rasa.'

'They were buying discarded embryos from fertility clinics, injecting the stem cells into people's faces.'

'You exposed them?'

'Alba did. A colleague—she had to suck fat out of housewives' thighs for a year before she was allowed near their faces. It took her another year to uncover the black market stem cells. We also exposed the Ribber Ranch, XmonkeyD and Slimonade.'

Kirsten had heard about all of them over the last few years: their nasty secrets being revealed and those involved being strung out during the subsequent trials.

'The thing about amazing runaway technology,' says Seth, 'is that it makes it easier to be evil. Government can't legislate fast enough to keep up. Alba is the self-appointed, independent watch dog.'

They quicken their pace down the stairs.

'So, there has always been talk about the Genesis Project. It's seen as, like, the ultimate black clinic. Like a human version of Reptilians: a huge clandestine society that actually controls the world. They're supposedly everywhere, especially in leadership positions.'

'The Queen-is-a-lizard theory, but no, well, lizards.'

'And local. It's a South African group.'

'So the Nancies are probably lizards. Or, whatever, non-lizards. You know what I mean.'

'According to the rumours, there would be a few strategically placed Genesis Project members in key political positions.'

'The president?'

'I've always thought she looked a little reptilian.'

They get to the parking basement, and Keke's motorbike is parked in its usual place. Kirsten opens the storage space at the back of the bike, takes out the inflatable helmet and key, and packs the insulin kit and Seth's backpack. She offers Seth the helmet but he waves it away. She puts it on, wincing as it inflates, and fastens the strap underneath her chin.

'But you don't believe it? I thought you'd like the conspiracy element, given your predilection for paranoia.'

'I don't know. Before today, I thought that if it existed, we would have some kind of proof by now.'

'Now we have the knife.'

In the corner of the parking basement, a car comes to life. Kirsten and Seth move quickly into the shadow of a pillar. It revs, its tyres squeal on the smooth concrete. It blasts warm air on them as it rushes past. Tinted windows. Kirsten releases her grip of Seth's arm.

'GP could mean anything,' he says. 'It could be from your dad's local bar. GastroPub. Gin Party. Geriatric Pints.'

'Getting Pissed.'

'Gone Phishing.'

'Green Phingers.'

'Gay Pride?'

'He wasn't stylish enough.'

They get on Keke's bike, and Kirsten starts the engine, revs. She accelerates gently, trying to get a feel for the machine thrumming between her thighs.

'Except that I've seen that insignia before, that diamond.'

'What do you think?'

'I think it's the only lead we've got.'

CRACKED COBALT

27

Johannesburg, 2021

There is a loud bang, as if someone had shunted a wheel, and the bike goes skidding, screeching off the road, and slams into a stationary 4X4. Spinning colours, heat and tar, tumbling, until they are still. Kirsten's left arm sparks with pain. She touches it gingerly with her other hand. Blue gleam (Cracked Cobalt). Broken.

Seth isn't wearing a helmet.

'Oh my God,' she says, trying to turn to see him, but he's also pinned to the tar. 'Oh my God. Seth? Seth?' She doesn't recognise the sound of her own voice. She tries to wriggle out from the bike, but only manages an inch. She looks around for help, but the street is dead. Seth groans, brings his hands up to his head.

'Are you okay?' she asks in the stranger's high-pitched voice.

He doesn't say anything for a while.

'Depends on your definition of okay.'

Kirsten sighs loudly, lies down. 'You can talk, which means you have a pulse. That's something.'

He gets up, tries to find his balance, staggers on the spot for a while before realising Kirsten is trapped under the bike. He comes over to her side, releases her. Once she rolls clear, he lets the bike crash down again.

'Something happened,' he says, 'to the bike. I heard it.'

He kneels to get a closer look, tries to spot any signs of sabotage, but he doesn't know what he's looking for. He always liked the idea of a bike, but liked the idea of being alive more.

'Donorcycles,' says Kirsten, wincing. 'That's what James says they call them in the ER.'

'Cute,' says Seth.

Using one hand, Kirsten deflates her helmet, opens the compartment at the back of the bike, retrieves their things. She checks Keke's insulin pack. Three out of the five vials are broken.

'Let's try get a cab,' she says, limping in the direction of the main road. The left leg of her jeans is hanging on at the knee by a thread, her calf is bloody and gravel-bejewelled. Her shorn head is bruised and dirty; she supports her injured arm as she walks.

'You look like you're straight off the set of *Terminator 8*,' says Seth.

'You don't look too bad yourself,' she says, gesturing at his newly bleeding forehead. There are sparks in her arm. She eases off her shirt, revealing a tank top, and ties it into a sling. Seth hands her his hoodie to wear.

'Is your arm broken?'

'I don't know. Think so. Never broken an arm before.'

Seth can't say the same.

'The pain is blue. Different shades. Right now it's Cyan Effervescence. I think that means broken.'

'You're one of those people,' says Seth. 'Those points-on-the-chicken people.'

She looks sideways at him.

'Those people that taste shapes,' he says.

'Taste shapes, feel flavours, smell words, hear colours, see sound... yes. My wires are crossed. I have no walls between my senses.'

'So that's why they wanted you,' he says.

'Hey?'

'All the kids that were abducted had some kind of talent, some aptitude, something that set them apart. Musical genius, edgy horticulturalist, uber-athlete, super-linguist...'

'What's yours?' she asks. 'What's your super power?'

'Maths.'

'Yuck,' Kirsten says. 'Sorry for you. You must have drawn the short straw.'

'Maths is the language of the universe.'

She looks at him with his fauxhawk, smudged eyes and eyebrow ring.

'Seriously.'

There are no cabs, so they catch a communal taxi instead. The passengers inside move up quickly when they see the state of the new fares. Even the driver seems concerned. Kirsten pays him double to expedite the journey and he takes the cash with an upward nod. It's a quiet trip. Kirsten can feel the glares cutting into her body, as if it isn't lacerated enough. A few passengers are exchanged en route: they swap a sweating businessman for a woman with blond dreadlocks and a see-through blouse, a couple of floral aunties clutching an over-iced cake inch their way out and in jumps a metal-mouthed schoolgirl in a uniform (Dried Cornflower). Kirsten catches the girl staring at her, so she smiles, but the girl quickly looks away.

It takes them fifteen long minutes to reach Parkview and they jump out when they get to Tyrone Avenue. There seems to be some kind of afternoon street party going on:

the road is strewn with streamers, and paper lanterns float above them on invisible wires. Small crowds are milling about, drinking craft beer and warm cider in dripping plastic tumblers. A food truck hands out hot crêpes and galettes. Warm air, acoustic tunes on the speakers, and the laughter of strangers. The cafés and restaurants spill their swaying customers out onto the pavements. Despite the sunshine, empty wine bottles act as candleholders, growing capes of white wax. As they pass the tables, someone says a toast and glasses are chinked.

'This is it,' says Seth, motioning to a florist with street art for signage that reads "Pollen&Pistils." Inside a petite girl with a beehive, her back turned, is wrapping a fresh arrangement of hybrid green arums (Neon Cream). They enter the shop, a bell jingles, and immediately her eyes shoot up to the back wall strip mirror, where she sees Seth's reflection.

'And in come the walking dead,' she says, spinning around with a giant pair of scissors in her hands. She is wearing glam 1950s make-up: dramatic eyeliner, striking red lips, beauty spot on powder-pale skin.

'Well,' says Kirsten, 'I know we're not looking our very best.'

The different colours and fragrances in the small room swirl around and Kirsten has to blink through them and step slowly to make sure she doesn't walk into anything. The back wall is a painted mural, graffiti-style, of an outdoor flower market, and this also affects her depth perception.

'I didn't mean that, honey,' she says, 'I'm talking about when You-Know-Who finds out you Called A Friend.'

'I didn't have a choice,' says Seth.

The girl palm-weighs the scissors, purses her ruby lips.

'Seriously,' he says, 'there's a lot more going on than you know. The bugsweep you sent...'

Her wide eyes flicker.

'I'm sorry,' he says, handing her the dead boy's locket.

She looks down and wipes the blades of the scissors on her red-and-white damask apron, leaving sharp lines of bright green (Cut Grass) that cut across her torso.

'Your current assignment?' she asks.

'We seem to have a bigger problem.'

She puts down the scissors, closes and locks the front door of the shop and turns the 'closed' sign to face the street. Automatic blinds shudder across the glass façade. Once the blinds are in place, she claps and they all disappear into darkness. She hits a button hidden from view under the counter, and a portion of the mural on the back wall starts rolling up.

They follow her down a tapering passage that leads to a security gate where she punches in a complicated code then has to stand on her toes to look into the small screen above the number pad. A red laser scans her retina and it clicks.

The door opens up into a large bleached-looking room

with a few shoulder-height cubicles. Bright lights, chipboard ceiling boards and cheap wooden veneer desks: not what Kirsten expects a rebellious cult's underground HQ to look like at all. A few people are dotted around, grinding quietly at their desks. They look up unseeingly as the three enter, then return to their screens. A few of them lift their chins at Seth.

They approach the back corner, where a typical office kitchen is attached: a basic sink, bar fridge, and coffee machine. A man springs up from a small Formica table tucked around the corner and Kirsten and Seth both jump.

'Sorry!' he says, 'I didn't mean to startle you.' He is a wiry man with a nervous demeanour and a pale moustache. 'I shouldn't have jumped up like that. I guess I'm a jumper. I think I'm just a little nervous. Very nervous. I wasn't thinking. Sorry.'

The flower girl doesn't make introductions and no one shakes hands.

'I'm the Lab Man,' he says, rubbing his palms on the back of his trousers. 'I'm the one who will be looking at your samples.' He speaks too quickly and finishes his sentences by putting his index finger to his lips, as if to stop himself from saying more. Seth takes the still-intact Fontus samples out of his bag and hands them over, along with Kirsten's bottle of pills. The florist raises her eyebrows at the pills but doesn't ask any questions.

'There's something else,' says Seth. 'I know it sounds insane, but I think I may have a chip, a microchip,' he rubs the back of his head, 'and I need it destroyed. We think it has some kind of tracker system...'

The man's eyes grow wide; he holds the samples to his chest, as if to protect them.

The florist bangs shut a drawer and glares at Seth. 'So not only do you bring a civilian in, but you send the target our fucking GPS co-ordinates?'

'I'm sorry. I didn't have a choice. The chip is the only clue we have. They'll find the shop, they won't be able to get in here.'

She stalks out, head down, speed dialling.

'So the chip,' says the man, 'the microchip, it's still in your... actual head?'

As opposed to his non-actual head? His theoretical head?

'Yes,' says Seth. 'You have a scalpel?'

The man gulps. 'I can't take it out. I don't do blood. I faint when I see blood. I'm haemophobic. Once, in high school, I fainted on the stairs because there was this big poster with a cartoon vampire on it, a blood donation drive. It was this big friendly kind of looking vampire, kind of like a Nosferatu-looking vampire, not a contemporary kind of sparkly good-looking vampire, but friendly, with a big toothy smile, and fangs. He had a cartoon speech bubble and it said "I vant to suck your blood." And I just fainted. There, on the stairs. Fainted, bam, just like that.' Then he remembers his finger and puts it to his lips.

Seth rummages noisily through the drawers but finds

nothing with which he'd be happy to cut open his head. He sighs, rubs his eyes. 'Fine,' he says to Kirsten. 'Fine,' he says again, more firmly, motioning to her bag.

She takes out the pocketknife.

'Do you have any alcohol?' she asks the Lab Man.

He shakes his head. As if on cue, the faux-florist comes back with a first aid kit, a half-empty bottle of whisky and some toasted sandwiches.

'Thanks,' says Seth, and she winks at him without smiling. Kirsten wolfs down half a sandwich, its gooey melted cheese golden lava on her tongue. It's one of the best things she's tasted in years. She feels a rolling brown spiral mow towards her, and just before it touches her it disappears. She gingerly washes her hands, uses hand sanitizer, and swabs the knife and the back of Seth's head with the booze. Her injury slows her down. Seth sits at the table and the man turns away, busying himself with the lab kit he has brought with him.

With her good arm, Kirsten begins to touch Seth's scalp. At first they both flinch at the feeling: it's too intimate an act for strangers. But we're not strangers, they both tell themselves. A slight sensation remains where they connect.

'So, what made you get into biopunking?' asks Kirsten. She's trying to distract him and he feels like telling her to just get on with it; he's not a child. He feels the cold blade against his skin.

'In high school I saw a YouTube video of the LSD experiments they did on British soldiers in the early 60s.

It's hilarious. Ever see those?'

Kirsten is concentrating too much to answer but the Lab Man starts giggling.

'I've seen it, I've seen it.' He smiles, nodding at them, then immediately looks away. 'LSD-25,' he says. 'Acid. Soldiers be trippin'.'

Seth smiles, despite himself. 'They were considering using it as part of their chemical warfare, to incapacitate the enemy, so they tried it out on the men. They go from these upright marching men with machine guns to complete jokers. They can't read the map and get lost even though the hill they need to find is right in front of them. They just walk around in circles and hose themselves. One guy climbs a tree to feed the birds.'

Kirsten finds the small thickening and quickly excises it, squeezing the chip out. Seth doesn't flinch; his only movement is to spin his ring. It's a much neater procedure than hers.

'The troop commander eventually gives up, and falls on the floor laughing.'

After applying pressure to stem the bleeding, she sprays it and covers it with the extra plaster she brought with her. Kirsten rinses the chip under the tap then hands it to Seth, who stares at it.

I didn't believe it until I saw mine, either.

'It was so powerful. A simple drug changed men trained to kill into fools. Affectionate fools. Imagine the lives that could have been spared in our wars. It kind of hit me in the face. That's what made me want to become a chemical engineer.' He hands it over to the Lab Man, who hesitates before taking it.

He holds it up to the light, taps its glass capsule with his fingernail then holds it close to his eye, looking at it through a magnifying glass.

'Very scientific methods,' murmurs Seth in Kirsten's ear, causing her to almost choke on the last bite of her sandwich. He takes a swig of whisky then offers it to her. She doesn't wipe the mouth of the bottle: they are double-blood-siblings now.

The Lab Man puts the chip on the tiled floor and steps on it. It doesn't break, so he steps on it again, this time putting more weight on it, and still it doesn't break.

'Very interesting,' he says, causing Seth to snuffle. He turns around, unsure of why they are laughing, then turns back to the chip. 'Superglass,' he mumbles. 'Super. Glass. Hmm.'

'Why is that interesting?' asks Kirsten.

'Because superglass was only put on the market in 2019,' says Seth.

'Yet I'd guess that the chip itself,' says the man, 'was created in the early nineties. But tracking biochips were only invented in 2007, so this isn't making sense. It's not making sense at all.'

'It must be, like, an early prototype,' says Seth. 'The

guys who made it were obviously far ahead of the crowd, but didn't share it. Technology wasn't as open source back then.'

'There is a code on here,' the Lab Man says, 'which could link back to the manufacturer.' He scans in the miniature barcode on the chip and reads out the numbers. Kirsten knows the colours by heart now, recognises Seth's numbers from the list.

'GeniX, it says.'

The Lab Man hands the chip back to Seth.

'Excuse me,' Seth says, holding up the chip, 'I need to go to the little boys' room.' Within a moment of him leaving, they hear the gush of water through pipes in the wall. *Good riddance.*

Seth comes back, and the flower girl sidles in.

'I've evacuated the office, and we now have security outside. Hopefully they'll be able to stop anyone from coming in.'

She gives Seth a hard look, and there's something close to an apology in his eyes.

'I'll let you know the results as they come in,' she says, stepping aside so that they can leave. They nod at the Lab Man and make their way outside, where there are still many noon-drunk creeps wandering around on the chunky pavements, enjoying the music and the open air. Seth and Kirsten survey the faces of the people around them. A man leaning against a broken algaetree streetlight acknowledges them with the slightest movement of his head. Kirsten hopes he is the security post.

A cab rolls to a stop in front of them, and the leaning man motions for them to get in. They hesitate, but then the driver flashes a card at them: a green rabbit. It happens so quickly Kirsten wonders if she imagined it.

They climb inside, and Seth gives the driver the address of TommyKnockers. Kirsten feels every bump of the drive; every pothole sends more blue sparks flying up her arm. She needs to talk to distract herself from the pain.

'Why the green bunny?' she asks. 'Seems a bit, I don't know, too fun and quirky for what you guys do.'

'No science journals lurking in your house, I can tell.'

'You don't have to be snarky. I prefer pictures. It doesn't make me dumb. It's how I see the world, in thousands and thousands of photos. Pictures fly at my brain all the time as if I'm some kind of five-dimensional dual projector. From reality, hyper-memory, from my senses... books are just too much of an assault... you wouldn't want to be in my head.'

'Mine neither,' says Seth. 'I see formulae and patterns and equations in everything. Sounds like a similar affliction.'

We're similar, in some ways, he thinks.

'We're similar,' she says, 'of course we are. We're twins.' It sounds strange to say it out loud. He finds it strange to hear it.

'Ever heard of the Fibonacci sequence? The Golden Ratio?' he asks.

'Of course. It's that pattern that keeps appearing in nature. And in beautiful things. Didn't know the Fibonacci part.'

'He was a mathematician. He discovered it by theoretically breeding rabbits.'

'*Theoretically* breeding? That doesn't sound like much fun.'

'I don't want to bore you.'

The nerves in Kirsten's broken arm hum.

'Tell me. I'm interested.'

'So in theory you'd start with one pair of baby rabbits. When they mature at two months, they have their own pair of baby rabbits. So it's just one pair for the first and second month, then an additional pair in the third month. How many pairs? Zero, one, one, two Then the parents have another pair. 3. By then, the first babies are mature enough to breed, and they have a pair, along with the parents. 5. Then 8, 13, 21, 34, 55... etc. In a year you'll have 144 rabbits.'

'So you just add the number to the number before it to get the next number.'

'If you wanted to suck all the beauty out of the equation then yes, I guess you could say that. So the sequence is fn equals fn minus 1 plus fn minus 2 where n is greater than 3 or n is equal to 3'

'Okay, you just lost me.'

'It's not important. I get carried away. The cool thing is that the ratio plays itself out in nature. Pinecones, pineapples, sunflowers, petals, the human body, DNA molecules. Like, a double helix is twenty-one angstroms wide and thirty-four long in each cycle. It's also in lots of different algorithms. So, handy in... software and stuff.'

'Hacking?'

'In theory.'

'You smartypantses like your theories.'

'Goes with the territory. Science, and all.'

'Ooh, "science",' she mocks, smiling. 'Using a strange and beautiful ratio to bring down the baddies. A green bunny.'

'It's the symbolism, more than anything.'

'I like it.'

'Any reason you chose bright green? The green number is three, so that kind of makes sense.'

'It's a nod at bioartist Eduardo Kac. He created artwork based on a transgenic albino green fluorescent rabbit called Alba. They bonded. Once he had finished his research, the corporation he was grinding for went back on their word and didn't let him take her home, and she died in the lab. It was sad. They were attached, after all that time. The corp became, like, the epitome of bio-bullies, and she's kind of our mascot.'

'Poor Alba,' says Kirsten. 'What did they splice her with, you know, to make her glow?'

'GFP of a jellyfish gene.'

Kirsten thinks of the beautiful jellyfish she saw at the aquarium, when she

learned of Betty/Barbara's death.

'I don't know, it seems wrong to me.'

'That's the whole point. He used transgenic art to spark debate on important social issues surrounding genetics, and how they are affecting and will affect generations to come. It was ground breaking, for its time.'

'And poor Alba lives and dies in a lab.'

'Yes.'

'Not cool.'

'Not cool.'

'And so... Fibbonacci, Kac... you pretty much have an obsession with bunnies?'

'Science does. Theoretical bunnies, anyway.'

The car stops, the driver cuts the engine. Seth looks past Kirsten, out of the car window, and says, 'We're here.'

She moves, but he puts his hand on her shoulder. Still, a

kind of vibration.

'Stay here, this will just take a minute.'

Kirsten watches him disappear down an alley, then lies down on the back seat, cradles her arm, and closes her eyes. *Keke, we are on our way. Keep breathing, keep breathing.*

Rolo sees Seth coming and begins to lift the red rope to allow him access into the club. Seth gestures to show he's not going in, and Rolo clicks it back into place.

'Mister Denicker,' he says in a low rumble, 'what can I do for you?'

'Good to see you, my man,' says Seth, and they click their fingers together, leaving two five hundred rand notes in the giant Yoruba man's palm. 'I need to see your—associates—again. The ones you introduced me to a few years ago.'

'You wish to make another purchase?' he enquires.

'I do.'

'The people themselves change. They have various addresses, and various contact numbers. Are you looking for heat, or spike?'

'Heat.'

'In that case, I suggest you contact Abejide.' He takes out his handset, which looks like a toy in his huge hands, and pushes a button. Seth's Tile pulsates. 'Tell him I sent you.'

Seth turns to go, when Rolo says, 'I gather you know, Mister Denicker, that you are being followed?'

LITTLE LAGOS

28

Johannesburg, 2021

Seth spins around, hand in pocket, but he can't see anyone in the alleyway. Rolo motions with his eyebrows that the interloper is ahead of them, around the corner to the right, effectively blocking his way out. He motions for a bouncer stationed inside to watch the door, and jerks his head for Seth to follow.

They enter the club and walk through the velvet curtains and over the plush carpet towards the restrooms. It feels like midnight inside. A woman in a snakeskin bikini dances lazily around a pole. Guests, swirling the ice in their drinks, nod at Rolo as he passes. The restroom is large and spacious, tastefully decorated in comparison to the club's gaudy interior. A man is swaying at one of the urinals.

They walk to the last stall on the left, which is always closed. Rolo takes a bunch of keys out of his pocket, squints at them, locates the correct key and unlocks the door, revealing another door in the wall where the toilet should be. He hefts his bulk through the narrow stall door and unlocks the next door, which swings out into the darkness of the back street of the club.

'Good evening to you sir,' he says, as if nothing was out of the ordinary.

'Good evening, Rolo.'

Seth glides in the shadows along the buildings until he reaches the car. He sneaks up to it and is about to jump in when he sees that the car is empty. He stays down, crouching next to it, pulls out his gun. As he moves forward, he looks into the car and sees that it is not in fact empty, but that the driver's body has listed to the side, a bullet hole in his temple. He glances around, but the evening is silent around him.

'Kirsten?' he says, knowing if the killer is near he will be giving his position away, but in the moment not caring. 'Kirsten?'

A hand shoots out from under the car, grabbing his ankle, and he yells with fright, pointing his gun at it. He realises a split-second before he pulls the trigger that he recognises the hand—it's the female version of his own.

'Kirsten!' he whispers. She starts crawling out; he tries to help her. She's ivory-skinned and beaded with sweat. He sweeps her into his arms for a moment then opens the driver's door and pushes the dead man out onto the street. He looks for a wallet but the driver's pockets are empty. Kirsten clambers into the passenger side, feels the warm blood seep into the seat of her jeans. Seth jumps in, locks the doors, and presses the ignition button. It's been a while since he has driven.

'Put your safety belt on,' he says, but Kirsten's numb fingers can't follow the instruction. He doesn't flick on the headlights until they reach a main road, and keeps checking for a tail in his rear view mirror.

'What happened?' he asks, keeping his eyes on the road.

'What happened? A boy with a nice face falls out of a window and a then man's brain is blown out of his skull.'

'Did you see who did it?'

'No. He saw something—'

'Who?'

'The driver. Saw something or heard something. He told me to hide. There wasn't any time. He would have seen me run. I rolled under the car. Then I just heard the shot and there were yellow stars everywhere. I saw his feet. The killer. Big. Black boots, like... workman boots. He circled the car, so slowly. I was trying not to breathe. Then he walked in the direction you disappeared.'

'One guy?'

'Yes. I think so.'

'He must have followed us from the flower shop.'

Kirsten keeps quiet, looks ahead.

'He was waiting for me, in the alley. Hopefully we're a little ahead of him now.' He fiddles with the air conditioning dial. It's not cold in the car but Kirsten is shaking. They travel in silence for a while.

Kirsten scrolls through Keke's drop-down list of contacts, looking for Marko. He isn't listed by name, so she looks for FWB, but doesn't find it. Most of the contacts seem to be in codes and nicknames. LoungeLizard; Open SAUCE; hotelbarsuperstar. Then she sees HBG and clicks on it. Hackerboy Genius.

KK> HBG, Kirsten here. You there?

HBG>> Whre is Keke, wth u?

KK> Missing. We need your help.

He takes a while to reply.

HBG>> Anything. For her.

KK> Is there any new info you have, that you hadn't shared with her yet? I have her FD.

HBG>> Not / lot. Ths fckers knw hw 2 cover thr trax.

KK> Chips were made by GeniX. Capsule was superglass.

HBG>> Ahead / thr time.

KK> Can you find out who had access to that kind of tech / early 90s?

HBG>> Short answer = no1, but let me look.

Kirsten looks across at Seth, who is concentrating on navigating the narrow roads crowded with pedestrians.

'Anything?' asks Seth.

'He's looking. He'll let us know as soon as he finds something.'

The roads are crammed with communal taxis of all different colours and states of disrepair. Reading the bumper stickers, Kirsten thinks she should photograph them some time and have an exhibition of taxi décor in Jozi. She considers all the mini-disco-balls, the hula girls, the fuzzy dice hanging on rear view mirrors she has snapped over the years. A cut-out picture of a car radio face Prestik-ed to the dash; a makeshift beverage holder made from an old plastic Castle lager beaker, held in place with an artfully manipulated coat-hanger wire; a handheld fan taped to the windscreen and wired into the cigarette lighter power source; a dog-eared picture, stuck in the sun-shield flap, of a young bride, perspiring in a synthetic fibre dress. *They all tell their own stories.*

People swarm around their car. Drivers steer one-handed, leaning on their hooters, heads out of their windows. A scuffle takes place a few metres away from them.

'Welcome to *Gadawan Kura* territory: Little Lagos,' he says.

'You aren't supposed to call it Little Lagos,' says Kirsten. 'It's un-PC.'

'Fuck PC,' says Seth. 'It has the highest concentration of Nigerians—and hyenas—outside of Nigeria.'

'And Malawians. And Zimbos.'

'Those guys don't count,' he says, 'too quiet.'

'African Slum of Nations.'

'That's more PC. More representative. Good one.'

They haven't moved for a while, so Seth parks with the intention that they walk the rest of the way.

'It's nothing short of insane to walk around here, but if we sit in this gridlock your friend's had it.'

Kirsten grabs the insulin kit, slings the handle over her arm and keeps it pinned to her chest as they manoeuvre their way through the throngs of people. Seth presses the button to lock the car and set the alarm, but has little hope for it to be there when they return. There are a few other white creeps around who look like locals—poor whites, thinks Kirsten—who don't stand out as much as she does with her new apocalyptic hairstyle, and Seth's smudged eyes and piercings. Having grown up in a virtually colour-blind society, it's a novel feeling to be so aware of the tint of her skin; she feels the glances from everywhere. They pass an informal marketplace, a few stalls on the side of the road that seem to be doing a great deal of business. Airtime; doorstops of white bread; *amaskopas*; paraffin sold in re-purposed, scuffed plastic soda bottles; yellow boxes of Lion matches; half-jacks of cheap brandy-flavoured spirits; spotted bananas. Leathery R50 notes travel from palm to palm and change is slipped deftly into warm pockets, never counted. They weave in and out of the streams of people, Kirsten shielding her broken arm, till Seth turns into a road without a name.

They make a few more turns, passing a house in mourning with a SuperBug warning on the door. The occupants' wailing sends streamers of powder blue out of the house and Kirsten tries to dodge them. Seth almost trips over a blind beggar with grey milk for eyes, and the stench of open sewers makes Kirsten retch in the direction of a greasy, defaced wall.

'Almost there,' he says, checking his Tile and grabbing her hand when she straightens. She lets him lead her further into the jutting maze.

When they arrive at the destination, it's not at all what Seth expected. A 1950s style brick-and-mortar house stands defiantly among its corrugated-iron shack neighbours. Chipped steps lead up to a small burgundy veranda: sun-brittle plastic chairs and a blue front door. Cracked black windows like broken teeth in the grimy façade.

'I expected… more of a… security system in place,' says Kirsten, 'taking their particular business into account.'

'They move around a lot. I guess there's not always time to put up an electric fence.'

They walk up the steps and are startled when something with matted brindle fur bolts straight for them, screeching, yellow fangs bared (Rotten Egg Yolk). They both jump. The animal gets to within a metre of them but is yanked back by its chain. A monkey.

'Jesus Christ,' says Kirsten, hand to hammering heart.

Despite the limitation of being chained to a pillar, it still tries to get at them, chattering and screaming in frustration. There is a raw patch of skin around his neck where the collar chafes; it seems there are frequent visitors to this house.

'There's your security system,' says Seth.

They knock on the door. Kirsten has the urge to wash her hands and wonders if the house has running water. And if they have running water, would it be acceptable for her to ask if she could use it? She isn't sure what kind of etiquette is expected in this kind of situation. She will smile and ask nicely, and hope to not offend protocol. Footsteps sound behind the door and a masculine voice says, 'Yes?'

'I'm looking for Abejide,' says Seth. 'Abejide.' The door opens, but there is no light on inside, and no one says a word. They take it as a sign to enter, and as soon as they step across the threshold, the door is slammed shut behind them and they are pressed against the wall, smoke-fragrant hands over their mouths, gunmetal clicks to their heads.

YIP, YIP, YIP.

29

Johannesburg, 2021

Someone flips the light switch and the image of the room jumps out at Kirsten. Cadmium blazes around five glistening, tight-muscled men; dark, oily, like sealskin. They wear layers of light, dusty clothes, wildlife-fur armbands, leather trinkets, and carry the biggest automatic weapons Kirsten has ever seen. Only two aim their guns at them; Kirsten guesses two AK47s are enough.

The youngest of the five pats them down, takes Seth's gun off him. Looks embarrassed when he finds blood on

Kirsten's jeans. She has the unreasonable urge to tell him it's not hers, but has a hand over her mouth. He snatches the insulin kit from her hand, sniffs it, and drops it on the floor. She protests and the muzzle of the gun gets pushed right into her ribs. Seth strains a little against the man holding him down. Not too much to warrant being shot, not too little to show he's not a pushover.

'What do we have here?' the man says.

'A couple of white maggots,' another says. He pronounces it mag-GOTS.

'You a cop?' he asks Seth, taking his hand away in order to let him speak. The animal teeth on his leather necklace click together, sending little circles towards Kirsten. Seth laughs.

'I think that everyone knows that cops don't come into Little Lagos.'

The man lets out three bars of a laugh, looks around at his colleagues. They flash their teeth. The moment is short lived; as soon as he stops smiling the others do too.

'Then who the fuckayou?' he asks.

'A punk,' says one of the other men. 'A fuckin' punk come to make trouble for us.' Seth can see he is the dangerous one: hopped up on something—tik? Nyaope? White Lobster?—and unable to contain his jerky movements. Not a quality you want in a man pointing a large gun at your face. Kirsten senses that he has killed a lot of people. *Bloodthirsty,* she thinks. She can almost smell the warm red metal on him.

The man with the tooth necklace, possibly the leader, narrows his gaze at Seth. He takes a hunting knife out of its casing on his thigh and runs it along Seth's face, his neck, then uses it to inspect his clothing.

'I think we should skin him,' says the aggro one, hopping on the spot. 'Skin him and feed him to the fuckin' hyenas.'

The other one chips in, 'They're hungry. They didn't get their chickens this week.'

'You know what that means?' he asks Kirsten, licking his lips, 'It means they'll eat your bones too. Crunch-crunch!'

Kirsten glares at him.

'And what's in this pretty little box?' the man who is gagging her asks, kicking the insulin across the room. The other man stops it with his foot as if it's a soccer ball. Again she objects but she's beginning to feel dizzy and the smell of the man's hand right up against her nostrils is distorting her vision.

'I'll tell you what it is,' says the mad one, lifting his foot. Seth tries to step forward but is thrown back against the wall. The man jumps on the bag with all his weight. 'It's broken!' He laughs.

A gushing of saliva in Kirsten's mouth. She tries to warn him but it's too late, and soon hot vomit is spraying through her guard's fingers, through her nose, and she is doubled over.

The man looks at her, horrified, and backs away.

'You have the Bug.'

'No, no,' she says, shaking her head, 'I don't,' and she retches again.

The other men also take a quick step back.

'You brought bad juju into this house,' he says. The others look worried, their fingers dance on the triggers.

Kirsten gets angry. She wipes her mouth with the back of her hand. '*I* brought bad juju into this house? Have you even looked in a mirror lately? You reek of death. You want to *skin us* but you say *I* brought bad juju into the house? Fuck you!' Then she turns to the others, 'and fuck you all too!'

They look at her and each other, not certain of what to do. She swallows and looks down at the wet stain on the floor.

'And I'm washing my hands now,' she growls, moving towards the kitchen sink, 'just try to stop me.'

She finds a hard bar of soap with which to scrub her hands. The tap spits water at her and the pipes groan overhead. Once her hands are clean, she splashes water on her face and neck. When she walks the few steps back into the open-plan lounge no one has said a word. She collects the kit and stands away from the spill of puke on the thin, cigarette-burn-patterned carpet, hoping to not get sick again. The man washes his hands too.

'Look,' says Seth, 'Rolo sent me. He said I should ask for Abejide.'

'Rolo sent you?' the leader asks.

'It's the first thing I would have told you if you hadn't jumped us.'

'Give me your phone,' he says.

'I don't have a phone,' says Seth. 'I wear a patch.'

'Smart man, hey? Then give me your tablet.'

Seth hands over his Tile. He pushes a few buttons, checks his bump history for Rolo's message thread, then gives it back to Seth, motioning for the others to lower their weapons, says something, perhaps in vernacular, that Seth doesn't catch. The aggressive man looks annoyed, probably on behalf of the hungry hyenas.

'I need bullets, and we need something for her, something easy to handle.'

'We don't sell lady-guns,' he spits.

'Good thing I'm not a lady, then,' says Kirsten.

He looks at her then laughs his strange, three-bar laugh again.

'Okay,' he says, and nods at the others. Seth expects them to print some guns in front of them, or have some printed already, but instead two of the men scrape the coffee table towards the side of the room and roll up the lounge carpet to reveal a huge trapdoor. It takes some effort to lift the piece of wood, and buried below it is a pile of all kinds of different guns in what appears to be no particular order.

Less like a gun store, more like a wartime weapons cache, thinks Kirsten, an old *uMkhonto Sizwe* stash. She is half expecting the man's arm to be blown off by a rogue landmine when he dips his hands in. He motions for Seth's gun and it is thrown to him; he catches it with one hand and inspects it.

'Z88?' he asks.

'Yes,' says Seth.

The man locates the correct ammo and passes a few boxes up.

'More,' says Seth.

He passes two more.

'Another one.'

The man shrugs and passes up another one. 'You taking on an army?' he asks, making the other guys chuckle.

'Could be,' replies Seth, serious.

'And for you?' he says, looking up at Kirsten.

'Do you have a compact semi-automatic?' asks Seth, 'like a CS45 or something like that?' The man shakes his head. He starts sorting through the pile to look for something suitable.

'Give her an AK,' says the one, and the others cackle again.

'What about this one? You like this one?' he asks,

showing her a big silver revolver: a Ruger. She frowns at it.

'Does it work?' she asks.

'It works,' he says.

'Then I like it.'

'We only sell guns that work,' he says, passing her bullets. 'We like—what is it called?—return customers.'

'You could have fooled me,' mumbles Seth.

'Abejide is very good with faces,' says one of the men. Kirsten thinks this is his way of saying their next purchase will run more smoothly, but then he adds a sinister, 'Never forgets a face,' and it sounds more like a threat than anything else.

'What are those things?' She points towards what looks like second-hand lipsticks.

'You won't like those,' he says, 'they for ladies.' He picks one up, twists the cap off, and pretends to apply lipstick in a wide circle around his mouth. Pouts and bats his eyelashes. Snickering in the background.

'They are magic wands,' he says. 'You didn't know we could do magic here?'

'How does it work?' she asks.

'Come with me,' the leader says, 'I'll show you.'

She's sorry she asked, doesn't want to go with him, doesn't want to know.

'Come,' he commands, and she follows, Seth right behind her. They walk down a passage and into another room with a crumbling back door. He opens it and they see reflective eyes looking back at them (Glowing Green). The outside light comes on automatically and there is loud laughing and yipping. Five, six, seven beasts trawling around in the patchy grass, scratching and sniffing, pink tongues lolling.

'Holy Hades,' says Seth. 'They weren't kidding about the hyenas.'

Yip, yip, yip, the animals say. Abejide calls one of them by name: an older female who has the lope and old eyes of a war vet. He whistles: six high-pitched calling sounds, and she comes forward, ribs patterning her side: perhaps hoping to be fed. Kirsten's stomach seizes.

Abejide points the magic wand at the animal and presses a button, sending a long blue thread of electric current into her body, whipping her up into the air with a surprised yelp then dropping her, in slow motion, onto the sandy ground, where she lies motionless. The other hyenas panic and try to run, but they are ringed in and bounce off the garden fence, shrieking all the while. The man laughs, and Kirsten feels ill again.

'See?' he says, 'I told you it works.'

The animal lies twitching on the ground.

'Did you kill her?' she asks, 'is she dead?'

'Na,' he says, 'she is a tough one. Survivor. Like you.'

They take the guns, the ammo and the lipstick-taser, pay

cash: a fat roll of R500 notes. It's all the cash Seth has, and it's triple the amount the weapons are worth. They go through Kirsten's slimpurse and take all her money too. No one says thank you. After all, it is more like a hijacking than a business transaction.

They've only been inside the house for an hour but it feels like days when they exit the front door. Dodging the rabid monkey, running down the steps, they both breathe the polluted air deep into their lungs. It's warm, and Kirsten gives Seth his hooded jacket back, bunches her new gun and taser into her bag. Her arm jars, but the adrenaline in her system dulls the pain.

The streets are quieter on their way back; most of the market stalls have been packed up and moved to another location, as if they never existed. It takes them a while to find the car and they both think the worst until they see it, abandoned-looking, on a road in which they don't remember parking.

They do a quick inspection: all four tyres are still attached, the engine and battery seem to be in place, and there is no pool of brake fluid under the car. Kirsten opens the crushed kit and finds one vial of insulin that survived the attack. She shows it to Seth, kisses it, then eases it carefully back into its pouch.

One, we've got one, Kirsten thinks.

One is all she needs, thinks Seth.

Kirsten sees a bump from Marko to check her chatmail.

HBG> Hey, hve something 4 u.

CAPITAL FUCKING F

30

Johannesburg, 2021

KK>> Sorry only replying now, we were held up.

HBG> Ws worried.

KK>> What do you have?

HBG> Sending u a pic.

An image pops up on her screen: a picture of three young students sitting on a grassy knoll. They look like students in every way: casual, hippie-style clothes, relaxed faces, a slight air of the arrogance of youth. Two leggy white men in stovepipe trousers, one in thick black-rimmed glasses, and a young dark-skinned woman gazing distantly at the camera. In the background, some kind of university insignia. A badge. They look vaguely familiar—has she seen this before?—but Kirsten can't place their faces at all.

KK>> Got it. University students, circa 1970s?

HBG> Yebo. Thr is a spec search u can do 2 look esp 4 files and images / hve bn deleted ovr & ovr again over time. This pic has been deleted ovr 6K times. Some1 doesn't want it on Net.

KK> Relevance?

HBG>> Kex didn't give me much 2 go on. I ws searching 4biddn files / 'Trinity'. These 3 known as The Trinity when they studied together. WITS. Tag keeps comng up.

KK> Trinity? As in Trinity Clinic?

HBG>> Looks like it. Then superglass & Fontus unrelated on paper apart from / obvious business relat, but dig deeper & c they r both subsids along / 100s other companies under holding company GeniX, trading as GNX Enterprises.

KK> All owned by the same creep?

HBG>> Same creeps. 3 creeps.

KK> Trinity.

HBG>> Registerd GeniX when thy wre still / varsity.

KK> What's / connection 2 Keke?

HBG>> You.

KK> ??

HBG>> Kex starts digging / keywords / threaten the company. My guess / thy hve hackbots automonitoring 4 anything like that, & find source & quash it.

KK> But Keke didn't have any of this info, only the list of barcodes.

HBG>> Et voila.

KK> So the barcodes threaten them. The list of abducted kids threaten them.

HBG>> Yebo, hence your hitlist, + any1 else who gets in / way.

KK>> We wouldn't have known there was a connection if they didn't react to Keke.

HBG>> Thy were too careful.

KK> Who R people in the photo / Trinity?

HBG>> I'm running thr faces / my FusiformG now. Will have a match in hour/so.

KK> An HOUR? Keke's SugarApp says only 5 hours left.

HBG>> It's going as fast as it can.

KK> Can we come over?

HBG>> Who is 'we'?

KK> Seth (no.5) and I?

HBG>> I dn't allow visitors. Esp 1s assoc / kidnapping & grim reaper.

KK> We hve nowhere else 2 go.

HBG>> Police?

KK> No police.

HBG>> Cape Town Republic? Mexico? Bali?

He is quiet for a while.

KK> Just till we can work out who the Trinity are / how 2 find Keke.

HBG>> U being follwed?

KK> Don't think so.

HBG>> Dn't think so? Tht's reassuring.

Kirsten logs out and gets Marko's GPS co-ordinates; directs Seth out of Little Lagos in between telling him about GeniX. When she tells him about Fontus, he hits the top of the steering wheel.

'*Shut* the front door,' he says. He has the face of someone who has just won the Lotto. Or found Jesus. 'I knew it!'

'You knew that the creeps responsible for abducting us are the same creeps you were grinding for?'

'No. I just knew they were dirty. I knew that they were fuckers. Fucking fuckers. Capital fucking F.'

'Look, that sentence didn't even make sense.'

'Fucking Fontus.' He exhales, shaking his head.

'Do you still think that the Genesis Project is a myth?'

Seth's mouth twitches, but he doesn't answer. He takes his bottle of pills out of his pocket, is about to take one, then throws them out of the car window.

*

Marko is drumming his fingers on his knees, then his desk, then his knees again. Hundreds of thousands of faces are flying through his FusiformG software, trying to recognise a pattern. He can't sit still. He stuffs a doughnut past his lips, but his mouth is so dry he chokes. He looks around his room, picks up a vinyl toy and pretends to shoot another toy with it. He makes laser sound effects then kicks the other toy over. In his head, crowds cheer.

The computer chirrups: it has matched one of the three faces. Marko looks at the screen and drops the rest of the doughnut.

'Go home FusiformG,' he says, 'you're drunk.'

*

Marko's place is more of a bunker than a house. *Fort Knox would have been more welcoming.* Kirsten studies the giant gate and 8m walls frosted with the glitter of electrified barbed wire. The kinesecurity cameras follow their movements to the gate. She buzzes the intercom but there is no answer. She buzzes again.

'You think he changed his mind?' she asks Seth. 'He really didn't want us to come.'

Seth is inspecting the gate. He pushes on it, as if to test the lock, and it swings open. Kirsten's glad—now they can get in!—but then her heart sinks. *Oh. Oh, this is bad.*

'It's impossible,' she says. 'It's impossible that they found him. That they got here before us. I was online with him fifteen minutes ago.'

'You sure it was him?'

They look around, notice some broken glass on the driveway, some damaged plants. Seth heads back to the car, unlocks it.

'What are you doing?' she says.

'Getting the hell out of here.'

'We have to go inside,' she says, 'it's the only way.'

'It's a bad idea,' he says, but closes the car door anyway. Once they step inside the property and are halfway to the house, the gate swings closed, and the lock mechanism clicks into place. The electric wire that circles the property like a malevolent halo begins to hum. They hear vicious dogs barking, but there is nowhere to run.

'It's a trap.'

THE UNHOLY TRINITY

31

Johannesburg, 2021

The dogs' barking is deafening now, but there's not a dog in sight. White spikes etch into Kirsten's vision and she has to close her eyes.

'It was him online, I was sure!'

'Maybe it was him, but with a gun to his head.'

Seth realises that the sound is a recording, playing on loop. There must be speakers hidden in the unkempt garden. The front door opens, the security gate is unlocked in three different places, and out walks a chubby young cappuccino-skinned man with tinted spectacles. He pushes them up on his nose and squints at his guests. He's carrying a game console that he touches, and the barking stops. Another button turns on calming white noise: a waterfall, birds, a rumble of thunder.

'Hello,' he says, 'sorry about the dogs, and the gate. I programmed it myself and I'm still ironing out some of the kinks. Or, I was. I'm a procrastinator. A paranoid procrastinator.' When they still don't move or talk, he comes out further along the driveway, looking left to right as if to cross the road. His hands remain on the console.

'I'm Marko,' he says to Kirsten, then blushes. 'Obviously.'

He's wearing a Talking Tee shirt a size too small that stretches over his doughy belly. It has a simple animation of a panting Chihuahua and says: 'My favourite frequency is 50,000 Hz'. When he turns around to lead them inside the back of the shirt says: 'You've probably never heard it before.'

'Come in,' he says. 'I've got something to show you.'

His room—the basement—is wall-to-wall glass screens, blinking projector lights, drives, processors, constant white noise, and the smell of powdered sugar. The walls are papered with posters of T-Rex jokes, incomprehensible maths formulae, and one with a picture of a pretty planet. It says: 'God created Saturn and he liked it, so he put a ring on it.'

Nerdgasm, thinks Kirsten, nudging Seth.

'Your kind of guy.'

He makes a ha-ha face. She spots a brooding woman on the wall, black and white, thinks she kind of recognises her.

'Vintage movie star?' she asks Marko. He momentarily stops smashing his keyboard with his stubby fingers.

'That,' he says, 'is Hedy Lemarr.'

Her face is blank.

'Lemarr was a remarkable woman and I will love her forever.'

Okay, that's not weird.

'She was the most beautiful woman in Europe in the forties, starred in thirty-five films, one of which was the first portrayal of a female orgasm ever, and a math genius. She invented frequency hopping spread!'

'That's Wi-Fi,' says Seth. 'Wireless internet.'

'Never heard of it,' Kirsten says, but is impressed nonetheless, specifically at the intensity of his geekdom. She is surprised he doesn't have a neckbeard, or giant gaming thumbs.

'So your timing is excellent,' he says, using his handset as a wireless pointer to open a browser on the main projection, revealing the photo of the college students and allowing the programme to run, showing which facial features were isolated to run a match.

'This FusiformG has the most amazing features baked

in. You won't believe the results. Who the creeps are, in the photo, I mean.' He pushes his glasses up again. 'It's huge. It's, like, cosmic. No wonder they're trying to cover it up.'

'Marko?' comes a feminine, distinctly Hindi voice from the top of the stairs. Marko rolls his eyes.

'Not now, Ma!' he says. 'I'm having a meeting!'

'Marko?' she calls, closer now.

'Ma!' he says, 'I'm busy!'

Gold-trimmed indigo erupts at the bottom of the stairs.

'I *thought* I heard voices!' She beams—a handsome woman in a sari bright enough to spike your eyes out, holding a silver tray full of deep-fried goodness. Smoky ribbons of scent: cumin, turmeric, cardamom billow towards them. Kirsten blinks, wonders briefly if she is hallucinating. Her arm seems swollen now.

'Marko, you should have told me you were expecting visitors. I would have cooked *dosa!*'

He blushes, stalks up to her, takes the tray, bangs it down on a crowded desk. A designer toy—a Murakami—falls over. Kirsten gently rights it.

'Thank you,' she says, 'I'm starving.'

'It's just a little plate of eats, nothing special.' The woman smiles.

'Thanks, Ma,' Marko mutters, steering her towards the stairs. 'I'll see you later, okay?'

'You're too skinny!' she says, pointing at Seth. 'I'm making beans, if you want to stay for dinner.'

Once Seth sees samoosas on the platter, he laughs out loud. It is refreshing to see an old cultural stereotype played out in real life. South Africa has become so cosmopolitan that it is rare to see, say, an Afrikaner farmer in a two-tone shirt wearing a comb in his khaki socks, or a coloured fisherman missing his front teeth. He celebrates this by eating a samoosa that burns his mouth. *Excellent.*

'As I was saying.' Marko sighs, then looks excited again: 'Cosmic.'

FusiformG automatically opens browsers on three of the other screens, one for each of the faces, and the first two identities are revealed: *blip, blip.* The software is still searching for the third face. Cross-referenced with hundreds of televised interviews, PR shots and virtual news articles. Kirsten and Seth stare at the matches.

'Shut the front door,' whispers Kirsten.

The first man, good looking, smiles back at them with his perfect teeth.

'This is—' begins Marko.

'Christopher Walden,' says Seth. 'Founder and CEO of Fontus.'

'Then,' continues Marko, 'Thabile Siceka, the Minister of Health.'

'No,' says Kirsten, in disbelief.

'The third face is taking a while... could be that the third person isn't as well known or photographed as much as the first two. Maybe the shy one, staying out of the limelight.'

'So, we have the CEO of one of the biggest, most successful corporates in the country, and the minister of fucking health. Industry, government, and what we can probably guess is some kind of academic, doctor or scientist. Reach and power to do anything. The Trinity.'

'The Holy Trinity,' says Marko.

'More like the Fucking Unholy Trinity,' says Kirsten.

'But we still don't know *why*. Why the kidnappings, why the murders,' says Seth, 'and why now?'

'We need to focus on finding Keke. She's got,' Kirsten looks at her watch, 'maybe three hours left before she—'

'That's if they haven't killed her already,' says Seth, and they both glare at him. He spins the ring on his finger. 'Where do we even start?'

The room is quiet.

'Marko?' comes his mother's voice from up the stairs again. 'Marko? Would your friends like a mango lassi?'

*

'There's one person that can help us find the Trinity HQ,' says Kirsten, as they jog to the car. 'Someone that's not involved in the Genesis Project. Someone who would want justice done.'

The gate opens and the barking starts again. Once they're on the road, Kirsten takes her mother's letter out of her pocket and reads it to Seth.

'Ed Miller is his name. There's an address. Melville. He has the packet of information. Everything we need to know about what the Genesis Project is and why we were taken.'

The car is redolent with curried potato and coriander. Marko's mother wouldn't let them leave empty-handed and packed them a Tupperware take-away, along with some gold-coloured paper serviettes, despite her son's embarrassed protestations.

Kirsten is quiet, anxious they won't find Keke in time, or, as Seth had said, worried that the worst had already happened. Tears sting her eyes but she blinks them away, opens the window to get some fresh air. It's a strange sensation to her: tears. Little lines like pins dance in the top half of her vision. She doesn't remember the last time she cried. Has she ever cried? She breathes in deeply, swallows the warm lead in her throat and looks out the window at the ChinaCity/Sandton skyline. Seth catches himself thinking about the future. He won't be able to go back to his ordinary life after this. What will he do? What will it be like?

That's if we survive today, thinks Kirsten, *which is looking increasingly unlikely.*

They stop at a red light in the middle of the CBD. A man dressed in filth appears out of nowhere and peers into the passenger side, giving Kirsten a shock.

'Jesus,' she says, in fright, 'I'm not used to seeing beggars anymore.' A gun appears in the ragman's hand.

Oh.

His wrist is inked with prison scrawls. A Crim Colony graduate. In other words: an ex-con, or in this case: a con.

'Out,' he barks, shaking the weapon at her. She tries to go for her handbag, reach for her own gun, but the man loads the mechanism and something tells her he won't hesitate to put a bullet in her brain. She puts her hands up.

'You have got to be kidding me!' shouts Seth, flames in his cheeks. 'Not today!' he shouts at the hijacker, 'not today! You can fucking *have* the car tomorrow, but not today!'

'Out,' says the man, his voice iced with violence.

'Fuck!' shouts Seth, hitting the steering wheel, 'Fuck you!' He gets out, slams the door, sending a lightning bolt of silver through Kirsten. Kicks the car door, kicks the tyre.

'I need my handbag,' says Kirsten to the hijacker, 'and that other bag. It's medicine. I'm keeping both bags, you take the car.'

The man is annoyed, looks around: this is taking too much time. Kirsten unzips the insulin, shows him, but he searches her handbag himself, takes her Ruger with a loud whistle, and her empty slimpurse. He throws both bags onto the road and Kirsten scoops them up off the tar, picking up the lipstick taser and keeping it hidden in her palm. The hijacker loses focus for a moment as he tries to start the car, lowers his gun-hand. Kirsten tasers him and is surprised by the force of the current. A thin blue line connects them for a second (Electric Sapphire then he slumps back.

'Holy fuck!' she says.

His gun clatters onto the road, his eyes roll back.

'Is he dead?' she asks.

Seth opens the car door, pulls the slack body out and leaves him on the shoulder of the road. It doesn't escape his attention that this is the second time he has pulled a limp body out of a car during the past six hours. He inspects the man's gun, a semi-automatic, and finds it empty. Throws it into the car. Passes Kirsten her Ruger.

'I don't know, don't care,' he says. 'Let's go find Ed Miller.'

CHEERIOS

32

Johannesburg, 2021

Kirsten presses the red button (Faded Flag) and a doorbell rings out, jarring in its cheer. Static. It's an old Melville house, with chunky whitewashed walls and a green tin roof. It has the look of an artist's residence: slightly run down, a little messy, decorated in a quirky way. The house number is a mosaic. If you look through the pedestrian gate you see a goat, made out of wire and beads, grazing in the garden. The rusted arms of an Adventure Golf windmill inch around. The black-spotted roses need pruning.

She presses the doorbell again, holds it down for longer. More static then they hear the phone being picked up. Crackling on the other end.

'Hello?' says Kirsten. 'Ed Miller? I'm Kirsten Lovell. You knew my mother?'

There is a pause then the gate buzzes. He opens the front door, cautious, sees her, and relaxes. When he sees Seth he looks nervous again.

'You can trust him,' she says.

'How do you know?' says the man she assumes is Ed Miller.

'He's blood of my blood.'

Miller stares at them for a while. He is wearing a creased Hawaiian shirt and ill-fitting chinos. Horrendous tan pleather sandals. He has a full head of snow-white hair that moves when he nods. He comes out to make sure the security gate is closed behind them, sweeps his gaze left and right on the street before he clangs it shut. Kirsten studies him. Can't imagine her mother dating a hippie.

'You have something for us?' she asks.

'It's not here,' he says. 'Too risky. They're everywhere. I put it somewhere safe.'

Kirsten closes her eyes, hears the ticking of time she doesn't have.

'It's close,' he says, 'I'll take you.'

His aftershave smells like something with a ship on the label. Small crunchy loops the shape of Cheerios float around him. He shrugs on a light jacket and takes a set of keys off the hook by the door. Seth grabs them out of his hand, startling him.

'I'll drive,' he says.

They climb into the beetle of a car. Miller seems too tall for it and hunches over in the front. Kirsten wonders what kind of person buys a car that is so obviously too small for them.

'Oh, wait,' he says, tapping his temple with the side of his index finger. He gets out of the car, walks to the garden shed. Ducks under the door and disappears into darkness. Kirsten and Seth look at each other. They don't have to say it out loud. They are both thinking: *Fuck*.

Miller steps out of the shed, back into the sunlight. He is holding a couple of shovels. He holds them above his head and shakes them, as if he has won a race.

'My mother said we could trust him,' Kirsten says.

'By 'mother', you mean, 'kidnapper'?'

She pulls a face at him. What choice do they have?

He returns to the car, folds the passenger seat forward and takes in Kirsten's long legs.

'Move up, honey,' he says, dumping the shovels next to her. He winks at her before he slams the chair back in place and climbs in. She kicks the back of his seat.

Seth starts the car. It's a prehistoric thing, and chokes twice before it comes to life. Miller smacks the dashboard twice.

'Good girl!' he shouts, making them both jump.

Kirsten is still staring at him, trying to imagine what on earth they had to talk about. She had thought of her 'mother' as a dry, sexless, beige, irritated woman. She can't imagine the two of them having a conversation, never mind a twenty-six-year-long affair.

'Which one to open the garage door?' asks Seth, looking at the rubber buttons on the ancient remote.

'Uh, the blue one,' he says, but nothing happens.

Pins of dread on Kirsten's skin. Seth is slowly reaching for his gun.

'I mean, the orange one. Sorry.' He laughs. 'Nervous.'

Seth clicks the orange button and the garage motor heaves up the door. They all exhale. Four and five, thinks Kirsten, easy enough to mix up.

The man beats a melody on his khaki-clad thigh.

'Left,' he says.

'Where are we going?' asks Seth.

'To the hidey-hole I came up with. Genius, if I don't say so myself.'

'Where?' asks Kirsten. 'We don't have much time.'

'We'll be there in twenty minutes,' he says.

Kirsten looks at her watch, feels the adrenaline pulling at her stomach. This had better pay off, or Keke is dead. Seth puts down his foot.

They pull up at a small flower farm on the outskirts of the city. The guard seems to recognise Ed and drags the gate open for them. The metal catches on the hard sand. Miller directs them along the powder dirt road, and they drive until it comes to an abrupt end. Seth, driving too fast, slams on the brakes and they skid a little, landing in some wild grass. They look around, as if wondering how they got there, sitting in a vast field of flowers.

Kirsten is exhausted, nervous, dirty, and hurt, surrounded by blue skies and blooms. The prettiness around her is not making sense.

'I don't understand,' she says, 'why here?'

'Why else? Your mother loved flowers,' he says.

'Loved killing flowers, more like,' she says. 'She killed every plant we ever had.'

'Okay,' he says, 'correction: loved *cut* flowers. I sent her some every year on her birthday. Lilies—' He sniffs. '— were her favourite.'

Kirsten remembers the huge flower arrangements arriving once a year. She had always assumed they were from her father, but realises now that would have been out of character for their relationship: there hadn't been a flicker of romance in it. She doesn't remember ever seeing them touch. She hadn't realised that holding hands was a thing couples did until she saw someone else's parents do it.

When the bouquets arrived her father would complain of hay fever. He'd throw out the flowers as soon as a single petal turned brown; inspected them daily until he found one.

'It's buried under that tree,' he says, pointing at a leopard tree a hundred metres away. Kirsten and Seth each grab a shovel, swing them over their shoulders. They must look daunting in their ripped clothes, their skin bruised with black blood.

'Whoah,' says Miller, feigning surrender. 'Settle down there, puppies.'

'Let's get a move on,' says Seth. The sun is sinking fast.

'Seriously, whoah,' says Miller. 'I'm gonna need to pat you down, cowboy.'

'No need,' says Seth, taking his gun out of its holster. 'I'm packing. So?'

'Well, will you be kind enough to leave it in the car, please?'

'Why?'

'Son, no offence meant,' he says, hand on hips, Hawaiian shirt restless in the breeze. 'But I don't know you, I can't trust you. A couple of weeks ago the love of my life was murdered for a reason I'll never understand. Then you two show up in your punk clothes saying you're the people Carol told me to expect. I'm hoping for the best, but I will not walk into a field in the middle of nowhere with a bunch of strangers with a gun. I am not armed. I think it's fair to ask you to leave your weapon in the car.'

Seth thinks about it, then shrugs: 'Fair enough.' He walks towards the boot but Miller stops him, putting his hand on the warm metal.

'It's broken,' he says. 'Hasn't sprung open in years. Just put it in the cubbyhole.'

He does what Miller says, gives Kirsten a quick questioning look. She barely nods. They rush to the tree. Miller falls behind.

'Which side?' Kirsten yells from under the canopy.

'Where you're standing!' yells Miller. The twins begin to dig. Kirsten struggles with one arm, but is able to use her foot for leverage. It hurts like hell. The ground is baked clay. Keke's phone beeps with a SugarApp warning. Code orange: three hours left.

'Are you sure?' asks Seth, swiping his brow. 'You sure it's here?'

They both look up at the same time, and find themselves staring up the barrel of his gun.

'You have got to be fucking kidding,' says Kirsten.

'We are who we say we are,' says Seth. 'We're the good

guys.'

'I know,' he says, 'Keep digging.'

They know he means for their graves.

BABY STARTER KIT

33

Johannesburg 2021

The heavy-set man, clad in charcoal jeans and polished workman boots, looks completely out of place in bright and bonny BabyCo. He is standing before a twirling display of sippy cups that plays a childish song and ends in a forced giggle. He wishes there are more customers so he can at least attempt to blend in. The cheerful products on the shelves seemed to age right in front of him. It is like browsing in a pastel-shaded ghost town.

He is excellent at his job, but this isn't his job; this is the antithesis of his job. If a polar opposite exists of what he was good at, this is it. But he is not one to shirk orders.

He grabs a blue silicone beaker with an animation of a sniggering snowman on it and slings it into his basket. He hopes no one he knows will see him in here. It will be difficult to explain. Another reason he gave in motivating for ordering this all online, but The Doctor said no. It is urgent, he said, and he doesn't want any kind of paper trail. Moving towards a new aisle, he jumps when a BabyCo-bot surprises him on the corner. The bot is clown-themed: wide eyes, red nose—grotesque, painted-on smile. A uniform of bright, clashing colours and a *hyuck-hyuck-hyuck* chuckle. Scary as hell. No wonder this shop is a graveyard.

'Congratulations!' effuses the robotic shop assistant. 'May I give you a hug?'

'Not unless you want your arm broken,' the man says.

'Pregnancy is such a special time. You and your baby deserve the very best!'

The man tries to walk past the bot, but it blocks his way.

'What can I help you with?' the clown says, glowing and *hyuck*-ing at him.

The man growls.

'We have great specials on disposable nappies!' shrieks the machine, lighting up. 'A pack of forty newborn-sized diapers for only nine hundred and ninety-nine rand! Get two packs for one thousand and seven-fifty!'

It assaults his ears with a tune.

The man pushes up his sleeves, cracks his knuckles.

Moves his head from side to side. Indulges in a quickie fantasy where he snaps the bot's neck with a flick of his wrist, and drags its body to the stuffed toy section, to later frighten some kids.

The daydream perks him up. He takes a deep breath.

'I need a...' What does he need? If he knew, he wouldn't be standing around here like a gimp.

'Yes?' says the bot, desperate to help.

The man realises his scarred arm is showing, and pulls his sleeves down. A scar like that has no place in BabyCo.

'I need a... starter kit. For babies.'

'Can you repeat that please?'

'A starter kit.'

'I'm sorry, I didn't get that.'

'Everything you need when you're... you know. Expecting.'

'You need everything?' the bot asks. 'I can help you with that!'

It spins around and starts taking products off shelves, scanning the barcodes on its chest as it goes. A packet of glow-in-the-dark dummies, an Insta-Ice teething ring, a self-regulating temperature taglet. A swaddling blanket puffed up with clouds and zooming with planes. The BabyCo-bot stops and its head swivels around to look at the man.

'You're going to need a bigger basket.'

UNLUCKY FIRELIGHTER

34

Johannesburg 2021

'You fucking viper,' says Kirsten, thinking of the twenty-six years of lies.

'*Au contraire*,' says Miller. 'I'm one of the most loyal members of the Genesis Project. Was born into it. Not a bit of traitor in my blood.'

'Did my mother know?' she asks.

Miller looks as if he is going to say something, then shakes his head. 'It's complicated.'

Seth spreads his feet, wields his shovel like a sword.

'Don't get uppity, whippersnapper,' says Miller. 'Dig.'

'Fuck you,' the twins say, at the same time.

The gun glints in the late afternoon sun.

'Where's the packet?' asks Kirsten.

Miller pats his pocket.

'You never gonna get it, sweetheart. It's over.'

To illustrate his point, he zips his pocket open and takes out a plastic wallet. He opens the wallet and pulls out what looks like a notebook full of bookmarks and stickies. It is wrapped up with an old fashioned flash-disk on a lanyard, like a retro ribbon.

'Inside this book is everything you need to know to bring down the GP,' he says. 'Do you think I would hand it over to you punks?'

The combustible smell of paraffin wafts towards them. Petrol-green pinstripes. He has pre-doused it. Turned it from a book, a holy grail, a weapon, into an unlucky firelighter. Kirsten imagines the pages and pages of handwritten details. Blue ink on oily paper. Who their real parents are, the Chapmans; what happened in 1991. Who their abductors really are. Why they were killed. And why she and Seth, and the other five children, were taken.

He throws it on the ground, among the wildflowers. Takes a matchbox out of his top pocket, lights a match, and drops it towards the book. The match moves towards the ground in slow motion.

'No!' shouts Kirsten, starting to run towards it. Miller shoots the ground next to her foot and she freezes. Puts her arm up in surrender. The match lands, nothing changes, then the front cover begins to slowly curl, pulled by an invisible flame. The fire gains momentum, and is soon hungry and crackling. They stand in silence, watching it burn, scorching the surrounding flowers. Kirsten feels as she is burning along with it.

'Get on your knees,' Miller says. 'Hands behind your heads.'

They fall on to their knees, their faces masks. Seth puts his hands behind his head but Kirsten is in pain. Miller allows her to cradle her broken arm. He walks behind them.

'You don't have to do this,' says Seth.

'Actually, I do,' says Miller, gripping the butt of his gun, placing his finger on the trigger. 'Doctor's orders.'

The colours of the sunset tinge the flowers orange and pink (End of the Rose). There is some poetry in being surrounded by wildflowers, and death at dusk.

Miller takes aim. Kirsten reaches into her makeshift sling, grabs her revolver, turns in a smooth arc and shoots Miller in the shoulder, sending him listing backwards. Shocked, he tries to regain his footing, aims the gun at her again, but she is faster than him and she gets another bullet into his torso. He begins to stumble, still trying to shoot her, but not able to lift his arm high enough.

Seth jumps up, grabs a shovel, and smashes the gun out of his hand. He falls forward, onto his hands and knees. Blood spreads over the flowers on his shirt and the ones under his body. He grunts from the pain then pulls himself up so he is kneeling in the flowers. He notes the irony of his position.

'Where are they?' demands Kirsten, gun cocked.

He laughs. 'And why would I tell you? An extra bullet isn't going to make a difference. In fact, you'd be doing me a favour. Go ahead, do it.'

She lowers the Ruger, kicks him in the stomach. He moans. She kicks him again. He falls onto his back and lets out a long, terrible sound. Seth wields his shovel as if to brain him.

'Tell us!' she screams, stamping on his crotch. He cries out, tries to protect himself, so she stamps on his broken hand too.

Seth waits for him to stop screaming, and says, 'We can draw this out for hours.'

'I have a knife in the car,' says Kirsten. 'A Genesis Project pocketknife.'

'Think of what that would feel like, punk,' says Seth. 'Death by pocketknife.'

Miller mumbles something.

'What?' says Kirsten.

'Okay,' says Miller, 'okay.' Blood is running out of his mouth now. 'You'll never be able to get in, anyway.'

'Where are they?' she asks again.

'ChinaCity/Sandton. A round building made out of glass. Called inVitro.'

Kirsten kicks him again. 'You think we're stupid? You think we're going to believe that?'

'Believe what you want. It doesn't matter. Your friend's probably dead by now. And, anyway, you'll never get inside. You need a member with you to bypass the biometric access. Every member has their own access code, and it has to be combined with that member's fingerprint. Impossible—' He coughs scarlet. '—to hack.'

'Then you're coming with us,' says Kirsten.

Miller spits rubies on the grass, shakes his head. 'You kids have no idea who you are dealing with here.'

Miller's whole shirt is red now; his eyes are getting glassy.

'I don't think he'll last the trip,' says Kirsten.

'Me neither,' says Seth, 'and he'll slow us down.'

Miller watches the darkening sky as Seth fetches the car and drives it over the flowers; they lever him into the back seat. His breathing is laboured, and there is a bubbling sound. Kirsten finds some cable ties in the cubbyhole and Seth ties Miller's wrists together, then his ankles. Kirsten hands Seth his gun back, returns hers to her sling.

'Big mistake, *honey*,' she says to Miller, 'thinking a woman wouldn't be armed.'

Miller gets paler as they get closer to the clinic. His eyes are closed, skin waxen. His Cheerios are fading. Kirsten is sitting in the back with him, Ruger pointed at his stomach, safety catch off. *He will die today. I have killed someone. I'll never be able to eat cereal again.*

Seth is driving as fast as the car will go. 'We won't be able to get in.'

Kirsten looks out of the window, as if searching the sky for an idea. With a sudden grunt, Miller launches himself at Seth, throws his arms over his head and hooks his ligatured wrists across Seth's throat. The cable tie cuts off all his oxygen. Miller's body is taut and his veins like ropes with the effort of the strangulation. His jaw muscles ripple, his teeth melded together with pressure and pink spit. Seth, purple-faced, takes his hands off the wheel and immediately loses control of the car. Kirsten screams and grapples for the gun and shoots in the direction of Miller once, twice, three times. The sound of the gunshots and the ricocheting is blinding. *Did she hit him?*

She can't see past the noise of the gunpowder blasts. The car is off the road now. Seth manages to wrench the noose away from his neck for a gasp of breath, then tries to force the car back onto the road, but it's too late. It veers wildly and they hit something and fly through the air. Airborne, she feels her cheeks lift, her arm spark. The weightlessness is terrifying, and then there's an ear-splitting almighty crash, her brain short-circuits, and everything goes black.

The twins regain consciousness at the same time. The front of the car is smoking; the boot has sprung open. Miller lies dead in the road in front of them, his bare skin lacerated by the broken windscreen. The smashed insulin kit lies beside him. Kirsten and Seth don't talk. They reach out for each other, touch hands. Kirsten can hear herself blink.

She starts scanning her body for injuries: wiggles her toes, pumps her legs, palpates her ribs. Apart from the pain in her already-broken arm she feels fine; or as fine as numb can feel. Seth is holding his neck. He gives it a few squeezes, then kicks at the door. It takes three hard kicks to swing it open. He gets out and wrenches open Kirsten's door, helps her out.

They mumble worried phrases at each other, touch each other's grazes with furrowed brows. Satisfied that they are not too badly injured, they go over to inspect Miller, to make sure he is dead. He is a red spectre: his skull is crushed and he has five bullet holes that they can see. His skin is etched with a patina of blood. There is no life in him. His Cheerios are gone.

Kirsten picks up the bag of insulin. Despite being atheist, she crosses her heart and says a quick prayer to The Net and any god that will listen. She goes to the boot and heaves when she sees the contents. Motions for Seth to come over. Seth doesn't seem surprised. He leans in closer, to get a better look at the day-old corpse's face. A battered face and a body dressed in a Hawaiian shirt and chinos. Some fingernails are missing.

The real Ed Miller.

When Kirsten checks the insulin kit she discovers that the only remaining vial is broken. The bag is wet with the precious liquid. No insulin remains for Keke. No medicine to stop her from going into hypoglycaemic shock, stop her from going into a sugar coma and dying.

How strange, thinks Kirsten absent-mindedly, *how sugar and death can be so closely linked*. She bites down hard to stop herself from crying.

The car is un-driveable. They try to hitch but no one will pick them up looking the way they do, so the pair give up and sit on the kerb, facing the road, wobbling knees pointing to the sky. Seth puts his arm around Kirsten.

'James,' she says.

'What?'

'James can come get us. He has a car.'

For some reason this fills Seth with dread.

'James might have insulin.'

Kirsten sends James their co-ordinates in tracking mode.

'Let's walk so long. It's not too far from here. Five or six kilometres?'

Kirsten checks Keke's phone. Her diabetes app timer says thirty-four minutes.

'Keke doesn't have that long.'

'Can you run? With your arm, I mean?'

Even if they do run, they wouldn't make it to the clinic in time. If they make it to the clinic in time, they won't be able to get in.

'I can try.'

'Good girl.'

They stand up and start jogging. Seth tries to flag down cars as they go. Kirsten is dizzy, and she feels every footfall deep in her broken bone. The jagged pain mounts and mounts, until the blue light blots out her vision and she has to stop and throw up into a patch of roadside ivy. A plague of rats scurries away. She wipes her mouth and starts to run again, almost falls. Tries again.

'Stop.' Seth catches her. 'Stop.'

She tries to wriggle free, tries to keep running, but he grabs her again, just in time, and she faints into his arms.

When Kirsten comes to, it takes her a second to remember where she is.

'Keke?' she asks, but Seth shakes his head. Twenty-one minutes left on the SugarApp. When it reaches twenty minutes it begins flashing a red light.

'You've done everything you can,' he says.

She stands up, trembling. 'No.'

As if on some otherworldly cue, a white van appears on the road and drives in their direction. Seth starts yelling, waving his arms, like an island castaway trying to signal a rescue chopper. Kirsten blinks at it, trying to figure out if it is real, or some kind of desperate inner-city mirage. The car drives right up to them and stops on the shoulder of the road. The driver gets out and Kirsten's knees almost buckle again.

'Kirsten!' shouts James, running towards her.

'James,' she says, 'James.'

'Where have you been? I've been looking everywhere!' He seems agitated, but becomes gentle when he takes in Kirsten's shorn scalp and make-shift sling. He hugs her gently on her right side, kisses her forehead, her cheeks, her shorn head.

'What have they done to you?' he asks, 'What have they done?'

Who? thinks Seth. *What have* who *done?*

'I'm okay. But... Keke...'

Seth steps forward. 'We need to leave right now.'

James looks at him, the shock clear on his face. He doesn't say anything.

'This is Seth. He's been helping me,' says Kirsten. 'I'll explain everything later. We need to find Keke. Immediately. She needs insulin. Do you have any?'

James releases her. 'We'll get some.'

He jogs over to the van and opens the sliding door. It is dark inside the back, and there is a silhouette of someone, sitting in the front passenger seat: a large man. Both Seth and Kirsten stop.

'Come on,' says James, beckoning.

There is a flash of light in Kirsten's mind that bleaches her vision. Some kind of terror, some kind of dreadful *déjà vu*, roots each to the spot. Seth shakes his head, wants to hold Kirsten back. Kirsten's whole body is telling her not to get into the car, but she reasons with herself: *Must Save Keke*. Also: *this is James; Sweet Marmalade.* James beckons again, and this time Kirsten obeys: head bowed, like a shy little girl. Seth swears under his breath and climbs in next to her.

James slams the door closed and gets into the driver's seat. The passenger is looking out of the window and doesn't acknowledge them. The car has a chemical smell to it, rectangular in shape. Dry cleaning? New plastic? No, neither shape is right. And then she gets it: paint. A new paint job. Just as James is about to start the car, she gives him the clinic's address. James and the passenger look at each other. He stops for a moment, as if he can't decide whether to press the ignition button.

The man scowls at him, and only then does Kirsten recognise him.

'Inspector Mouton!' she says, not understanding the connection. He purses his lips, gives a nod in her general direction. Has James been so worried about her that he called the cops? Has Mouton agreed to help him find her?

The engine starts; the doors all lock automatically. She tries to open her door, but it won't budge, as she has known it won't. Child-lock. There is the distinct aroma of turmeric in the air.

Seth's Tile vibrates with a bump.

FlowerGrrl> Hey, hope u OK. Hope you get this. Results in. Ramifications huge. Hve already called emergency meeting with YKW. Hero u. Biggest bust in Alba's history. Fontus going down in big way. All yr previous fuck-ups forgiven. U officially now Rock Star. Whn can u come in? We hve a few bottles / Moët wth yr name on.

SD>> Results?

FlowerGrrl> Oh, U R there! Alive. :) Sending report now. Come in ASAP!

Two separate PDFs come through. The first is the report on the Fontus samples: Anahita and Tethys clear, Hydra with lots of red tabs, showing irregularities. Seth recognises the main chemicals: ethinyl estradiol; norgestrel; drospirenone; mestranol; ethynodiol—the same active ingredients you'd find in a contraceptive pill. James casts a backward glance, but keeps driving.

The next PDF is the analysis of Kirsten's yellow pills,

and he sees some more red tabs. Confused for a second, he checks that he is looking at the right report and not the Hydra analysis, but it's the correct one. The red tabs highlight various chemicals, all of which Seth recognises from his time at Pharmax. Diazepam, Sertraline, Doxepin. *The fuck?* It's a zombie pill. He starts as he remembers James is the one who fills her prescription for her.

James speeds up and weaves through the traffic, causing them to sway in their seats at the back. He swears under his breath and skips red lights. Smacks the steering wheel with his palm.

Seth bumps Kirsten.

SD>> Who's the beefcake?

KD> Cop. Mouton. He worked my parents' case.

SD>> WTF?

KD> ??

SD>> U know those pills u had?

KD> Yebo?

SD>> Tranquilisers.

KD> No way. I got them from James.

Kirsten digs in her handbag for her lipstick magic wand, and slips it into her pocket, along with her pocketknife. When the front entrance of the clinic is in view, Inspector Mouton pulls off his long sleeve shirt. Kirsten's eye is drawn to the skin on his arm. It's marbled, shiny. Burn scar?

They pull into the parking space closest to the giant glass entrance, and James and the inspector get out. Kirsten tries her door again, but it's still locked. She jimmies the handle, knocks on the window.

'James!' she calls. 'It's on child-lock!'

The realisation hits Seth just before it does Kirsten, and he puts his forehead in his hands. She doesn't understand his reaction, and then all of a sudden she does.

The memory comes back to her like a swift punch to the stomach, slams her back into her seat, takes all the air out of her lungs. She sees it as if she is back in that moment, that terrible moment, when the light went out of her life. A moment so long buried in her subconscious she'd think it would be decayed in some way, but it's not. It's cruelly vivid and so clear Kirsten can taste the colours.

She is playing a game with her twin brother on an emerald lawn in the front garden of a pretty little house. She remembers the building: rough ivory paint that scratches your skin if you brush up against it, curlicue burglar bars in the windows, cracked slasto leading up to a light blue (lemongrass-smelling?) front door. A brittle little letterbox on a pole with two red numbers on it (Lollipop)... red means two, so maybe it is twenty-two? The garden is bursting with colour, enough to make Kirsten giddy.

The sun is shining brightly but it is uncharacteristically cold that day, and they are dressed in warm boots and brightly coloured jackets: peppermint for Sam and mandarin for her. Her mother—her real mother—is leaning on the doorframe, watching them. She is pale and slim in a charcoal polo neck. She has on her gardening apron, and dirty gloves. A smear of soil on her cheek. Young, beautiful, with a long, thick braid of red hair. Kirsten gives her a toothy grin, and she responds with a smile and a thumbs-up. The phone rings from inside the house, and her mother peels off her gloves and goes to answer it.

Despite the warmth of the jacket, the skin on her hands is red when she looks down at them. Sam passes her something: a toy horse. No, a little pony, pink with a grubby white mane and tail. One of his action figures astride. A Thundercat. She zooms the pony over the grass and makes the appropriate sound effects, laughs. Sam doesn't smile. Something has caught his attention in the street and he looks past her, frowning. He stands up on his chubby legs, toy still in hand, held against his round stomach.

A black kombi has pulled up and all of a sudden there is a blond-haired little boy right there, on their pavement. He seems only slightly older than they are. He beckons to them with his hands, his sweet face promising something fun and exciting. She babbles excitedly, starts to go towards him, but Sam puts his hand on her shoulder, wanting to hold her back. He looks at the boy then back at the house, for his mother, but the doorframe is empty. Kirsten keeps walking and is soon beside the rosy-cheeked stranger. Sam calls out:

'Kitty!' and runs to catch up with her.

As he reaches the walkway beside the kombi, the door slides open and a giant man swoops over them and there are meaty forearms squeezing the air out of them. Before they know what has happened, they are struggling in the car. The other boy, stricken, is shouted at and jumps in last, and the door is slammed shut. From light to darkness, like that. Like that, the light in her heart went out. Nothing but darkness and a shocked wail in her ears. She realises the wailing is coming from her. In the dim interior she sees the blond-haired beckoner also crying, his face contorted with silent tears.

The face she knows so well. James.

THE ULTIMATE BLOODLESS REVOLUTION

35

Johannesburg, 2021

James opens the sliding door, flooding the car with light. Dust motes dance in the white air. Inspector Mouton stands beside him, gun drawn and pointed at the twins.

'Is that necessary?' James demands, anger gravelling his voice.

Mouton ignores him.

'Come with us,' Mouton says to Kirsten and Seth. 'Come quietly and no one gets hurt.'

'Fuck you,' the twins say in unison. Kirsten can't even look in James's direction. She sees where the car's paintwork has been touched up. James is the one who tried to run them off the road on the way back from the seed bank. James hid the letter from her mother. James tried to incapacitate her with pills.

Her heart is in shock, as if she has just been stung by a jellyfish. A swarm, a smack. His betrayal is a deep blue venom spreading throughout her body.

'Your friend is very sick,' says Mouton. 'You don't have much time. If you come with us, we'll give you the medicine she needs.'

'Go!' Kirsten says to Seth, 'I'll see to Keke. You get out of here.'

'No way,' he says. 'I've only just found you.'

'The deal is for both of you,' says Mouton. 'Just one of you is useless to me.'

Keke's phone starts vibrating and wailing, the SugarApp counter is at 0: 'DANGER ZONE.'

'Fine,' says Kirsten, 'we're wasting time. Let's go!'

Mouton halts them, pats them both down, takes their guns, including the sling-smuggled Ruger. He finds the pocketknife and magic wand. Puts the knife in his pocket and looks at the lipstick, undecided. He's about to inspect it when James makes an agitated sound.

'Come on,' he says, 'we need to move.'

Mouton hands the tube back to Kirsten. 'Go.'

He pushes the pair in front of him. They walk into the main entrance, which the regular security detail has deserted, and head to the elevator. James tries to take Kirsten's hand but she stands as far away from him as she can, squashing herself into the cool corner. The mirror, meant to make the small space seem bigger, reflects their taut faces and the result is claustrophobic.

Worried that she will get sick again, Kirsten closes her eyes and breathes into her corner, resting her forehead on the mirror. Her breath and sweat mist up the glass, veiling her reflection. Mouton inserts a wafer-key and they start moving down—past ground level and two levels of basement parking listed as the bottom floors—and still further, until they are deep in the ground and Seth can almost feel the weight of the earth above them.

'Kitty,' says James.

Shut the fuck up, she wants to say. *Your words are poison darts.*

'Let me explain.'

'There is not an explanation that would make this okay.'

'Van der Heever said to bring you in or he'd kill you.'

'And you believed him?'

'I know what he is capable of.'

'And yet you are delivering us to him.'

'Don't you see? I didn't have a choice.'

Kirsten sneers at him. 'I can't believe I ever let you touch me.'

'How long have you worked for the Genesis Project?' asks Seth.

'It's not like that,' answers James. 'That day, in 1988, when you were taken—'

'You mean when you took us,' says Kirsten.

'Just like you did today,' says Seth. 'Deja-fucking-vu.'

'After that day,' says James, 'I kept tabs on you. I made sure you were okay. I watched you from afar. Watched you grow up, as I grew up. I loved you—I did, I loved you—from the very beginning. We were meant to be together. Don't you see? We're a family. A different kind of family... that day we met—'

'Oh my God,' says Kirsten, '*everything* was a lie.'

They step out of the lift and stand before a massive security door, like something out of a high tech bank. It reminds Kirsten of the Doomsday Vault. Mouton keys in a five-digit code and puts his thumb to the scanner pad, two green lights glow (Serpent Eyes) and the door unlocks with a decisive pop. Kirsten lifts her hand to her face and narrows her eyes to cope with the intense light.

Everything is white: a passage with many inter-leading doors is made up of clean white floor tiles, white painted walls, a whitewashed cement ceiling. They walk along the passage and make a few turns. Every corner looks the same and Kirsten wonders how they'll ever find their way out again. They are rats in a 4D maze. She takes as many photos as she can with her locket. Some of the doors seem to lead to more passages; others open up to deserted labs. Huge machines whirr away. Ivory Bead. Wet Sugar. Coconut Treat. A hundred shades of white. Stuttering holograms of static. Glass upon glass upon glass.

The employees seem to have left in a hurry: Seth sees half-drunk cups of tea, open desk drawers, an out-of-joint stapler, an abandoned cardigan. Air sanitiser streams in through the air vents, sounding like the sea. It reminds Kirsten of being on one of the ghost ships floating endlessly on the Indian Ocean, many of which she explored and looted. Why had she been so captivated by stories of the Somali pirates? Because she had known all along, had a deeply buried awareness, that she, herself, had been kidnapped. Her life had been seized, snatched, carried off. It left her an empty vessel, unmoored. Haunted.

'That book I gave you,' says James, 'The fairy tale. "Hansel and Gretel". I gave it to you for a reason. Do you understand, Kitty? It was for a reason. I have a file on your real parents. I've tried to give it to you a thousand times, but every time I... I knew if I gave it to you we'd end up here.'

At the end of a nondescript passage Mouton pushes them into a room. The sound of a dog barking shocks them. A beagle rushes to Mouton and nuzzles his shin with a low whine and a wet nose. Mouton opens a drawer, takes out a treat, and feeds it to the hound. Gives her a cursory pat on the head, gives her loose skin a gentle shake. Locks Seth's and Kirsten's guns away in a safe full of meticulously arranged weapons.

Kirsten recalls the image of dog hair on Betty/Barbara's jersey, remembers the journo telling her that Betty/Barbara's flat had dog food bowls, but no dog. Seth looks up, at the opposite wall, and Kirsten raises her eyes too. They stand and stare.

Pinned, stapled, and tied to the vast wall are hundreds of objects. Rings, coins, photographs, pieces of jewellery, dead flowers, frayed ribbons, candy, baby shoes, old toys. Like a vast artwork, a collage of found objects, except they know as they are looking that these objects were not found, but taken. Special things stolen from the people he has killed. *Objets d'amour.* Not just a regular serial killer's bounty of murder mementoes. Not just a random hairclip or sweater or cufflink, but tokens of genuine affection. Layer upon layer of love, lost.

A love letter engraved on an antique piano key. A muddied toy rabbit. An Olympic gold medal. She sees the holograph photo-projector she gave to her parents. Both feel their rage build. The beagle barks. Mouton ushers them out of the room and raps loudly on the adjacent double door. A voice inside instructs him to enter, and they tumble in.

The room can't be more different than the bleached Matrix of the way in: soft light, warm colours, wood and gold, linen, organic textures. It's someone's office. No, more intimate than that: someone's den. Keke is lying on the couch, as pale as Kirsten has ever seen her. She runs over, puts her hand over her mouth to see if she is still breathing, and she is, but the movements are shallow. How long has she been unconscious? Her nano-ink tattoo is so vivid it looks as if it is embossed, and her body is slick with perspiration. James hands her a black clamshell kit (New Tyre) that she unzips. Three brand new vials of insulin stare back at her. Kirsten fumbles with the case with shaking hands, can't seem to co-ordinate her fingers. Eventually she gets a vial out, then looks for syringes, needles, but can't find them. She hadn't even considered this part: that she would have to load the syringe and inject her friend. Her trembling hands are all but useless.

'Let me do it,' says James. He finds something that looks like a pen in the side pouch, snaps the vial of insulin into it, and presses it against Keke's thigh. He clicks a button and Kirsten hears the hiss of the jab, watches as the vial empties. He puts the back of his hand to her forehead then measures her blood sugar, pressure and pulse with his phone.

'She's going to be okay,' he says.

Kirsten pushes him out of the way and grabs Keke's hand, bunches it into a tight fist around the magic wand, and covers it with a blanket.

'We wouldn't have let her die,' comes a voice from behind the mahogany desk. Dr Van der Heever swirls around in his chair and Kirsten recognises the icy irises behind his black-rimmed glasses (Wet Pebble).

'You,' says Kirsten. The word comes out the colour of trailing seaweed.

The doctor nods at Mouton, who forces Seth's hands behind his body and clicks handcuffs on him. James takes Kirsten's arm out of her sling to handcuff her. He does it as gently as possible, trying not to hurt her. She winces and squirms at his touch, as if his skin burns hers. There is a neat, metallic click, a perfect aqua-coloured square. She doesn't see the second click, the bracelet for her injured arm, and James squeezes that same hand. She glares at him and he looks away. Slowly she tests the cuffs, and it's true: he has left one open.

The doctor notices her hostility.

'Dear Kate, don't blame James,' he says. 'He had no choice but to bring you in.'

'There's always a choice,' says Kirsten.

'True. His options were: find a way of bringing you two in, or see you die. He has seen Inspector Mouton's... convincing... work. He chose to bring you in.'

'Mouton has been the one killing for you? A policeman?' she asks the doctor. Then, to Mouton: 'You killed those people? A sick woman, a young mother?'

'He was simply following orders. He is extremely good at his line of work.'

'Plus he gets to clean up the mess when he walks in as an inspector. I bet he's really good at covering his tracks,' says Seth.

'Just one of his many talents,' says the doctor.

'Why?' asks Kirsten, 'Why the list, why the murders?'

Doctor Van der Heever pauses, as if considering whether to answer.

'It's complicated,' he says, pushing his glasses up the bridge of his nose.

Keke's breathing seems to get deeper; her sheen is disappearing.

'The truth is,' says the doctor, 'the truth is that deletion is always a last resort. We did everything we could to stop it from getting to this stage. Unfortunately, people don't always know what is good for them. Or their daughters.'

'You mean my parents? My so-called parents?'

'Your—adoptive—mother. After being loyal for over thirty years she suddenly decided that she wanted to tell you about your past. She was a brilliant scientist, a real asset to the Project. Her decline was most unfortunate. If she had just been quiet, as she had been all these years... so many lives could have been spared.'

'Including hers?'

'Including hers. Your father's. And your cell's.'

'What? Cell?'

'Your mother deciding to tell you about the Genesis Project compromised the cell. We don't take chances. Compromised cells are closed down, their members removed from the programme.'

'Killed,' says Seth.

'Deleted is our preferred term.'

'I'm sure it is,' says Kirsten.

'Every generation,' says the doctor, interlacing his fingers in front of him on the desk, 'the Genesis Project selects seven very special infants to join the programme. We are very rigorous when it comes to this selection and hundreds of babies all over the country are considered. They need to match certain—strict—criteria. They must be absolutely healthy, highly intelligent, and have some special talent or gift. Also, during their gestation, their parents must have at some time seriously considered family planning—'

Kirsten: 'Family planning while pregnant? You mean… abortion?'

'Abortion, or adoption. They must have gone as far as signing the papers: a demonstration that they were not 100% committed to raising the child themselves for whatever reason.'

This stings Kirsten and Seth equally: they were not wanted in the first place anyway. When they discovered they had been abducted a little flame had ignited in their hearts: they were once loved, once cherished, before they were stolen away. Now that flame is snuffed out. Not one, but two sets of parents who didn't truly want them. Kirsten knows she shouldn't be surprised. After all, in the original story, Hansel and Gretel's parents lost them in the woods on purpose.

'Why?' asks Kirsten, 'why would the Genesis Project steal children?'

'The Project is concerned with far more than seven little children. In fact, the clonotype programme was really just a small hobby of mine in which the others indulged me. Our vision is far more all-encompassing than that.'

'You wanted to clone us?' asks Seth.

'Not clone you as such... more like, try to isolate the genes you carry that makes you... different. Special. Then we could recreate those genes in a lab and, well, graft them into new babies being born. Can you imagine?' His eyes sparkle. 'Can you imagine what our country could be if all our citizens were healthy, clever, strong, creative?'

'So that's what the Fontus thing is about,' says Seth.

The doctor throws him a sharp glance.

'GeniX. Eugenics. You audacious motherfucker.'

Van der Heever shifts in his chair. 'The word *eugenics* has become unpopular of late.'

'Perhaps because it's an archaic, racist, ethically reprehensible practice,' says Kirsten.

'What we do isn't racist,' he says.

'Really?' asks Kirsten. 'Is that why you are using the country's drinking water to practically wipe out South Africa's black population?'

'No,' says the doctor, 'not the *black* population. The *poor, uneducated* population.'

'This is post-apartheid South Africa. Most of the poor people *are* black.'

'Merely coincidence.' The doctor shrugs. 'Many non-whites are rich. In fact, very rich, not so?'

'Coincidence?' says Seth. 'We have that fucked-up legacy because of people like you who dabble in social engineering.'

James manages to get Kirsten's attention.

'Listen,' Dr Van der Heever says. 'Fertility rates are plummeting the world over. It's a well-known fact that in first world countries infertility is most prevalent in the educated and employed strata—we may even go as far as to say—the intelligentsia. The higher IQs go, the less chance of procreation. We also have the Childfree Movement: Ambitious couples are choosing to prioritise their careers and lifestyles over starting families. And yet the world's population is still mushrooming out of control. People with limited resources, limited faculties, are reproducing, putting a huge strain on the world's—finite—reserves.'

James wiggles his finger to draw her eye down, then, barely moving, he points at his shirt, the couch, his jacket, then touches his hair.

'It's a catastrophe waiting to happen,' says the doctor. 'So, the three of us—'

'The Trinity.' says Seth.

'The Trinity.'

Kirsten, frustrated, looks away, but James keeps staring at her. When she looks at him again he does the exact same thing. Shirt, couch, jacket, hair. He actually points twice at the couch, which she missed the first time around.

'We met in varsity,' says the doctor, 'took the same ethics class in first year. The debate question was: should South African citizens be required to obtain a permit before they procreate? This is, after all, what people do in Europe and other such countries, when they want to adopt a pet, an animal. There is a battery of psychological tests, a home screening. The system works well. The whole class was in an uproar: of course not! everyone yelled. What about human rights? The constitution! But the three of us argued in favour of the hypothesis. Human rights on the one hand, quality of human life on the other.'

Shirt, couch, couch, jacket, hair.

Seth wonders how many times the doctor has given this impassioned speech, how often he rehearses it in the shower, or while shaving.

'When tap water became undrinkable, it came to us. It was such an elegant solution. Dose only the state-subsidised drinking water, and leave the more expensive waters pure. If the privileged citizens drink Hydra for whatever reason, and find they have problems conceiving, they have the means to get help. Fertility clinics abound.'

'It's cruel. Barbaric.'

'Nature is cruel, Miss Lovell. Do you know that the

embryos of sand tiger sharks kill and eat their siblings in utero? It's the epitome of survival of the fittest. You can't fight evolution.'

'Children may be the only gifts a poor family has.'

The doctor laughs. 'Ah, now you're being sentimental. What about the burden those 'gifts' cause the family, and the country? The planet? What about those children who have to be brought up in dire circumstances? They fall through the cracks. Before we started implementing The Programme the situation was reaching breaking point. Hundreds of babies being born every day and South Africa's education system was broken.

'Do you know what a broken education system does? It puts people on the street. Criminals. Beggars. Infants were being hired for the day by professional street beggars to garner more sympathy from drivers. There were newborns for sale, advertised in the online classifieds! Other babies were lost on crowded beaches never to be claimed, left in dumpsters, or worse.

'In May, 2013, I was having a personal crisis. Wondering if my work would ever make a real difference. In that month two abandoned babies were found: one wrapped in a plastic bag, burnt. The other was stuck in a sewage pipe—his mother had tried to flush him down the toilet. A healthy newborn! And you talk to me of barbarians. The bottom line was that children were too easy to come by, often unwanted, abused, neglected. The Trinity vowed to take a stand against their suffering. It was—is—incredibly personal. We all have our own stories. Christopher Walden was brutally sodomised—raped—by his priest at a church camp. He managed to escape to a nearby house and use their telephone to call his parents. You know what they did? Told him to stop making up stories and go back to camp. Then they called the priest and told him where he was.'

The doctor walks over to Mouton.

'Mouton,' he says, now with compassion in his voice. 'Show them your arm.'

For the first time, Mouton is hesitant to obey orders.

'Show them,' says the doctor. 'Help them to understand the work we are doing here.'

Mouton sets his jaw and lifts the sleeve of his shirt to reveal the entire burn scar. It travels from his wrist to his armpit. A swirling motif of shining vandalism.

'That's not one burn. It's not from a once-off childhood accident. Marius's father used to hold his arm over a flame for punishment every time he cried, because "Men Don't Cry". A candle, the gas stove, a cigarette lighter, whatever was handy at the time. It started on his first birthday.'

Mouton pulls his sleeve back down. Shirks his shirt into place.

'My scars aren't so obvious,' says Van der Heever, 'my father preferred the crunch of breaking bones. That, and psychological abuse. Once, my dog, the only friend I had, followed a farmworker home. My father was furious. That night I put out extra food out for him, for when he came home. The next morning, when he returned, galloping and barking and happy to see us all, my father shot him in the head. The dog had been disloyal, he said. It was to teach me the value of loyalty. I was six years old.'

He takes a breath, lifts his glasses then rubs the bridge of his nose.

'I'm sure you can't imagine that now. It was before your time. Babies were seen as... expendable. Too many to go around, and most born to undeserving parents. Abuse was inevitable. Unchecked procreation was a scourge on our society. I knew when I heard that story about the baby being flushed down the toilet... I knew then that my work was vital.'

Shirt, couch, couch, jacket, hair. Blue, brown, brown, grey, yellow.

'Don't you see?' he asks, 'what we planned so long ago, what we have been working towards, is finally starting to come to fruition. Peace and purity. By tamping off the birth rate we have solved a host of societal ills. There are no more abandoned babies. Schools now have enough books and tablets and teachers and space for their learners, and children are looked after and cherished. Fewer uneducated people means less unemployment, less crime, less social grants. More tax money to invest in the future of the country. Better infrastructure, better schooling, better healthcare.'

Blue, brown, brown, grey, yellow, thinks Kirsten. *49981*. It's the code, she realises: the code to get out.

'Don't you see?' he says again, this time more urgently,

pride like fever in his face. 'We did it! We are responsible for the ultimate bloodless revolution!'

NEXT STOP: CYBORGS

36

Johannesburg, 2021

Keke stirs on the couch, but settles down again. Van der Heever is tireless.

'If you put your emotions aside for just a moment and look at the results, morally and ethically speaking, it's accepted that the welfare of the many should take precedence over the welfare of the few, and as such, sacrifices needed to be made. We were not, contrary to what you may think, barbarous about it, as many eugenicists have been before us… unwitting patients waking up, in pain, only to realise that their uteri had been removed. Our solution was much more humane. Cleaner. In fact, we believe that once it becomes clear what has happened here, other countries will follow suit, and soon we'll have a global population that is both under control and more efficient.'

'Next stop: cyborgs,' says Seth. 'That's not a world I want to live in.'

'Dear boy, if the population of the rest of the world keeps growing as it is, there will no longer be a world to live in. We are safeguarding the future for all.'

'For some. For those you deem fit. Others you deny a future altogether. How many cells are there?' asks Kirsten. 'How many people's lives have you stolen?'

'A dozen, maybe more. An infinitesimal portion of the population. Genesis members, however, are in the thousands. They're in every strata of South African life.' He lifts his palms to the ceiling, as if he is some kind of prophet. 'How else would we be able to pull this off?'

'I still don't understand,' says Seth, perhaps trying to buy more time, 'the point of the clone project. So you isolated some interesting genes. Then what?'

'You wouldn't believe me if I told you.'

'Try me. What was the point? To splice a little army for yourself? Take over the world?'

'The point was to create a superior race.'

'So not unlike Hitler, then,' says Kirsten.

'To the contrary, dear Kate. It was never about me, never about power. I've never liked the limelight. A superior race would get ill less often, work harder, be more intelligent, less violent, have more talents, and lead more fulfilling lives. It was to make the world a better place.'

'But how would it work,' asks Seth, 'in your sad, imaginary world? Deserving parents would get their license and then come along to you for a designer embryo? You harvest their eggs and sperm and make a few little tweaks, remove any genetic abnormalities, add some extra brains or blue eyes. Ask them if they'd prefer a boy or a girl. It's bespoke IVF. You're fooling yourself. You're not making the world a better place. You're in the designer baby business, a fertility quack. There is nothing new or noble about that.'

'You don't understand how far technology has come.' The doctor smiles.

'Okay, you straight-out clone them, then.'

'Cloning is now old tech. It was never very successful. The ratio of live births wasn't good at all. We started with cloning because it was the best technology we had at the time, but now... now we have other means. Besides, cloning is still dependent on the pregnancy and birth being successful. There are just too many things that can go wrong. Too many variables we can't control. So... we cut out the gestation period.'

'Wait,' says Kirsten, 'what?'

'You've cut out the gestation?' says Seth. 'As in, you grow them in artificial wombs, in the lab?'

Kirsten pictures a room filled with transparent silicone

wombs and feels like throwing up again.

'We experimented with that, but it wasn't a viable solution in the end. It was difficult to get the exact... nuances of the environment right.'

'Right,' says Seth. He is genuinely interested now. 'Okay, now you have to tell me.'

Dr Van der Heever's lips curl up into a smile; there is a snap in his eyes.

'We print them,' he says, not being able to keep the pride out of his voice. 'We print babies.'

THAT'S WHAT FRANKENSTEIN SAID

37

Johannesburg, 2021

'You print babies,' repeats Seth. It's not sinking in.

'That's impossible,' says Kirsten.

'Oh believe me,' Van der Heever says, 'it is.'

The doctor gets up from his chair and motions for them to follow him. He activates a door hidden in his bookshelf, which swings open, and he steps through. Mouton pushes them forward from behind, leaving Keke on the couch in the den. Soon they are standing in the white cube of a pristine lab (Immaculate Conception), the brightness highlighting the dirt and blood on their clothes and skin, adding to the surreal quality of the moment.

Kirsten looks down at her hands, fingernails black with grime, but is distracted by a small cry in the corner. She studies the row of incubators against the wall: a stack of empty Tupperwares. Has she imagined the sound? Is she imagining this whole thing? Is she lying unconscious somewhere, at the scene of the earlier car accident, or in hospital, having this bizarre dream?

A nearby machine, monochrome, spins. It looks like some kind of body scanner.

'We were already printing fully functional organs in 2010. It was the natural progression to print a whole body. All you really need is good software and some DNA. And stem cells, obviously, which there's no shortage of in our game. We've printed over a thousand healthy babies, and we have a 100% success rate. No more failed fertility treatments. No more mothers dying in labour, no more birth injuries or foetal abnormalities. Just screaming healthy newborns with 10 out of 10 Apgars, every time.'

'But you can't print a beating heart,' says Kirsten.

'Ah, that was one of the most challenging parts,' says Van der Heever, touching his chest, 'but a quick current to those heart cells and off they go—galloping along. It's a beautiful thing to behold.'

Seth says, 'I think that's what Frankenstein said.'

The doctor indulges Seth with a smile.

'Where are they, then? The babies?' asks Kirsten.

'A lot of them have been adopted out. As you know, the demand for healthy babies nowadays is astronomical.'

'You sold them?'

'In a manner of speaking.'

'So you cause a nation-wide fertility crisis and then set up a designer baby factory,' says Seth. 'Genius.'

'What about the rest?' asks Kirsten.

'We evacuated them when we got confirmation that you were coming in.'

'You evacuated the whole building,' says Kirsten.

The doctor nods. 'I couldn't take the chance you'd not... co-operate with us.'

'I wouldn't "co-operate" with you if my life depended on it.'

'That's what I thought you'd say.'

Another soft sound from the corner: a cooing. Transparent bubbles float playfully towards her. Kirsten blinks forcefully to wipe them out of her vision.

'That's why,' says Van der Heever, 'I had to up the stakes.'

He walks to the corner incubator, opens the top, and gently lifts a newborn out from inside. He carries the baby back to them like a proud relative. It's swaddled in a blanket embellished with planes and clouds that float in the sky. The baby squirms, tries to break free, shouts, and then fixes Kirsten with an intense stare. She knows she should feel revulsion. The doctor can barely contain his excitement. He raises the baby up, like a trophy, like the prize he'll never get from his peers.

It looks… It looks just like—

'James, Kirsten, meet your progeny. Congratulations. It's a baby boy.'

WHITE HOLE

38

Johannesburg, 2021

'No,' says James, breaking his silence. 'It can't be.'

'What have you done?' whispers Kirsten.

'You came to me for help,' Van der Heever says, 'you wanted to have a baby.'

'Not like this,' she says.

'I know it's still a novel idea to you, but this is how *all* babies will be made in the future.'

'No,' says Kirsten, shaking her head.

'There's nothing wrong with him. He's a perfectly healthy baby!'

'You're saying he's ours? Mine and Kirsten's? You used our DNA?' asks James.

'That's what I've been telling you! All your best traits, with none of your problematic genes. We switched off two for cancer, and one for dementia, I believe. He'll have Kirsten's hair, your eyes. Your fine motor skills, and Kirsten's artistic talent.'

The baby starts fussing, his skin blooms pink. The doctor motions for James to take off Kirsten's handcuffs, and as he does so, she feels his fingers slip into the back pocket of her wrecked jeans. A set of small keys: for Seth's handcuffs, she guesses. She takes the baby from Van der Heever without thinking, just scoops him up with her un-broken arm and rocks him, inhales the warmth of his skin, kisses his forehead. The baby calms, gazes up at her, barely blinking. She can feel him, smell him, and in that moment she knows acutely this is no dream. This baby—her baby—is real. Her whole body stupidly longs for the bundle in her arms.

'Why did you do this?' Kirsten keeps her voice low. 'Why bring us in and tell us everything? Why didn't you just have us killed, like the rest?'

The doctor puts his hands behind his back, strolls towards the empty incubators, leans against one of them.

'I'm getting older now. Softer? My health isn't what it used to be. It's too late to switch off the genes that are causing my heart to fail. My career has always been all consuming. I'll continue working but it's time for me to start taking some time off. Play golf. Travel. Watch my grandson grow up.'

'You can't be serious,' says James. 'You think we can just forget all this and play Happy Families?'

'Grandson?' says Kirsten.

Van der Heever's eyebrows shoot up. 'You haven't told her?'

'Why would I tell her?' demands James. 'Why would I tell anyone?'

His words hang in the air: the outburst makes Kirsten's head spin.

'Father?' She looks at James. 'He's your *father?*'

'Not by choice,' spits James. 'I broke all ties with him as soon as I had an idea about what he was doing. But this… my imagination didn't go this far.'

'Not your choice,' says the doctor. 'Indeed. It was *my* choice.'

'What?'

'My choice, to be your father. You were the first of the 1991 seven to be chosen to be incorporated into the clonotype programme. You were the first to be… taken.'

Kirsten thinks of the list, pictures it in her mind, sees the code of the last person on the list: number seven. Sees the colours, and recognises Marmalade's date of birth. So he was also abducted, she realises, was also a victim. Abducted then used to lure the rest of us. Bait. A toddler version of Stockholm syndrome.

James blinks.

'I am one of the seven?' he asks, amazed. 'I am not biologically tied to you? We don't share the same blood?' Something dark and heavy lifts off his shoulders; a shadow escapes his face.

'I did... care for you,' says Van der Heever. 'I didn't make the same mistakes my father made, with me. You were always well cared for.'

'You abused me,' says James.

'I never lifted a hand to you.'

'You used me as a lure,' says James. 'I was a child.'

Kirsten gazes at the baby who has now fallen asleep in her arms. His energy, like James's, is orange (Candied Minneola). Fresh, tangy, sweet. Mini-Marmalade. She feels a rush of tenderness.

'So, you now have a choice,' says the doctor. 'You can take your baby, walk out the door, and never look back. As long as you keep the Genesis Project a secret, no harm will come to the three of you. We will be watching over you—'

'Surveilling us,' says James.

'Yes, surveilling you. And making sure you are safe and that life is... easy.'

'What's the catch?' asks Kirsten.

'No catch, if you are willing to co operate.'

'And if we aren't?'

'Then we'll take the baby back.'

'Like you took us,' says Kirsten.

'Like we took you. For the greater good.'

'I have a hard time believing that you're just going to let us walk out of here,' says Seth. 'What are you not telling us?'

'I said I would let Kirsten and James go, with the baby. You, on the other hand, we can't release. With your history, your contacts at Alba... we just can't take the chance. I'm sure you understand.'

Seth nods.

'No,' says Kirsten.

'It's a good deal,' says Seth. 'If I were you, I'd take it.'

'No way,' she says.

'It's not like it would be the end for you, Mr Denicker. You would work for us,' he says to Seth. 'A chemgineer of your ability would be a great asset to The Project. You would choose your hours; we'd pay you handsomely. Not that you'd need the money. Everything down here is complimentary. And you'll have an extremely beautiful companion in that journalist who also needs to stay.'

'But I have to live... underground—literally—for the rest of my life?'

'For the foreseeable future, yes. Until people come to understand and accept our work. It's not as dreary as it sounds. Think of it as... living in a high-end hotel with every one of your needs met.'

The doctor takes a clicker out of his lab-coat pocket and switches on a hologram in front of them. It's like a hotel brochure in 4D: there is a picture of a beautiful suite, impeccably furnished, followed by other images the doctor clicks through.

'We have a heated swimming pool, sunlight rooms, halls of trees for nature walks. Movies, games, room service 24/7. As a bonus, you'll have a personal assistant who will make sure that your every need is fulfilled. Mouton, remind me, what is the young lady's name again?'

'Fiona,' says Mouton. 'Fiona Botes.'

Seth's face flushes.

'The finer details will all become clear once you settle in.'

The doctor switches off the projection.

'You'll also have access to all of this,' he says, gesturing at the lab equipment. 'Everything you need. We have equipment you wouldn't believe exists.'

'But I'll be your prisoner.'

'That's looking at the cloud, instead of the—rather significant—silver lining. I'm giving you—giving all of you—a way out. A unique mercy. I'd advise you to give it some serious consideration.'

'Five-star prison, with benefits, or death,' says Seth. 'I guess I'll take prison and see how it works out.'

'You can't work for them!' says Kirsten. 'They represent everything you hate.'

'Did you not hear the options presented?' asks Seth. 'You'd prefer me dead?'

'Of course not. I just thought... I just think you'd prefer it, over this. Over them.'

'Then you overestimate my moral compass. Or underestimate my will to stay alive.'

As they re-enter the den Kirsten sees Keke's eyes flutter closed. Without warning, James leaps at Mouton, tries to bring him down, scrabbles for the gun in his hand. Mouton roars. Kirsten whisks the baby onto the couch, needing both hands free to unlock Seth's cuffs. The doctor, now behind his desk, calmly opens a drawer, takes out a shiny pistol, snicks off the safety mechanism. Mouton, outraged to see that Kirsten had Seth's keys, aims his gun at her and fires.

The shot knocks her to the ground and she feels a sudden heaviness in her chest, and a sick warmth spreading. Her hearing is muted but she can hear the baby crying, as if he is behind a wall. She can't see, can't breathe. Her breastbone is on fire. A mint-coloured lightness; a searing sadness. The baby—her baby—wails.

This is what it feels like to die.

She expected relief, if anything. Instead it feels as if her heart is being stretched, shredded. She tries to reach for her child but she can't move. She waits for the eventual blackness, blankness of death, but it doesn't come.

She senses movement through her closed lids and opens them. Her vision is blurry: the animated shapes of James and Mouton are still struggling in silent slow motion, the white figure of the doctor has his pistol pointed at them. Keke on the couch.

She can't see Seth. Where is Seth? She feels her heart beating, so she knows she is still alive. Things are coming into focus. She's pinned to the floor. She tries to move again and that's when she sees him: her brother, slack-mouthed, white-skinned, lying on top of her.

'Seth?' she says, but can't hear herself. 'Seth?' but he doesn't move, and then she knows that the warmth and the crushing weight is his. Knows that he had jumped in front of the bullet meant for her heart and had trapped it in his own instead. She shuffles under him, uses her good arm to try to ease his body off hers, tries to get free. Her sense of hearing starts to return and the baby's screaming slashes her vision. She hunches over Seth, tries to find his pulse, but there is too much noise and too much yellow adrenaline singing through her body, numbing the pads of her fingers. She begins CPR, just as James had taught her.

1 and 2 and 3, she says to herself. *1 and 2 and 3*.

Blue sparks travel up her injured arm and lodge in her

clavicle, shock her jawbone. She continues the compressions: wave after wave of jagged Pollen Yellow and Traffic Light Red and Fresh Sage Leaf Green. Van der Heever keeps his gun aimed at Mouton and James as they struggle.

'Stop it!' shouts van der Heever. 'Stop it immediately!' but the men carry on their clumsy wrestling. 'This has been my life's work. It cannot end today!'

No one pays any attention to the flailing doctor.

'This lab will self-destruct as soon as my heart stops beating. Do you understand that? Do you realise what is at stake?'

Kirsten looks up momentarily, sees his face is taut with anguish, and feels nothing for him. She turns her attention back to Seth, only then realising that there is no blood. She sticks her finger into the bullet-hole and finds it dry. Kevlarskin. Tries for a pulse again, and finds it. Out cold, but alive. The baby screams and screams from the couch. Mouton is eventually able to throw James to the ground. He stops resisting when he looks up into the barrel of Mouton's gun.

'Let me reiterate,' says the doctor, taking a calming breath, 'If I die, we all die. There are explosives in every room that were designed specifically to blow this place to dust. We cannot risk anyone finding any evidence here. I have a one-of-a-kind pacemaker in my heart: if it stops beating, the pacemaker sends a signal to the bomb and detonates it.'

This seems to calm the room. Kirsten crawls over to the baby, gathers him up, tries to comfort him. Puts a pants-polished knuckle into his mouth to suck on. Van der Heever follows her with his pistol. James moves to stand up and go towards her, but Mouton shakes his gun and says 'Uh-uh,' motioning for him to stay where he is.

'You said you wouldn't harm her if I brought her in! I had to believe you. I'm asking you as the person you raised as your son...'

'You were never my son,' says the doctor, giving Mouton the signal to shoot them both. Mouton takes aim at James, and Kirsten shouts 'No!'

Before Mouton squeezes the trigger, Keke presses the button on the magic wand that Kirsten had tucked into her fist earlier and tasers him in the back. He yells out, his body convulsing with the current, letting off a few shots into the ceiling then into the wall.

She tasers him again, knocking him off his feet, unconscious. The doctor fires at Kirsten but she ducks, and the bullets land in the gilded frame of an oil painting. Keke points the lipstick at Van der Heever. Just as James gets Mouton's gun out of his hand and points it at the doctor, the doctor turns his pistol on him.

'If I die,' he says again, 'we all die.'

Keke hesitates, perhaps not sure what the taser would do to the incendiary pacemaker. Kirsten cries out as the doctor shoots James in the shoulder. James clenches his jaw and pulls the trigger, twice, and Kirsten sees two black apertures appear in the doctor's white coat. The force of the shot pushes him back a few steps, and he looks at James in astonishment.

'You were never my father,' says James.

Somehow, the doctor has enough strength to grasp his trigger, and he shoots James again, this time in the chest, causing his body to fall backwards and collapse at an awkward angle. Now, battling to stand, Van der Heever aims at Kirsten and the baby, but Keke moves quickly and tasers him before he has the chance to fire, and he falls down onto his knees, then onto his front. Kirsten crouches over James.

'It wasn't your fault,' she says, putting pressure on his wound. 'It wasn't your fault. You were four years old.'

James's face crumples.

'You were four!' Her hands, slippery with blood, slide off his torso. 'Hold on,' she says, putting them back in place. 'Just hang on,' she says.

She tears open his shirt, front and back, grabs his medical bag, claws it open, empties the contents onto the floor beside her. She finds some Platelet-Plasters, rips the backing off with her teeth, and sticks them onto the entry wound. She knows it won't help.

'Kitty, you know your Black Hole?' he says, 'That cold... emptiness...'

'Don't talk,' says Kirsten.

'You have always been the opposite of that, to me.'

'Sssshhh.'

'Whatever the opposite of a black hole is. A white hole?'

'Yes, a white hole,' whispers Kirsten past the stone in her throat.

A white hole: the opposite of a vacuum. The opposite of nothing.

The ability to escape.

Kirsten realises they're sitting in a pool of red. Sees he's fading. James puts one hand on her arm, the other on the baby.

'You were always that. You were everything,' he says, and the light goes out of his eyes. She shakes him, tries to wake him, but he is gone. She doesn't say that white holes don't exist.

'I love you too,' she says to his still body, 'I love you too,' and for the first time in her life that she can remember, huge sobs crash out of her mouth and she is wailing, tears mixing with blood.

A shrill siren stings their ears.

'We need to go,' Seth says to Kirsten, grabbing her arm, lifting her off the floor, away from James's still body.

'We can't leave him here!'

'This building is going to blow up,' says Seth. 'We won't get out in time if we take him.' Kirsten looks at Keke, sees how grey she still is, feels her own strength leaking out of her body. Despite losing so much, she still wants to live. They leave the office, but stop almost immediately when faced with the colourless maze of passages and rooms.

'I don't know where to go,' whispers Keke. 'I was carried in. I was barely conscious.'

Kirsten looks at the photos she took with her locket. The pictures get them halfway but then they are lost. The siren blares. She looks around, tries to think, but all she can see are the bombs in the walls. She looks down at the ground.

'Can you see that?' she asks Keke, pointing at the floor tiles (Toaster Waffles).

'What?'

'Scuffmarks.'

'It doesn't mean anything,' says Seth.

'Breadcrumbs.'

'What?'

'Hansel and Gretel. It's a trail of breadcrumbs. There weren't any marks coming in,' says Kirsten. 'Marmalade... was walking behind us. He marked it for us.'

They follow the grey marks on the floor, turn a few corners, and find the exit: the huge vault-like door. It's locked. Keke, panting, sinks to the floor. She is perspiring heavily again.

Shirt, couch, couch, jacket, hair, thinks Kirsten, and punches 49981 into the number pad. One of the two red lights turns green, and the door remains locked. They both see the small biometric scanpad at the same time, know that it's for a thumbprint.

Inky dread, mixed with neon nerves: Kirsten hands the baby to Seth, tells him to wait with Keke. She follows the scuffmarks back to the den. She doesn't look around at the devastation, the bodies, tries to remain clear and focused. She leans over Mouton's vast torso, finds her pocketknife in his jeans.

As she pulls the knife free his bear claw grabs her wrist. She screams white bolts, and knees him as hard as she can, landing a good one in his stomach, but he hardly flinches. He grunts and starts pulling her body towards him—a meaty tug-of-war. She screams, kicks. The siren screeches zigzags.

She uses her fractured arm to elbow him in the face, breaking his nose so that he can't see. They cry out at the same time and he loosens his grip. Kirsten launches forward, scooping Mouton's gun off the floor and turning on her back, taking aim from between her knees. He roars and lunges at her, but she is quicker than him and gets two shots in and rolls out of the way before he crashes down next to her. She shoots him again, and again, until she has emptied the magazine; until she has no doubt that he is dead.

How much time does she have left? She has no idea. She is hyperventilating, trying not to shake. Picks up the pocketknife again and springs the blade.

Kirsten starts to cut off James's thumb. She can't saw through the long bone, she doesn't have the strength or the time, so instead she cuts deep around the bigger knuckle until the joint is exposed, then digs the knife into the joint and pops the thumb out. The horror of what she is doing does not escape her, but she can't afford to think about it now. She files it away somewhere close and dark. She grabs the digit and runs. She doesn't think of the mutilated hand left behind, the body, the face, the lips. She thinks about getting to Keke, to Seth and her baby, and getting out in time. Staying alive.

The alarm increases in intensity; she is sure only seconds remain. Kirsten flies out of the room, intent on the exit, but halfway down the first corridor she hears something that stops her. Barking. Then beneath the siren: a snuffle, a whine, a whimper. She takes a few more steps. There is no time to save the dog. If she goes back for the beagle they would probably all burn. The dog scratches and whines. All the swearwords Kirsten knows explode in her head, splattering the inside of her skull. She turns around, runs back to Mouton's memento room, and gathers up the dog that is sitting waiting for her as if she knew she would come.

With the dog in her arms she hurtles back down the corridor, reaches the security door where Keke is lying on the floor. She holds the thumb to the scanner while she punches in James's code again. Both lights turn green and the door jolts open.

She puts down the dog and levers Keke up, supports some of her weight with her good shoulder and gets her through the door. Seth carries the baby, and a gun. The elevator is disabled, so they jog up the stairs, losing count of the flights—flights and flights of stairs—going as fast as they can, the dog at their heels.

They all lose the rhythm at different times, causing them to stumble, waste split seconds. Keke stops with only a few more steps to go, sways and falls, causing her and Kirsten to tumble down half a flight, sending the dog into a flurry of barking. Keke doesn't get up. Seth passes Kirsten the baby, picks up Keke and throws her limp body over his shoulder for the last few stairs.

They trip out of the front door. Kirsten glances down at the baby to see if he is okay. He frowns back. She tucks him further into her body to protect him. The blue gleam from her broken arm is gone. They get to barely a hundred metres away from the building before an ear-splitting roar occurs behind them that hurls them up into the air and crashes them down again onto hard concrete. The baby wails.

JOURNAL ENTRY 9

12 May 1989

Westville

In the news: *I am happy. Truly, wonderfully happy.*

What I'm listening to: Madonna's 'Like A Prayer'

What I'm reading: 'The Alchemist' by Coelho. Don't really get it. Sure I'm missing something.

What I'm watching: Rain Man

Today P and the kids 'surprised' me with breakfast in bed for Mothers Day. At 'terrible two' they are a handful—I call them my adorable monsters—but on days like this I could just eat them up, they are so cute and charming, on their best behaviour. Sam had made me a 'card'—a fingerpainting of our family standing outside our house—and Kate gave me a necklace she had made by stringing dried pasta shapes together. I stuck the painting up on the fridge and wore the necklace the whole day.

P went around the garden cutting some of my favourite flowers and put a big bunch in a vase for me. (Poor garden!) It was very sweet.

I love watching the kids learn and try out new things. I love it when they say new words. They really are a handful—you can't leave them alone for a second (just this week: Sam dropped my brand new hand-held vacuum cleaner into a bucket of water, and Kate climbed INTO the fridge and closed the door. Last week Kate cut up a dress of mine to make 'ribbons!' and Sam jumped out of his pram and smacked his forehead on the tarmac. One of them flushed a plastic car down the loo and flooded the bathroom). Some days—most days—I just collapse on the couch after getting them into bed.

I have started taking them to the river every now and then, for swims. I take snacks like Provitas and little cubes of cheese, and some CapriSuns and then we call it a picnic. It is a great way to get rid of all their extra energy so that they are tired and calm when P gets home from work, and they adore it. Especially Kate—she is such a waterbaby! I really have to keep an eye on her. They have matching costumes and these bright orange inflatable armbands and they love to splash. Sam is very protective, always keeping an eye on his 'little' sister. He gets this worried frown when he thinks she is floating too far away and when we call her ('Kitty! Kitty!' he says) then she'll turn back, smiling her funny, naughty little smile. God, my heart bursts. I love them.

My shrink says that we can probably start weaning me off the anti-depressants. I'm not in a hurry. I never want to go back to that dark place again.

Oh! I almost forgot. The strangest thing happened yesterday. I was grocery shopping with the little ones—NOT the easiest thing in the world—but they were on their best behaviour and sitting nicely together in the trolley while I passed them things (not eggs, from experience). A woman who was walking past us looked intently at me and I smiled back. I thought, we must look funny. Like I had gone shopping and taken two toddlers off the shelf and put them in my trolley. Imagine it was that easy: you just go to a shop and choose which adorable monsters you want. 'Hmm, yes, I'll take this one and this one.' They would need barcodes! And what would the return policy be?

But then later I realised that she had smiled at me because she had recognised me—she was the nurse at that family planning clinic that was so kind to me and held my hand! I wonder what she must have thought, seeing us together. I wonder how it made her feel.

A DIFFERENT KIND OF FAMILY

Epilogue: six months later

Westville, KZN, 2022

Kate sits in her hired car, parked a little way away from the river, under the glittering dappled shade of willow trees. She takes off her safety belt, adjusts her tender back in the chair. Her left arm is slightly paler and thinner than her right, still recovering from being in the exoskeletal cast she had to wear for months.

She breathes in the muddy green smell of the river (Wilted Waterlily): a smooth, undulating smell. Balmy Verdant. Rolling Hills.

Keke urged her—citing her 'condition'—to take the isiPhapha speed train from Joburg to Durban, but she wanted to drive, to take her time, to think. To appreciate the journey.

Keke has just won another journalism award for her coverage of the Genesis Project. She always tells people she doesn't deserve them, that Alba deserves all the credit, but they just call her 'humble' and love her all the more. She's getting job offers from all over the world: most notably, Sweden, where they have offered her an eight-figure retainer for a year's contract. She and Marko are considering it, but only when she is fully recovered. In the meantime she gets weekly Tupperware takeaways from Marko's mother, who insists that good Indian food, specifically *dosa*, can cure any affliction. Keke is sure she'll hate the cold, and Kate knows it will be difficult for Keke to leave her post of Godmother to Baby Marmalade. She doesn't want to give up her partial custody of Betty/Barbara the Beagle, either.

God, Kate has missed driving, the freedom of the open road to the thrumming soundtrack of your choice. Stopping for a hydrogen refuel—not as pungent a memory as petrol—and greasy toasted cheese in a wax paper envelope. Flimsy paper serviette. Vanilla whipped Soy-Ice in a hard chocolate coating that you get to crack open with your teeth. Noticing, inside the store, that all the Fontus fridges are gone. Kirsten imagines them yawning in recycle tips, stripped of any valuable metal, or re-purposed as beds or dining-room tables in townships. Most likely, though, they have just been bleached and re-branded with S/LAKE decals: Bilchen's "100% pure" bottled water, Hydra's supposedly incorrupt replacement.

Alba's secret underground identity has been blown wide open since they disclosed the information they had on Walden and his company. They are instant heroes, and the logo of the green rabbit silhouette has gone viral. True to hypothetical bunny breeding, they have multiplied overnight. Virtual stickers, 3D wallpaper, hoverboard art, graffiti stencils, and playful holograms: Alba is everywhere.

They receive offers of funding from various (apparently non-evil) corporates. Keke has heard rumours of a splinter group forming, with new 'unknowns': a secret faction that can still do the same job without worrying that their mugs are splashed on every news tickertape (and Talking Tee) in the country.

Kate winds her window down further, allowing more of the clear air into the car. After tossing out the air-freshener at the car rental agency (Retching Pink) she had driven the first hour with all the windows down to try to flush out the fragrance. Artificial roses: the too-sweet scent painted thick vertical lines in her vision. Her sense of smell seems to be in overdrive lately, and the shapes more vivid than ever.

It is a superb day: warm, the humidity mitigated by a cool breeze, and the sky brighter than she has ever remembered seeing it. The branches of the weeping willows stroke the ground, whispering, as if to soothe it. She can smell a hundred different shades of green in the motion of leaves.

A woman pops up in the distance, walking towards the river. She has handsome silver hair, a thick mass of it, twisted up and fixed in place with a clip and a fresh flower.

A stained wicker picnic basket in her hand. She is tall and moves in elegant strides: not rushing, nor dawdling, her sense of purpose clear. She doesn't look around for a good spot; she knows exactly where the good spot is.

She sets down her basket, lays out the picnic blanket, smoothes it down in a practised movement. Once she has removed her shoes she sits with her legs out in front of her, crossed at the knees, leaning back on her hands with her eyes closed and her face to the sky.

The woman takes her clip out and lets her hair tumble down like mercury. Kate unthinkingly touches her own short hair, rakes her fingers though the awkward length of re-growth. The woman relaxes like that for a while, then sits up and opens her basket, bringing out a plastic plate and knife, a packet of crackers, cheese triangles. A small yellow juicebox.

Kate snaps a photo of her with her LocketCam, then retrieves the cooler-box from the back seat that she had packed that morning. She takes out a dripping bottle of iced tea, a packet of Blacksalt crisps, and a CaraCrunch chocolate bar. Watching the woman by the river, she opens the foil packet and starts to eat; then she remembers the bright green apple in her bag (Granny Smith), and eats that too.

So this is what her real mother looks like. Not just her non-abductor mother, more than just her biological mother, but her real mother. She can feel it. She sees Seth/Sam in her body language, her straight nose. But the hair and the eyes are hers.

She looks at her reflection in the rear-view mirror, touches the new streak of grey at her temple (Silver Floss).

'We have the same hair, and eyes,' she whispers to herself.

She feels a welling up in her chest, an inflating of her ribcage, and breathes deeply to stay calm. Warm tears rush down her face; she is used to the feeling now, even welcomes the release. During the past few months she has made up for a lifetime of not crying.

The woman looks so peaceful, so at ease with the world: a trait Kate hasn't been lucky enough to inherit, but she hasn't always been like this; she has also had her dark days.

James kept an eye on the Chapmans during the past twenty years, even kept a file, which he had left in his SkyBox for Kate. She found the access code in the "Hansel and Gretel" book he had bought for her a lifetime ago. It had been there all along. The file contained a comprehensive log of the Chapmans' lives: the different jobs they held, the close friends they had, and the holidays they went on. The grief counsellor they consulted. They never moved house—they still live at 22 Hibiscus Road—as if they thought if they moved, they would lose all hope of the twins finding their way home.

Anne Chapman still visits the river almost every day, the spot where she used to sit in the shade while the twins splashed around, and then later, their subsequent children: another son and daughter, born five years after Kate and Sam, spaced three years apart. The children, now grown, visit often, and the family looks like any normal, happy, loving family. It would be difficult, seeing them laughing and joking at family dinners, to guess at their sad and fragmented past.

Kate's yearning crowds the car. How she would love to meet her mother, grasp her hand, taste her cooking, ask her about the years before the kidnapping, and after. But looking at her, seeing how content she is, how restful her spirit seems, she knows she can't do it. It would be like smashing a shattered mirror that has taken decades to put together. Its hold is tenuous, gossamer, and she won't be the one to re-splinter it.

No fresh heartbreak.

She has a new life, thinks Kate, like I do now. She thinks of Seth at home in Illovo with Baby Marmalade: how good he is with him, how gentle. Seth who wants to keep his Genesis name, instead of 'Sam,' says it doesn't suit him, and he is right.

He has a new life too, despite not changing his name. She pictures what she guesses they are doing now, sitting on the couch in front of the homescreen, Baby Marmalade asleep in his arms, Betty/Barbara the Beagle snoring in her usual spot, her snout on Seth's lap. The wooden floor littered with nappies and wipes and teething rings and toys.

A different kind of family, James said.

An unusual family, but a family nonetheless: waiting for her to return home, and anticipating its new addition.

She thinks of her Black Hole, which is still there but has been sewn up to the size of her skin-warm silver locket. It's the smallest she can ever remember it being, but it yawns when she thinks of James.

She watches her mother pack up, shake the blanket, fold it and put it away, then start walking back in the direction from which she came. Kate reaches for the door handle then stops herself.

No. No. But when that feels too harsh, she allows herself a concession, thinks: *At least: not today. Maybe tomorrow, but not today.*

After a few steps, her mother turns, looks directly at the car in the distance. Kate can't see her expression. A moment goes by; she turns back and continues her walk home.

Kate takes a few breaths with her head back and her eyes closed then snicks her safety belt in and starts the car, swinging it into reverse. Her back is aching again, her ankles puffy. She adjusts her position, rubs her swollen belly.

'Time to get you back home, little one.'

Born seven months apart, her babies will be almost like twins. A different kind of twin.

She pops the car into drive, and puts her foot down.

ACKNOWLEDGMENTS

When I decided to publish this book in 2015 I assumed
I'd sell twenty copies to my family and friends
and then everyone (including me) would forget about it.

Little did I know that 'Why You Were Taken'
would be the one that lit a fire in my life:
the sales, feedback and reviews were the kindling
I needed to kickstart my indie author career, and the book
is where it is today because of my loyal readers.

Thank you.

WHEN TOMORROW CALLS

• SERIES •

1. Why You Were Taken (2015)

2. How We Found You (2017)

3. What Have We Done (2017)

…

ALSO BY JT LAWRENCE

The Memory of Water (2011)

Sticky Fingers (2016)

The Underachieving Ovary (2016)

Grey Magic (2016)

ABOUT THE AUTHOR

JT Lawrence is an Amazon bestselling author, playwright & bookdealer. She lives in Parkhurst, Johannesburg, in a house with a red front door.

STAY IN TOUCH

If you'd like to be notified of giveaways & new releases, sign up for JT Lawrence's mailing list via Facebook or on her author platform at www.jt-lawrence.com

Printed in Great Britain
by Amazon